Chi-Town Blues

City Blues

D. J. Herda

Published by Elektra Press, LLC, 2020.

This is a work of fiction. Similarities to real people, places, or events are entirely coincidental.

CHI-TOWN BLUES

First edition. September 1, 2020.

Copyright © 2020 D. J. Herda.

ISBN: 978-1393569732

Written by D. J. Herda.

D. J. HERDA

D. J. Herda

Elektra Press, LLC
Salt Lake City

Library of Congress Cataloging-in-Publication Data is available on file.
ISBN 978-0-9991573-9-8

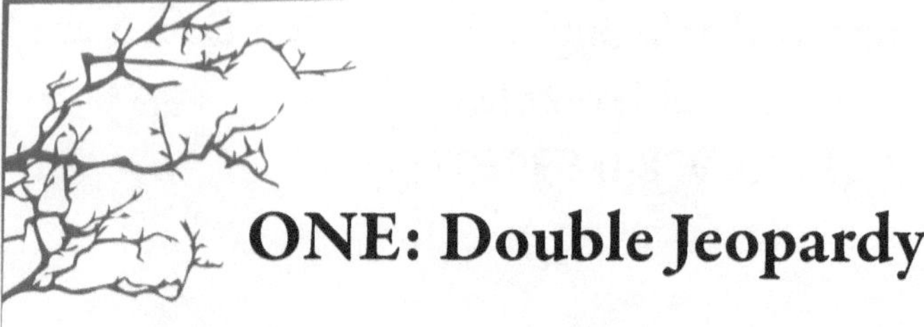

ONE: Double Jeopardy

A COCKROACH POKED ITS head out from beneath the bureau across the room. Several times it peeked out, paused, and sniffed the air like a golden retriever getting a fix before it scurried back to safety.

Bastard!

"Yes, Mrs. Martinowicz," I said. "I mean, no." The insect was proving to be a welcomed diversion to the endless harangue falling from the woman's lips. She droned on for an hour, pausing only long enough to ask a quick question, never long enough to hear an answer, and then asking it again a few minutes later. She'd enjoyed a happy childhood in Poland, selling flowers to the peasantry in her dear, since-deceased grandmother's shop. She eventually moved to America, met and married her husband, and lost him only two years ago. A yellow tear formed in the corner of one eye, beading up to enormous proportions before scaling its way slowly down a complexion so parched and crinkled, you could have read the Preamble in it.

"You know, excuse me, Mr. Joseph, sir, such a beautiful, such an elegant name as that ... excuse me for saying that the trouble with this American people is all this, this ... fooling around that so many people ... and the *women* ... do. It's a *sin*, excuse me, how these old hags who could scare the Frankenstein, how they smear all this makeup stuff all over their faces and they put on these short dresses, these skirts, and it's a sin how they chase after some men, now, isn't it? But, you know, Mr. Joseph, sir, I feel sorry for them, because they're all empty people inside ... with this sexy business and all. And I can't *stand* empty people. I can't *stand* people who don't use the brains the good God gave them. Excuse

6

me for saying it, Mr. Joseph, sir, darling, but I just can't *stand* no *empty people!*"

"Mrs. Martinowicz ..." I pulled my legs back beneath my chair and stood up. "I'll take it."

Mrs. Martinowicz patted the ball of yellow hair tacked to the back of her head. "Then you don't want it, no?"

"No. I mean, yes, I want it. I'll take the apartment. I'd like to rent it. Starting today."

"Oh, my God, can you believe it? Such an elegant young gentleman like yourself to want such an old place like this. That is a gift from the God. Believe me, sir, a gift from the God. Most people today, these empty-headed people, they don't want no old place like this. But you know what, Mr. Joseph, darling? They are all for show, these people. They all want to say, 'Look at me, what I got on the outside,' and inside ..." She made a circular motion with her finger. "They are all just empty people inside."

"I have to go now, Mrs. Martinowicz. I'm on my lunch hour from the bank. I don't have many things to move in here in the way of furniture and all. Mostly clothes. A few boxes. I could do it tonight easy, if that works for you. Around six?"

I handed her the security deposit and the first month's rent and observed how she signed her name, *Mrs. Josephine Martinowicz*, on the receipt, which she folded twice and handed to me. I'd had some training in handwriting analysis and found it fascinating, studying people's natures and comparing that to what their writing revealed. It was more than a pastime with me. It was a vice.

"Then, Mr. Joseph, sir, I see you tonight at six, and I give you your key then, no?"

"Sounds great. I'm looking forward to it. Oh, and one more thing. About my mail ..."

She held up her hand and led me out the door to the front of the building. "Right here," she said, pointing to an aging steel box standing guard over the steps leading up to the street and my future happiness. "This is your mailbox. I'll give you the key for that tonight, too. It's Apartment 1-B." She pointed to a label on the front. "See?"

I saw.

My mind raced as I hiked the stairs leading to the walk.

What a hole! Who would have imagined? Me, *a rising, button-down-collar man at the First. A junior officer. But, then again, it won't be intolerable. For a while. That's all it will take. If everything goes well, I'll be settled in by Saturday. Within a few short weeks, I'll be* rich.

And then I'll be gone.

THE LAST TWO PEOPLE filed out of the department except for a couple of tellers and Lynn, an assistant accountant who looked up, caught my eye, and waved from across the room. I smiled and waved back as she swung around in her chair and buried herself in a file cabinet. *Good kid.* I opened my bottom desk drawer and pulled out a stack of mimeographed sheets. Slowly, I ran my finger up and down the list, stopping finally at account number 74775.

"Martinowicz," I whispered.

Quickly my fingers followed the line of print after her name. *Address?* Four East Maple, Chicago, Illinois, 60606. *Telephone?* 312-659-1121. *Credit Rating?* AAA. *Loans in Force?* None. *Amount on Account?* $673,244.

"No lunch, Joe?"

The voice startled me. "*What?*"

"I say, aren't you going to lunch?" Mr. Cox learned over my shoulder. I wanted to close the sheaf of papers before me or set them print-side down on my desk. But neither would do. That would surely make him suspicious. No, I'd just have to sit tight and hope for the best. Just wait for whatever happened.

"Oh. No, no." I pointed to a wrapped sandwich sitting next to my phone. "I thought I'd just eat in today. You know, catch up on a little work. I want to run some figures I've been working on. For a mortgage that one of our customers is applying for." I hoped he wouldn't notice the sweat forming on my brow. "I figured I'd use the 5660."

"Bernice?" Fred turned toward the computer sitting in a room across the hall. "If she can't do it, nobody can. Of course, you have to treat her right, you understand. Just like any woman. You can kick her around a little and push her to the limit, get her fired up as all hell. Then, just when you think the love affair is over, you give her a pat on the processor, tickle her BIOS, and she'll purr like a kitten." Fred winked.

"Oh ... yes, *sir*." I forced an awkward laugh. "Very good, sir. I'll have to remember that one."

"Well, I'm off now. Be back in an hour in case anybody asks for me."

That would be a first, I thought. I followed the hollow sound of his hard-soled shoes down the corridor and across the hall. Pause. More sounds, followed by the slamming of the elevator door as the fiberglass-and-steel cage whisked its occupant to the 14th-floor cafeteria. My pulse suddenly dropped twenty points, and I took my first breath in a minute-and-a-half. I patted the sweat rolling down my temples.

Stupid, Joe. Very stupid. If you're going to do this thing, you have to do it right. No chance for slip-ups. Absolutely none. Otherwise, don't do it at all. I'm not going to spend the next thirty years of my life in Joliet because you fucked up. Uh-uh!

I glanced around before returning to the list, copying all the information I needed and shredding the rest. Then I got up and keyed a user-name into the computer. I punched some figures in, entered the access code and the password I'd seen Fred use a thousand times before—*asshole!*—and updated the information for account number 74775. After that, I went across the hall to Internal Security. As I expected, the department was vacant except for Marge.

"Hey. Hi, Marge."

"Joe. How are you doing? "

I shrugged. "Oh, you know. Busy, busy. Like they say, no rest for the wick—..." I caught myself. "—*uhh*, weary."

Some other time, she might have tempted me to stick around awhile. You know, sling a little hash. Marge had the smoothest curves and the sweetest smile I'd ever seen. Strawberry blonde mane, teased just enough to make it stand out from every other woman on earth but not enough to make her look cheap, you know? And when she walked, her firm, well-rounded buttocks swayed poetically—the kind of sway that tells a man she's a woman of vast experience ... all *carnal*. And not averse to putting it to use.

"Say, I need to use Bernice for a bit. I have to scan in some new customer signature cards. Alright by you?"

She threw her shoulders back and motioned with her arms, her bosoms shifting precipitously. "Let me know if you need any help."

I had to struggle to remember why I was there. In fact, for a brief moment, I was tempted to feel her out on the whole thing. You know, in a "just-kidding" sort of way. Tell her I had a plan for making a quick bundle and ask if she'd be interested in joining me. Something like a junior partner. With senior assets. Something in the way she smiled told me she wasn't exactly above it all. And she'd be good company along the way. *Guaranteed*.

But it was too risky. I knew that. There was too much at stake. Too much riding on everything going smoothly. I needed a foolproof plan, one hundred percent. And that meant no one else could know what I was up to. After all, there were a million Margaret Maddings down in Mexico. Plenty to last me for the rest of my days. And with the money I'd soon have, I'd be able to sample each and every one of them.

I turned the scanner on, punched in the account number, and waited as the machine whirred into action. On the oversized screen appeared the name, "Josephine Martinowicz." Below it was a scan of her signature. I revised the name on the file, deleted and resigned the signature line, and saved everything back into the computer. I ran a copy onto a new thumb drive that I slipped into my pocket. Now, the file read, "J. Martinowicz" with a signature that matched.

My signature.

Next, I made a slight altercation to her mailing address: From "Four E. Maple St., Chicago," to "Six Playa del Real, Acapulco."

Okay, I mused, *maybe not all that slight.*

I signed my name as a witnessing officer of the bank and stepped over to the printer where I slipped a dozen blank withdrawal slips into the hopper. I watched mesmerized as the printer spit out the new slips just as the elevator bell rang. I turned to see two tellers returning from lunch. I closed out the account and walked back toward Marge, eyeing her cautiously so as not to arouse suspicion. Well, that's done," I said, smiling. "Thanks. Catch you later."

"You get what you were after?"

"*Hmm*?" I paused, trying to gauge the meaning behind her words. "Oh, yeah. Sure. Thanks, again. No problem."

I turned to leave when she stopped me short. "Just a minute."

Oh, crap. I stopped and looked back, arching my brows.

"Yes? Anything wrong?" *Shit. Why did I say* that. *It was practically an open invitation to start her thinking. And wondering.*

"I was wondering."

Crap!

"Do you have plans for dinner tonight?"

"*Dinner*?" I let out a soft breath and thought for several seconds, taking in suddenly the flush of wildflowers wafting in from some illusory window overlooking some make-believe meadow covered in imaginary blooms. Confused, I shook my head. "No. No, can's say that I have. Why?"

"I was just thinking. Why don't we grab something together? Nothing fancy. Maybe Gino's for pizza and a beer?" Her eyes glistened, shimmering like those of a cat on the prowl.

I shrugged. *Why all of a sudden?* I wondered. I thought for a brief moment that she might somehow have gotten suspicious, and then I stuffed that crazy notion right into the shredder. Besides, what could go wrong with a harmless dinner with an even more harmless coworker?

"Besides," she added, "I received some good news this morning, and I don't feel like celebrating alone."

"Oh? What good news?"

She smiled—that cat again—and I could swear I heard her purr.

"*Uh-uh.* I'll tell you tonight."

I smiled and nodded. "It's a date."

"Great. Let's make it at eight. I'll meet you there."

I took her in more closely, the eyes, the crooked smile, the kind of cockiness that comes from a woman who's just a little too sure of herself just a little too soon into a relationship. *Any* relationship.

"Sounds like a plan," I said as she leaned across her desk, laying her hand on mine, the chasm between her breasts exhorting me home. I swallowed. "But, *uhh*, that's a little late, isn't it? Why don't we make it seven? Before the crowds. That line starts to form pretty early."

She smiled wider, a wickedness to her grin, as she squeezed my hand. "Eight," she said again, more firmly this time. "And don't keep me waiting."

I must have raised my brows because she released my hand and sat back in her chair, crossing one shapely pin over the other, her skirt hiking up provocatively. "I don't know," I said, pressing my point and shifting my head to one side for a better view. "Eight is a little past my bedtime."

"You can make an exception tonight. It's Friday. Besides ..." She popped her mouth into a perfect "O" and slid her tongue across her lower lip. "I'll be sure to make it worth your while." She threw me one last provocative wink, her eyes locked on mine as I headed back toward the executive suite.

I entered the office and slid back behind my desk, feeling for the deposit slips in my pocket. *It had been all so simple. In with a wink and a smile. A minor change to a customer's signature card. Out with a handful of signed withdrawal slips and a dinner date. What could have been easier? It was all so perfect.*

Too *perfect.*

Except that it hadn't been too perfect at all. In fact, it was a little unnerving, even though I'd fantasized about it for months. Sitting across a table in a cozy booth entombed by ancient fresco walls and a ceiling painted with swirling cherubs, a single candle in an old Chianti bottle lighting the table, two people flirting shamelessly. I wondered why I'd never thought of it before. Except I'd always felt that dating someone at the office was a bad idea. You know what they say about shitting where you eat.

But even if it *had* been a bad idea, it wasn't any longer. After finishing our coffee, she asked me where I lived, and I told her around the corner on Maple. She broke into a devious smile.

"What?" I asked, wondering what she found so amusing.

"I know," she said. "I checked the records."

So we climbed up the steps of the café and out onto Rush and rounded the corner at Maple just half a block from where I lived. We slipped down the stairs to my flat like two kids on a scavenger hunt and rolled around in bed like a couple of acolytes from the Church of Perpetual Heat. And after I'd scrubbed every lingering glint of color from her lips and fondled those magnificent breasts and stroked her where it was appreciated the most and she'd zeroed in on her target for the evening and had me begging for release before she lay back—the sweat on her chest, her belly, her thighs glistening and her bosom heaving ... well, after a couple of hours of that, I dozed off and slept the sleep of the dead.

Until five the next morning. That's when I rolled over and reached out to find her ... *Gone!*

Popping up onto my elbows, I peered out of the bedroom toward the front door. She had stopped there, pausing to fasten the last of the buttons on her blouse, when she looked up.

"Sorry. I didn't want to wake you. You were sleeping so soundly. I was going to slip out and call you later."

"That's okay." I took her all in, ran my eyes across her from head to toe. She still looked good. "Where are you going?"

"I've got to get home."

What? My eyes popped open wide. *Home? Oh, shit!* That's *why I'd never come on to her before. How could I have been so stupid! Of course. That's why she'd always seemed so unapproachable! Because she* was!

"To ... to your husband?"

She grinned. "To my pro. My neighbor Dee and I take tennis lessons on Saturday. She'll get suspicious if I don't show."

I took a deep breath and exhaled, shaking as many cobwebs from my head as I could without spilling out what little remained of my brains. "Will I see you again tonight?"

She shook her head. "I've got plans tonight. Business."

"Oh."

"But you'll see me tomorrow morning at Francie's. For breakfast. At nine. *Sharp.* I don't like cold blintzes."

I sighed. *Blintzes.*

"Then maybe we can catch that Pissarro retrospective at the Art In-stitute before going to my place to watch an old Bogie movie and make love in front of the fireplace."

Oh!

Suddenly, she strode halfway back toward the bedroom door, her movements so quick I thought she was going to pounce on me when she stopped. "And, just so you don't forget ..."

She reached down, hiked up her skirt, and slipped her tangerine panties down first one long, limber leg and then the other before flipping them toward me. Turning her back, she bent down at the waist, lifted her skirt again, and flashed me before standing back up and straightening out.

"Hey, wait a minute!"

She turned back and raised her brows.

"You never did tell me what we were celebrating last night. Remember?"

"Oh, that's right." She crossed the kitchen and led me back into the bedroom where she maneuvered me onto the bed, opened her mouth, and slipped her tongue between my lips. I let out an instinctive groan as she ran her hand across my shorts. "I got a promotion at the bank. And a raise. I start training for my new job Monday morning. Isn't that incredible?"

"Wow. Yeah," I said, reaching out, swiping at her and coming up with an armful of air. She blew me a kiss—actually blew me a fucking kiss, can you believe it?—and turned toward the door. "Hey!" I called as she reached for the knob. "What new job?"

"Oh. Meet the bank's new analyst for Internal Affairs. *Security Division*."

The rest of that day, Saturday, was just exactly perfect. I couldn't have asked for anything better. *Prayed* for anything more. I was now the proud diddler of the bank's new security officer. Suffice it to say I did not go easy into the night. I couldn't take my mind off her for a moment. And it wasn't good. Was her promotion at the bank just a coincidence? Was she just kidding around with that Internal Affairs Security Division stuff? If so, why, *how*? That would have meant she'd found out about my scheme and was toying with me, seeing how far she could string me along before dropping the big one. Whatever that might turn out to be.

But why would she go to all that trouble instead of just confronting me? Just laying everything right on the line?

To cut herself in on the deal, I thought. *That's why. To rattle my cage just enough to make me feel I had to take her in as a partner. As if I have no choice.*

But what would have been so wrong with that? I'd already considered the idea of inviting her along with me. Mexico was a big, cold, strange place on your own. Two people together would make it a lot cozier. What difference did it make who thought of it first ... or *how* much she may have learned about what I was up to?

And then *that* possibility played a number on me. *Because if she has figured it out, just how perfect a plan could it be, and how long would it take before someone else at the bank figured it out, someone who hadn't just fucked my brains out, someone who maybe had a solid reason for whistle-blowing on me? Someone* else *with Internal Affairs?*

And then I realized I was being foolish. She *couldn't* have known what I was up to, she *couldn't* have. Even if she'd gone into the computer room right after I'd left and somehow managed to check out what I'd been up to, she couldn't possibly have found out anything that would have tipped her off. Sure, she might have noticed Mrs. M.'s change of address, but that would have been highly unlikely. And even if she had, so what? Even if she saw the old lady's new identification card, how could *that* tie me to anything out of the ordinary?

No. No. It was all just a coincidence. She'd been working at the bank longer than I had. She was probably just due for a promotion and a raise, and Internal Affairs just happened to be the next available position. Internal Affairs' Security Analyst. Big fucking deal. So she was a trainee. Starting Monday. No, that's not why she asked me to dinner and then came back to my apartment to fuck my brains out. That wasn't the reason at all.

But, then, what was? How could someone I'd seen nearly every day of my life for the past six months suddenly come steamrolling along, panting after me like there was no tomorrow? And why last night of all nights? What was it about last night? Why hadn't she made her move sooner? Why wait until after I'd pulled the I.D. switch? Another coincidence?

And how was it that she handled herself as if she'd planned everything in advance to be absolutely perfect? Everything she did, everything she said. All rehearsed. Thought out. Ordained.

Are you kidding me? If she'd been a German Panzer tank during World War II, the allies would still *be fighting to liberate Europe.*

Yes, I'd hit upon something. She knew. Exactly *what* she knew, I wasn't sure. But whatever it was, it was too much for my own good. Unless I took her in on it with me. That was a possibility. But if she decided not to come along, *then* what? It would be like a signed confession. "I, Mr. Joseph Darling, do hereby confess to attempting to swindle Mrs. Josephine Martinowicz out of her entire life's savings and would have done so, too, except for my own stupidity."

She had to know. She just had to.

But, no, I decided. She couldn't possibly. I'd been too careful, too cautious. I'd planned out everything down to the tiniest detail. It would be impossible for her to know. I was being paranoid. She was who she was, period. No pretense, no illusion.

So, by the time Saturday evening rolled around, I'd pretty much run all my wildest fantasies through the wringer and put my suspicions to bed. There was no conspiracy, there was no advanced knowledge. There was only us. Just the two of us. It was kismet or something. Just one of those things that happens, just one of those crazy, incredible, unfathomable, inexplicable, intoxicating, mesmerizing, infatuating, mind-boggling things.

Damn!

I sank into an old, tattered chaise lounge that had been making people squirm uncomfortably since 1822 and switched on a lamp by my side. *Quarter to six.* The last rays of the sun slipped behind the brownstones lining the street across from my new digs. And as I picked up the pair of panties I had placed next to me, I sniffed them once more, reliving a night I'd not known for a long, long time.

As in *forever.*

I hoisted my *attaché* case onto my lap and opened it. From an inside pocket, I removed the stack of withdrawal slips. In the open space marked, "Amount Withdrawn," I carefully printed the figure, $9,000 on one of them and tucked the rest back inside the case. It was not an arbitrary amount, nine grand. I knew from experience that withdrawals of $10,000 or more triggered a teller to fill out a Federal Transfer Form before the withdrawal could be authorized. Federal forms meant more bank scrutiny, more bank signatures, and more bank *witnesses*—none of whom I was particularly anxious to invite to the party.

Moving my pen across the slip, I stopped at the space marked "Address" just above the signature line. I printed "Six Playa del Real, Acapulco, Mexico." I checked the box marked "Non-cancellable Bank Transfer," slipped the paper into a pre-addressed and stamped envelope, and sealed it. Within a few days, I would be nine thousand dollars richer. Within two weeks ... well, it was easy enough to calculate. I could probably have grabbed it all, drained the old lady's account, and left her with nothing, but there was no sense in being *greedy.* Besides, I didn't have anything against her personally. But, when my ex and I had split, the bitch had left me with a headful of erotic memories and a handful of debt. No, I was going to stick to my plan and take just enough to allow me to live the way I'd hoped to grow accustomed to living for the rest of my life. Give or take a year or two. And if that meant spending the rest of that life as an ex-pat in a foreign land, so be it.

When I had first gone to work at the bank as an assistant vice president, I was clearing $500 a week. Which, you understand, is not horrible. But, with eight other full- and two part-time officers on the payroll, advances were sure to be slow ... *if* they came at all. And I am not big on spending my days rusting in the rain.

The idea of running a grift on Mrs. Martinowicz had come only after I'd told her where I worked. *Why, that's where I bank*, she said. On a hunch, I followed up. Now, that alone wasn't enough to stir me to action. But, when I found out the old lady was a widow with no family in the world that she knew of, I would have been a fool to let it ride. After all, at 76 years of age, her days were numbered. She'd never spend all that money. And who better to benefit from her financial fortunes than her darling new tenant, Mr. Joseph? Her *cat*?

So, I slipped on my coat and hat and went outside to the mailbox. I felt like kissing the envelope goodbye before dropping it through the slot but instead slipped it into the hole like any average person mailing a check to the telephone company or paying off his bookie.

By Monday morning, the bank would receive the withdrawal slip and run it through the computer. The giant machine would shoot a shower of sparks around the room before determining that there was more than enough cash on account to cover the withdrawal.

Next, the slip would be routed to Internal Security, where someone—maybe even Marge—would run the paper through the scanner to compare the signature line to the one on file. The two "J. Martinowicz" lines would be identical—I had made sure of that.

Finally, the slip would wend its way to Auditing, where a non-cancellable bank draft for $9,000 would be issued to the account holder and the funds, transferred to a bank account I had opened in the name of "J. Martinowicz in Acapulco. Once I received word that the money had arrived and been deposited in my account, I'd be ready for the next test, a transaction transferring $270,000 to *Margaritaville*. I'd over-ridden the computer's log so that monthly statements would no longer go to Maple Street but instead to Acapulco, where Mrs. Martinowicz had recently purchased a retirement villa and planned to relocate permanently.

Meet Mrs. Martinowicz.

Of course, such a significant transaction would trigger the Federal Funds Transferal Act and require a form be filled out and signed by Mrs. Martinowicz in the presence of an officer of the bank before that officer mailed a copy of it to the Feds for their records.

Meet an officer of the bank.

I mean, why leave such a mundane, time-consuming task to someone as old and slow-witted as Mrs. Martinowicz when I could save her the effort. I hate seeing old people exposed to undue duress. I really do.

As soon as I received word that my Mexican account was swollen to the tune of more than a quarter million dollars, I'd pack up my gear and hop a plane for the land of milk and honey. Or *cervezas* and *senoritas*.

Whatever.

By then, I'd have an account tipping nearly $280,000 before Mrs. Martinowicz ever woke up and smelled the *kolachki* and realized something had gone wrong. By then, I'd be hell and gone from my Maple Street digs, from the bank, and from the good ol' U.S. of A.

And Mexico, I was careful to have checked in advance, has no extradition treaty with the United States for any crime short of murder.

So, as evening pooled its resources, I girded myself against the onset of one more Saturday night alone in Chi-Town. I walked down the street, turning north on Rush where I let my eyes feast on the full-color girlie-show placards and the flashing neon lights of the strip bars and the black-and-white cutouts outside the blues clubs, each of the buildings dark and depressing on the outside and blazing on the inside with only God knew what. I stopped only once to chat briefly with Fat Max, who worked for one of the nudie dance clubs as a "grabber."

"Hey, man. Doncha be walkin' on by like dat. Don' you know what beautiful dings is wigglin' an' a-wrigglin' just inside dees doe? Come on, my main man. Gib yoself a treat, Homes. No cover, no 'mishon. Jes you an' duh li'l ladies doin' what cum natchel, dig?"

I dug, smiled, and slipped him a buck, I don't know why, and then I wandered on down toward State Street and a small burger joint I'd visited a couple times before. It wasn't exactly what I had a taste for. But with less than a hundred bucks and a one-way ticket to Acapulco in my billfold, it would have to do.

And then, before I realized it, it was Sunday. And there she was, just as she'd said she'd be. She was wearing neatly pressed white slacks, appropriately scuffed tennies, and a white linen shirt that did little to conceal the fact that she was braless. A red, white, and blue nautical belt and expensive-looking earrings completed the ensemble. I felt myself begin to pant and regretted the fact that we weren't alone.

"Hey," she said. "Right on time."

"Hi. You look fantastic."

"You, too. Here," she said reaching down to the chair next to her. "I brought you something."

"You did? What?"

She grabbed a Sunday paper, still unopened. "*Chicago Tribune.*"

I laughed. "So I see."

"Don't laugh. I couldn't make up my mind whether to bring the *Trib* or the *Sun-Times.* But I finally figured you for a broadsheet man."

"And just how did you come to *that* conclusion?"

She thought for several seconds. "I'm right, aren't I?"

I smiled and reached out to squeeze her hand. "Yes. Absolutely."

She laughed, loud and guttural. "I just knew someone hung like you could never be a tabloid man. I'll bet you like to look beneath the fold, too." She laughed again, loud enough so that several people turned to look. She lowered her voice. "Sorry."

"Don't be." I stretched my palm toward hers and peered into two eyes peering back. "God, I missed you."

She paused only briefly. "Me, too."

I took a feigned breath. "So, how was your lesson?"

She cocked her head. "What lesson?"

"Your tennis lesson. Yesterday morning."

She shook her head. "I don't know."

"You didn't go?"

She squeezed my hand tighter. "Yes, I went. But I couldn't concentrate. I couldn't think of anything but *you*." She leaned forward, her nipples straining against the cool thinness of the fabric, my organ struggling to keep pace.

"Oh, my God," I said softly.

"What?" she asked, tilting her head toward me.

"This could get complicated."

"I think it already has."

I paused, breathed in and out for real this time, and shook my head. "If only you knew."

We spent the rest of the morning wandering the crypts of the museum, stopping for lunch at *Terzo Piano* and topping it off with a chocolate truffle tart and espresso. If breakfast hadn't turned the trick, lunch had.

"Did you know," she said, leaning into me with her most conspiratorial tone, "that Pissarro was an Impressionist until he transformed himself into a Neo-Impressionist at the age of 54?"

"No."

"It's true. He was so brilliant, Cezanne regarded him as a father figure; Gauguin referred to him as a genius. Even Renoir claimed he was a genuine artistic revolutionary, which is true. Of course, he studied under Seurat, Signac, and the other great Impressionists of the time and took the best of each of their techniques to weave into his own artistic tapestry."

I stared at her half amused, the other half stunned.

"I just thought of it," she said, running her finger across her plate and painting a layer of chocolate across her lips, "because of Seurat's

Sunday Afternoon on La Grande Jatte. You remember the huge painting? The one he created using pointillism?"

By the time we got up to leave, I was overwhelmed. What set out as little more than a devastatingly stunning woman with a vivacious sexual libido had turned out to be a walking enigma of science, history, art, and only God knew what else. Who would have guessed?

We caught a cab back to Francie's to retrieve our cars, and I followed her to her brownstone on North Wellington. After nuzzling with her in the kitchen, she opened a bottle of Rioja, and we made love for the rest of the afternoon to a backdrop of Bogie and Bacall. As the darker side of midnight crept upon us, I knew I was in trouble.

All the way home, I kept replaying in my mind my questions to her. *Why? Why now? Why us?*

And replaying her replies.

"It just wasn't right before. I was involved with someone else. It's against bank policy. I didn't want to get hurt."

And when I reminded her that, if anyone saw us out together, she could still lose her job, she said she'd risk it.

That's when I knew.

The next few days were excruciating, like being in a candy store owned by your dentist. Marge spent all day working her main job and breaking in another girl while training for her new position at night. A few telltale smiles here and there, a sexy glance now and again, but no touching, little talking, nothing to tip anyone off to anything serious going on between us.

I understood. Pretty much. I mean, it wasn't only our jobs at stake. If anyone found out I was planning on taking off for good and bringing her along, my entire world would come crashing down around us.

Me.

By the time the following Thursday evening unveiled itself, I was a frayed bungee cord ready to snap. My stomach turned cartwheels. My head whirred.

Nerves. Or maybe that fucking Philly cheesesteak sandwich with those greasy fries I inhaled for lunch.

Either way, I couldn't let it slow me down. I had less than twenty-four hours to finish stuffing my suitcase with everything I owned in the world, catch some shuteye, and grab a cab out to O'Hare for my flight in the morning. Then, just four hours later, I'd be home free.

And then the thought struck me. *How? How would I be home free? And home where? In Acapulco? Without her? I could still invite her, of course. Maybe afterward. Maybe a couple of weeks later. Or a month or two. Once all the dirt that was bound to blow up had died down. But a month or two without her ...*

And then another thought struck me. *Why not just stay put. Don't go anywhere. Get the money back from Mexico and replace it in the account. Make it look as if it had never left. I had the know-how and the opportunity to do it.*

I couldn't believe what I was thinking. My perfectly crafted plan was unraveling like a giant ball of twine. What had started as a lark had turned into a nightmare. The harmless little theft of a few thousand dollars that no one would miss had suddenly become my life flushed right down the toilet.

Could I give her up? I mean, if I told her I wanted her to join me and she said no? Could I go ahead with my plans anyway? Would I be able to function without her in my life? Could I be really satisfied alone?

Damn straight I could! I didn't plan this thing for the past two months only to watch it all wash down the drain because of some sexy little skirt, some empty-headed dame with more cutes than common sense who can turn me on with the flash of a smile. Uh-uh. *No way, mister. Get over it.*

Except she wasn't some empty-headed dame, and she *did* turn me on with her smile. I realized that suddenly. And she had more intellect, street smarts, and social breeding than anyone I'd ever met before. And I *still* didn't know what I was going to tell her about why I wanted her to join me. Or where. Or why we could never come back. Hell, I didn't even know if she'd say yes. She might have family in Chicago—she never did say. She might not be comfortable living in a third-world country. Christ, I didn't even know if she liked *frijoles*!

But, I couldn't just give it all up. Not now. I had already put through the second withdrawal, and after checking the old lady's account, sure enough, it had triggered the requisite 1053 Transferal Form signed, of course, by "J. Martinowicz." I had given Security a copy of the form to send to the Feds before the bank's closing that afternoon. By noon the following day, the First Bank of Acapulco had e-mailed me that a transfer of $270,000 was pending, noting that the funds would be available for withdrawal the following day, Friday.

No, no, I couldn't back out now. The only sensible thing was to wait until morning and proceed as planned. And try to keep my mind off her.

Then, as I stuffed my last knit shirt into the satchel and struggled to close the clasps, I heard a knock at the door.

I froze.

Who could that *be?*

My heart raced, my palms itched, my temples pounded—beating so hard I didn't just feel them, I *heard* them ... really *heard* them, for God's sake. I looked around. It wouldn't do to have anything lying about that might give me away. But everything appeared normal, so I shoved my case under the bed and paused. To the sound of silence.

I let out a deep breath. Had I been mistaken? I must have been. Perhaps it was a knock at the door of the apartment upstairs. I checked my watch. Nearly 10:30. No one would come calling at 10:30. Not at 10:30 at night they wouldn't. Not on a Thursday evening before a busy work day.

I listened some more. The only sounds in an otherwise silent sanctum were the steady *klickety-clack* of the roaches as their little feet skittered across the Formica countertop in the kitchen.

Bastards!

I was just in the process of bending down to pull my satchel out from under the bed when I heard it again. Louder, this time, more insistent. I shot up, my eyes bulging. This time, there was no mistaking it.

"*Fuck!*" I spat. I had slipped up. I *knew* it. I had missed some tiny, nearly inconceivable detail and would now have to pay for my carelessness.

But that was impossible. I'd followed my plan down to the letter—even so far as giving my boss at the bank a prescription from my doctor, ordering me to Arizona for six weeks of rest and relaxation for an asthmatic condition I'd been faking for a few weeks. My "doc" was a friend, a guy I'd gone to school with, not a real doctor but a pharmacist—close enough. I slipped him a fifty and told him I needed a break from work. That was all it had taken. My boss bought it hook, line, and sinker and actually expressed his deepest sympathies and concerns. He even put me on medical leave so I could continue drawing a paycheck, which I conveniently instructed our Accounting Department to send to a drop-box in Tucson where it would be forwarded to Mexico.

"You lucky son-of-a-gun," Fred announced when I'd told him of my misfortunes. "While we're here, suffering through another bank audit, you'll be basking in the sunshine by the pool, flirting with all those pretty girls!" I smiled to myself. Little did he know.

The knock sounded again, louder than the last. It was Mrs. Martinowicz come to say goodbye. *That* was it. To wish me luck ... maybe even refund me half my rent. That would be fine with me. I could use a little extra traveling cash.

I let out another deep breath, straightened my tie, and walked across the kitchen to the door. I lifted the latch, but Mrs. Martinowicz was nowhere to be found.

"Mr. Singleton? Joseph Singleton?" the taller of the two men asked. He wore a suit like a Maxwell Street bum and smelled like a cut-rate undertaker. His eyes were cold, glossy, black. His lips were dry and white. I couldn't tell whether or not he had any color at all to his pallor.

"Yes," I said.

"Mr. Singleton, I'm Lieutenant Cartwright. I think you know why we're here."

I froze. Could I have heard right? Was he a *cop*? I glanced at the second man, a uniform, and realized what was happening.

I furrowed my brow. "I'm sorry. There must be ... some mistake."

The man shook his head. "No mistake."

"But ... what's this all about?" I really didn't want to hear it, but I figured it would look bad if I didn't at least *feign* a modicum of interest.

He squinted down at a piece of paper he'd been holding. "Mr. Singleton, we're here to take you down to the station with us."

"Me? For what?"

His face was chiseled marble as he ticked off the list. "Let's see, we're talking grand larceny, grand theft, embezzlement, forgery, bank fraud, mail fraud, and an attempt to flee the scene of a crime. Will you grab your coat and accompany me, please?"

"*What*?" I said again, this time my furrowed brow genuine. "You've *got* to be *kidding*."

I mean, attempted fraud I could see. But I hadn't done that other stuff. Not all of it, not yet, anyway. How could anyone arrest someone for what he was *planning* on doing? And how would they even know? It's not as if I'd taken out an ad in the *Chicago Tribune*, for God's sake. How could they possibly pin all those charges on me? It was *insane*.

The man shook his head again. "Afraid not. Mr. Singleton. Please. If you don't mind. This shouldn't take long."

Long? Oh, no. Not for him. But probably forty-to-life for me!

He held his arm toward the door, and he said something unintelligible, either to me or to the uniform, I wasn't sure, although I imagined it went something along the lines of, "You have the right to remain silent. If you choose to give up that right, anything you say may and will be held against you in a court of law. You have the right to speak to an attorney and to have an attorney present during any questioning. If you cannot afford an attorney, one will be provided for you by the court at the expense of the government ..."

I never actually heard the words. I was too stunned. He could have read me the Mexican Magna Carta for all I knew. For all I *cared*. Somewhere along the line, I had miscalculated. It was the perfect crime—with one tiny flaw. But *what*?

I gathered up my wallet and grabbed my watch, and I slung my coat across my back. Lieutenant Cartwright took me by the arm and led me to the door, and I felt the sudden chill of the evening across my face.

"This is some mistake," I said. "Some *big* mistake."

"I don't think so," he said. "We've got her nailed to the wall."

I stopped. *Her!* My blood froze, my heart raced. *Did he say* her?

He led me up the stairwell and out into the night, where we paused at the curb for his partner to walk around and unlock the door to the prowler.

"Tell me," I said. I knew I shouldn't have. I knew it was stupid, against all advice any attorney might have given me. I knew it was wrong to say anything, but I *had* to find out. I *had* to know.

"What?"

"How?"

He paused. "How what, sir?"

"How did you find out?"

"Oh, that? Your coworker called and tipped us off."

"My ..."

"Coworker. A Miss Margaret Madding. She gave us a call when she noticed an impropriety with one of the bank's accounts."

Goddamit, I knew she was too good to be true. I just knew it was a setup from the start! My one fucking chance to foul things up, and I fell for it hook, line, and sinker. And me, practically ready to give it all up, throw it all away, just to be with her!

"You know," I said, not sure yet of from where the words were coming, "I don't know what she told you, but in my book, this looks more than a little like entrapment."

Meet Perry Mason.

"I don't think so," he said. "We've got all the proof, all the documentation."

"Of what? I mean, I didn't actually *do* anything. Oh, maybe some fooling around here and there, but nothing major."

"According to Miss Madding, you apparently did plenty. You were the brains behind it all."

I froze, the anger welling within me. "Did she tell you that? Did she say that?"

I thought back to our first night together, when I'd looked at her in the glow from the fluorescent lights seeping through my bedroom shades, how I couldn't tell if she had the face of an angel ... or the devil. Now I knew.

Cartwright opened the rear of the car before the uniform came around to the passenger's side. "Are you ready?"

"Yeah," the cop said. "Is that her?"

Cartwright looked up toward the building, second floor, to a window with a light behind a silhouetted figure that slowly pulled closed the curtains. "That's her," he said. "3-B."

"Couldn't be on the first floor," the cop groaned. He labored his way up the steps to the solid wooden door on the landing, brushed some webs out of the way, and pushed it open.

"What's going on?" I asked.

The lieutenant never took his eyes off the window. "Jack's going up to get her."

"Her? You mean Mrs. Martinowicz? For what?"

"To bring her down, of course."

Fucking great. It wasn't bad enough one woman in my life had turned against me. Now a second was coming down to nail the coffin shut. Things just keep getting better and better. I can't wait *to hear what she has to say about her Mr. Joseph darling now!*

Several moments later, the cop emerged from the building, helping Mrs. Martinowicz down the steps and over to the curb and the waiting car. When she saw me, she smiled; when she looked at Cartwright, she frowned.

He told her that she was under arrest for embezzlement, collusion, and bank fraud.

He thinks she's *in on it, too? How could she possibly embezzle her own funds?*

She sighed, frowned, and looked up like a child caught with her hand in the cookie jar. "Tell me, please, officer. Will I have to go to jail?" she asked. He replied that most likely not, considering her age, *provided* she returned the money to the bank.

She demurred. "But the money from the interest the bank paid me is mine. They shouldn't make me pay that back, no? That money is from my investments."

"Your investments," he said, shaking his head, "were the bank's money in the first place, remember? The bank was paying you interest on the money you stole under false circumstances. It's like stealing from the bank twice. You can't do that, Mrs. Martinowicz. Life doesn't work that way."

I felt like shaking my head, asking if he minded if I turned up the volume or switched to another channel, one with subtitles in English, *anything* to understand what the hell was going on. But they hadn't slapped the cuffs on me yet; they hadn't shoved me into the back seat of the cruiser, either. They hadn't even read me my rights. Had they? Something strange was going down, and I figured the best chance I had of coming out on top was to keep my mouth shut until someone addressed me. Someone did.

"So," Cartwright said, "I take it this is the woman you've been investigating? The one with the account at the bank?"

I raised my brows. "Her? Oh, yeah. Yes. Sure is. Absolutely."

"Just making sure."

"Yeah. No doubt about it. It's her all right. But tell me, lieutenant, how did you catch on to her so quickly?"

The lieutenant told me that Margaret had notified them that Mrs. Martinowicz had made arrangements to withdraw her funds a little at a time and transfer them to Mexico. That's when she got suspicious as to how a little old lady from Poland, with no job and a meager social security income, could have amassed so much money in such a short period of time. That's when she ran a check on the woman's account and learned about the loan scam.

"Loan scam?"

"Miss Madding wired the bank in Acapulco to hold the funds until we called for them. I assume that's when she enlisted your help to ensure Mrs. Martinowicz wouldn't find out what was happening and skip town before we could build a case against her."

"My help. Yes. Of course. But tell me, just how *did* she get all that money? I mean, Mrs. Martinowicz. I'm a still a bit fuzzy about that part."

"Do you want to tell him that," Cartwright asked. The woman shook her head. He said he didn't think so and turned back to me. "Apparently Mrs. Martinowicz here got the idea to doctor several fictitious bank loans, using several of her friends and relatives to pose as applicants. After they had received substantial loans using the phony docs she'd supplied to them, they turned the loan money over to her in exchange for a payoff of a thousand dollars each. Then she deposited that 'loan money' into her account, which, over the eight or ten years of running the scam, had grown into quite a nest egg."

"So," I said, "the part about Mexico ... she was transferring her funds there?" It paid, I realized, not to play *too* dumb.

"She'd just started doing so when Miss Madding discovered the transfers and called us. A little sleuthing, and we were able to tie everything back to her."

I looked at the woman and craned my head. "Is that what you were planning, Mrs. M.?" I asked.

She shrugged. "I don't know nothing about no transfer to Mexico, but I am not sorry one *bit*. That president of the bank, he is a dumbbell. Excuse me for saying so, Mr. Joseph, darling, sir, but he is empty-headed. I never liked him one bit. He treat me like an old lady. He treat me like a dummy, so I show him who is the smart one and who is the dummy."

"But ..." I heard the words slip out of my mouth without being able to stop them. "But, you knew that setting up a loan scam was wrong. You knew it was wrong and that someday you'd be caught. Didn't you?"

"Caught? Caught what? No one lost anything. When my friends get their loans, they pay a fee to the bank. Then I pay them for their trouble, and they go back to Poland for a visit for a while, and no one is hurt. You know that, Mr. Joseph, darling, I can't hurt nobody. Nobody except the dumb people like the bank president and that little fellow who used to live here before you move in, such a little fellow and a drunk and with the women all the time. The women for the sex. It's such a shame."

I glanced at the lieutenant who was making some notes, his lips moving as he scribbled. I tried glancing at what he was writing down, but he turned away before I could see.

"Do you ... do you think she had some ... help?" I asked, motioning toward her. "I mean, do you think she had an accomplice or something? A partner?"

I hadn't wanted to ask, but for some reason, I was suddenly fascinated. The old lady had actually pulled off a scam worth more than I'd ever imagined. And would have gotten away with it if I hadn't bumbled along. Yet, at first glance at least, she didn't seem to have the brains to boil a pot of coffee.

Cartwright looked up. "*Nah*. She's strictly a lone wolf," he said, turning toward the woman, "aren't you Mrs. Martinowicz?" She shook her head and looked away. "It seems she didn't need any help. For her, pulling off the scam was no big deal. Not for someone who once worked for a bank in Poland ... as an Internal Affairs Officer in the Fraud Division."

"*What*?"

"So," Mrs. M. said, "what happens now?" She tugged on his overcoat sleeve. "I'm sorry, what did you say your name is, again?"

"Cartwright," he said. "Lieutenant Daniel Cartwright."

"Oh, that is a good name. Such a elegant name, Mr. Daniel, darling. I am so fortunate to live the good life with such wonderful people around me. First Mr. Joseph come to me looking for a place to stay, and now you. I tell you, Mr. Daniel, sir, I thank my lucky God to find people like the two of you in this world. But tell me something, tell me something, Mr. Daniel. Do I have to go somewhere now or can I go back upstairs and feed my cats?"

He told her she'd have to accompany him to the station, and he helped her into the back of the prowler. He said they'd probably keep her in the holding area until they could get the night judge to bind her over for arraignment, after which she'd most likely be released on her own recognizance; so, she'd be back home and sleeping in her own bed by midnight.

"With my cats?"

He nodded. "With your cats."

She asked if she could go back upstairs to retrieve her shawl, and he told her it wasn't necessary, that the officer would be happy to turn up the heat in the cruiser. "Won't you, Officer Carlisle?"

Carlisle looked from one to the other. "Oh, yeah, sure, thrilled. Nothing I like better than running the heater full blast in the middle of August."

I watched as Carlisle slammed the back door and walked around to the driver's side. I turned to Cartwright. "So, you don't really need *me* anymore, do you, lieutenant? Now that you have Mrs. Martinowicz's confession."

"I'd still like you to come down to swear out a complaint on behalf of the bank. Then you can go."

"You mean that's why you ... I mean, that's the reason you ..."

"We need your complaint on behalf of the bank to bind her over." I told him that, since Margaret was more knowledgeable than I, perhaps she should be the one to sign off.

"She's on her way to the station now," he said. "You can sign a joint complaint and make things official. That will wrap things up on our end."

"And ... Mrs. Martinowicz? Will she really be okay? I mean, you're not going to throw her behind bars or anything like that, are you? I don't know that her old heart could take it."

"We'll treat her with kid gloves. Look, she made a mistake in judgment. She's an immigrant American. Once the funds are returned from Mexico and she signs over her account back to the bank, everyone will be satisfied, including the D.A. I don't expect there'll be any more to it than that."

Thank God, he thought. *Thank my* lucky *God.*

Following the affairs that were unfolding, my biggest remaining concern was what Miss Margaret Madding was going to say when we collided at the police station. Was she going to stick to the story she originally told Cartwright, or was she just setting me up to turn me over to the D.A.? How much did she actually know about my activities, my plans? And why, if she knew as much as it appeared, did she just let me off the hook?

I got part of the answer when I laid eyes on her. I expected her to turn on me. But she was cordial, pleasant, businesslike. One employee to another. And she stuck to her story. Almost as if she really *didn't* know the extent of my involvement. Maybe she had checked up on Mrs. Martinowicz, found out about the bum loan applications, and saw that the old lady had already transferred half her funds to Acapulco. And that she had rented a villa there in her name. And was planning on leaving the country for good. At least, that's the way it must have appeared.

That was it. Margaret actually *did* think Mrs. M. was the only guilty party here. She really *did* believe the old lady had done everything I'd actually set in motion and was planning on skipping out for good with her account. How could she possibly think anything else? Everything I'd done was in the name of J. Martinowicz!

On the way out of the station, Marge asked if I needed a lift home, and I told her thanks. And for the next several minutes, the communication between us was an abyss, a black hole of emptiness. I didn't know what to say, and she wasn't exactly in a chatty mood. So when she pulled up outside my place, I leaned over, gave her a quick peck on the cheek, and thanked her.

"For what?"

I shrugged. "Oh, I guess for including me in your report to the police, saying I had a bigger role to play in the apprehension of Mrs. M. than I actually had. I mean, you really could have taken all the credit. You're the one who figured this whole thing out. I didn't have anything to do with that end of it."

"Oh, I don't know if I'd go as far as to say *that*."

I looked at her, my brows furrowed, my lips pursed.

"*Hmm?*"

"I said, I don't know if I'd go so far as to say you didn't have *anything* to do with it."

I sat there, waiting for an explanation, and when none came, I asked her what she meant.

"Well, if it hadn't been for you changing Mrs. Martinowicz' signature card from 'Josephine" to "J" Martinowicz and updating her residence from Maple Street, Chicago, to Acapulco, Mexico ..."

I sat in deathly silence as she rattled off every single move I had made in the litany of missteps I had taken on my way to pulling off the Crime of the Century. And when she was finished, I sat, mouth agape, hands sweating. *How did she know? How* could *she have known?*

"Once I began checking up on Mrs. Martinowicz' banking history," she continued, "I stumbled across a series of suspicious loan applications made by her friends and neighbors, each of whom had a Polish surname and each of whom ended up defaulting on their loans after disappearing into the woodwork. I guess she provided each one with a one-way ticket back to the Old Country. That's how I knew she'd never had any intention of transferring her funds to Mexico and skipping out."

When I told her I still didn't get it, she explained how only a fool would risk a perfectly successful scam like hers by pulling up stakes and leaving the country right in the middle of a winning streak. It would have been financial homicide. "So, I began looking for someone else behind the transfers, another party, someone who knew her well enough and could get close enough to her to learn certain things about her lifestyle and personal habits. Someone with access to her banking records."

"Someone like me," I said.

She nodded.

I shook my head.

"What's the matter? Stunned?"

"More like ... *stupefied*."

"Why? Don't you think I have the brains to put two and two together and come up with embezzlement?"

I shifted uncomfortably. "That's ... *such* an ugly word."

She forced a smile. "Well, how about *theft*, then. *Better*?"

I was trapped, and I knew it. I shrugged. My mouth opened and, after the awkward passage of several electrically charged moments, a single word flopped out.

"Fuck."

She smiled. "Later, darling. We've got a lot to do before then."

"What?" I peered over at her, her eyes fixed on the road. "What are you talking about?"

"About what you have to do, and soon."

"Like what?"

"Like, going back to finish packing and then getting some rest. We've got a flight to catch tomorrow at eleven."

"What?"

"Has this rain impacted your hearing? I said we've got a flight to catch to Mexico tomorrow morning, so you'd better get some rest."

"Look, here," I said finally. "I'm grateful for what you did and all. I really am. You didn't have to help me out. You could have told Lieutenant Cartwright everything."

"You're welcome."

"But ... we can't exactly go riding off into the sunset together ..."

"It's dark out, and it's raining," she said flatly. "Besides, we're traveling by air."

"I mean, what if we *did* go off to Mexico together?"

"What if we did?"

"You'd always have something over my head."

"So?"

"So, what's to say that one day you wouldn't use it against me? I mean, you'd always have that power over me."

"True." She glanced at me before returning her eyes to the street. "So, what's your point?"

"My point is that this can't possibly work."

"Why not?"

"I just told you."

"That's just silly. Everybody knows a wife can't testify against her husband on a felony rap. Not even in Cabo San Lucas."

"Acapulco," I said.

"Cabo. My family has a villa on the cape overlooking the bay. Or *did* have. When mom died last year, she left it to me. It would be a shame to see it go to waste."

"So, this is how you see things ending? The bad guy gets the girl and the glitz and the glamor, and everything turns out for the best?"

She thought for several moments. "Yeah," she said, "something like that."

"And the good girl ends up with some jackass who just happened to be fortunate enough to have her fall in love with him and save him from the gallows?"

"Pretty much," she said.

"So, in other words, crime *does* pay. Is that what you're telling me?"

"I'd prefer to think of it a little differently. I'd prefer to think of it as you recognized from the moment you laid eyes on Mrs. Martinowicz that something about her was fishy, and, as an officer of the bank, you felt it was your duty to investigate. And you were right. So, you shifted some funds around to prevent her from absconding with the bank's money and taking a hike. That's a small enough risk to take in saving the bank a bundle. You'll probably get a handsome reward. Maybe even a medal."

"We both know that's a bunch of crap."

"Do we?"

"I'd have to have a pretty creative imagination to talk myself into believing *that's* how this all went down."

"But, darling, you *do* have, remember? After all, you talked yourself into believing you had a fool-proof plan, didn't you? And that you were poised on the brink of success?"

"Okay, okay, I confess. I blew it. All right? Satisfied? I overestimated my criminal talents."

"That's the understatement of the decade."

I paused, thinking, puzzled, defeated. "So, what's next? Do I throw myself on the mercy of the court here or what?"

"In this particular instance, yes. Just think of me as the judge."

I nodded. "And ... you're going to give me a suspended sentence providing we get married so that we can live happily ever after in Cabo San Lucas. Is that about it?"

"That's about it." She pulled the car to a stop, unfastened her safety belt, leaned over, and slipped her arms around my neck. "Oh, there is one more thing," she said, pulling me closer.

I looked into her face, the street lights dancing in her eyes, her hair shimmering like spun gold. "Yes, your honor?"

She moved so close to me, I could smell the tantalizing scent of her lipstick. "Don't ever pull a fool stunt like that again."

TWO: Fisher of Men

JOHN LOOKED AROUND, up-shore, down-shore, all around. Nothing. Not a solitary shrub. Not another person. Nothing. He shrugged. Perhaps it would pass, this growing pressure deep down inside his bladder. Maybe he needed to take his mind off of it and just concentrate on the task at hand.

I shouldn't' have had that fourth cup, he thought. But he knew, even in his four a.m. stupor, that the lake would be cold, the winds would be bitter, the water whipped into froth, icing everything in its path.

It was that fourth fucking cup.

It was not John's idea of a good time, coming to the lake so early in the morning—in fall, just days before the first snowflakes began their assault on Lake Shore Drive, mere weeks before classes resumed at Chicago's Columbia College. It was not his idea of fun at all. But when his uncle had called the night before and said he was going smelting and would he like to come along ("They're running big-time!"), well, John naturally clenched his fingers around the receiver, fought off the lump that had sprouted in his throat, and stammered, "Sure. Love to. What, *uhh*, time are you going?"

John loved his uncle dearly. And his uncle? He loved fishing. Well, not fishing, exactly. More like *catching*. There was a big difference between the two. Fishing, to John's uncle, was a means toward an end that was, simply enough, bringing home the bacon. Never mind how you got from Point A to Point B. It was arriving that made all the difference.

John's uncle wasn't a spit-and-polish fisherman; he was not of the catch-and-release school of thought. He had never tied a fly in his life and never could see the value of standing in the middle of a rolling trout stream, throwing cast after cast into the wind in the hopes of snagging a small brookie or a rainbow or even a giant brown and reeling it in for the sport of it all. To John's uncle, it was a simple fact: you fish to catch. The more you fish, the more you catch. The more you catch, the better your life will seem when you look back upon it only moments before expiring, wheezing up your last breath because of lung cancer or angina or maybe even something as mundane as getting run over by a bus: *Jesus, but I've caught a shit-load of fish. It's been a good life!*

That was pretty much how John's uncle saw it. And John knew that, if his uncle said the smelt were running, then, by God, the smelt were running. John liked little more on the face of God's green earth than the taste of freshly caught smelt freshly fried in a pan and served up with a little salt, pepper, and enough seafood sauce to float a small armada. And if he occasionally had to go through hell to get it, so be it.

The wind whipped up suddenly—a growling, sudden gush sweeping across the lake and across John and across the entire world, making the boy's teeth rattle—literally chatter out loud—so that in order even to catch his breath, he had to turn sideways to its fury. "Fuck!" he said finally. His uncle looked up at him, that same vacuous stare John had seen a million times before.

"What?"

"*What*, what?" John couldn't believe his ears. He couldn't believe his uncle could even think about asking such a foolish question. "What? It's fuckin' cold out here, that's what! Jesus, who's idea was this, anyway?"

His uncle laughed. Besides catching fish, John's uncle liked nothing better than showing off his toughness. He had served proudly in the U.S. military as an infantryman stationed in Italy during the waning days of World War II. He had caught some shrapnel in one arm at some battle or another, Antietam or something, and John thought he remembered his uncle saying that he'd caught some in his head, too, which is exactly where the doctors decided to leave it for fear of causing complications should they have decided on going in to remove it. So, they installed some sort of metal plate inside his uncle's skull to prevent the shrapnel from shifting, and they left it there. And now John wondered if it had somehow managed to work its way in deeper, like a worm tunneling through the decaying carcass of a once-living creature, until finally it had reached the soft innards of the man's cranium, itself, turning his uncle into an avocado.

"Aren't ... aren't you ... *c-c-c-c-cold*?" John shivered.

His uncle laughed again. "*Naw*. Cold is all in the head."

John pictured the metal plate slowly but steadily decaying.

"Tell you what," John's uncle said as he strained to see his watch in the near-light of near-morning. "It's almost five. Old Man Feeney will be opening the bait shop soon. Why don't you walk on over and get yourself a cup of hot Java. That'll warm you up. When you get back, we'll check the net and see how we're doing."

John didn't have to be asked twice. He tugged at his coat collar until it hid his ears, and then he turned windward and followed the shoreline north, shielding his head from the incessant pounding of the wind and spray so that his face cranked to one side like an owl. He walked like that, head skewed sideways against the cold, when he felt himself stumble across the edge of the pavement and turned to face the glowering windows of Old Man Feeney's bait shop. He quickened his pace and reached the wooden steps, hiking them three at a time while grabbing for the knob that led to the heated confines inside. He twisted it. He twisted it again.

"Shit!" he spat. He looked around before glancing at his watch. Two minutes to five. "Shit!"

John peered through the glass pane rattling against the wind, peered through the door and into the shop where the lights glowed an eerie yellow-green, and the coffee machines sent plumes of steam funneling surrealistically toward the ceiling. He looked away, huddling lower into his coat so that a passerby might mistake him for a huge turtle. He shivered, which made him recall that he still had to pee, and he looked around for some sign of a rest room. He peered back inside the shop and saw a closed door against the back wall.

"Thank God," he said softly before pulling back into his shell where he stood quietly except for the shivering. He stood there counting off the seconds, too cold to pull his hand out of his pocket to check his watch. *What if he doesn't open on time?* John thought. *What if he doesn't open at all? What if he had an emergency or something and had to take off and won't be back until tomorrow?*

These were not mere rhetorical questions. Old Man Feeney was a loon, pure and simple. His reputation preceded him up and down the lakefront.

It'd be just like the old fart not to open up at all on the coldest fucking day of the year. It'd be just like him, goddamn it.

It *would* have been like him, but when it came time for Old Man Feeney to open shop, John heard the unmistakable sound of footsteps followed by the soft clang of metal-on-metal as the iron bolt slipped to one side. Suddenly the knob turned and John's heart leaped as the door opened wide.

Now, Old Man Feeney—John knew from past fishing trips he'd taken to Lake Michigan with his uncle—was a year or two older than Moses and a lot more ornery. John once watched the old bastard drop a pot of coffee in some poor kid's lap before throwing the kid out of his shop for making such a mess. Still, Old Man Feeney today would be a welcomed sight, no matter how much of a shit he could be.

John slipped halfway through the door and stopped to shake off the cold. As he looked up, his jaw fell slack and his eyes glazed over until they looked like the shiners he used for bait whenever he and his uncle went walleye fishing in Wisconsin. He shivered. Less from the cold than from what lay before him.

My God!

She looked up at him ... curiously at first, then more comfortably. She craned her head gently to one said and smiled through dainty white teeth, each set perfectly into a turned-up mouth like so many matching pearls clinging to some widowed dowager's neck. She batted her eyes—actually batted them, for Christ's sake.

"I ... I ..." John heard somebody say, and then he realized it had been he. His eyes brushed her lips—red, deep red, crimson, the color of a fire engine after it has been freshly washed but not yet dried. She smiled past a complexion so sweet, it had to have come from a pitcher of cream risen to the top, soft and white, with just a blush of peach.

But her eyes ... oh, her eyes. Those two limpid pools of aquamarine, the color of Lake Michigan on a calm summer's day; the color of a sapphire caught glistening in the sunlight; the color of a Taos sky on a cold, crisp, January eve. It was those eyes that caught his attention, caught his desires, caught his very heartstrings and sent them tumbling toward her until he could feel their two bodies touching, beating, pounding in unison. He smelled the jasmine in the air, heard the nightingales sing, felt the silk of her anointed skin. More, still, he realized something else:

Jesus, she's built like a brick ...

John knew right then and there that he would have to have her. She didn't have to say a word. She wouldn't *ever* have to say a word. And if it turned out that she never ever *did* say a word, he would still possess the world in all its glory.

I'd kill for a shot at those tits!

"Aren't you cold?" she said.

John stirred. Fear beat at his chest. Terror stalked his brain. He wasn't positive, but he thought for one split second that he felt his heart stop beating. She had spoken to him. She—this apparition of joy, this vision of perfect loveliness, this goddess of all goddesses, this monument to love and light and life.

What a fucking body!

The girl giggled. "I'd just better get you a hot cup of coffee, mister," she said, and she turned, jiggling her way across the room. John felt himself take one step after her, heard the door slam closed behind him, and stared. She was poetry in motion, a perfect body to match a perfect face. A twenty-four-inch waist set between 34-inch hips and a 38-inch chest ... 38-D, even! Give or take a letter or two.

The goddess hesitated as she reached the counter, and then she looked back at him and smiled once more before ducking down and skittering through the passageway only to emerge upright on the other side, looking more radiant and perfect than before.

"Well, come on," she said, her voice oozing honey, draining sweet nectar lightly squeezed from a comb so that it dribbles its golden mellifluousness down your forearm. "I won't bite."

John took several steps across the cracked black-and-gold speckled linoleum that somehow, after 57 years, still managed to pass for a floor and slid down across a vinyl-covered stool that matched, in age and overall condition if not in cleanliness, the flooring. He stared at her chest—he couldn't help himself—at the promise of the untold wealth at which those two magnificent mounds portended, watching first one stupendous globe strain tightly against the pink chintz of her uniform and then the other as she turned halfway away from him to pour a cup of steaming coffee, then halfway back as she reached for a saucer and a spoon. He managed to lift his eyes only milliseconds before she turned full toward him, placing the java on the counter between his outstretched hands. She smiled. He smiled. They both smiled.

He looked down at the cup, managed to thread one trembling finger through the hole, and lifted it slowly off the counter. Slowly, deliberately, wantonly his vision, his apparition, his goddess leaned forward, resting her weight against her forearms, pressing lightly against the counter's edge. She reached out and grasped his wrists.

Setting the trembling cup back down, John looked up—up and in, up and deep down within that chasm of hope, that sink-hole of joy, that glorious crater of delirium in which those two grandiose globes were opened wide for inspection, opened to reveal the swollen ripeness of their bounty, two honey-do's ready for the harvest. They were the biggest boobs he had ever seen, and he was positive they must have been the sweetest tasting.

Gradually, the faint scent of jasmine on a moonlit night swept past him, and he heard the voice of an angel incant, "Do you take cream?"

John couldn't believe his ears and blurted out suddenly, "Oh, God, yes!" He stopped short. His eyes widened, and a sudden rash of red washed over his face. "I ... I mean, *y-y-yes*. I'd love some ... cream ... if it's not too much ... trouble."

She smiled at him, pausing far longer than one would have thought necessary while staring into his eyes, capturing them, taking them prisoner, ensnaring them for all eternity, pausing far longer than anyone would have expected a waitress to do before finally releasing his wrists from her grasp, and, still smiling, turning away to fetch the creamer.

Suddenly, John felt a new surge race through his body, a swelling deep down within, felt his manhood straining against all decency, straining and coursing, ready to race, raring to go ... and felt his bladder begging for release. He shifted his weight uneasily to one side as his vision of loveliness returned, set the pitcher before him, and said something softly, too softly for him to make out, before smiling once more and turning away to go fiddle with one of the coffeepots. John raised the cup to his lips and took a sip, then another, then a third, his lips lingering at the edge of the cup, his nostrils taking in the heady aroma, the heat rising from the black brew, a heat that nearly matched the one he felt burning within his loins. All the while he sipped, he watched the goddess move her derriere first this way, then that, its perfectly formed twin globes matching in symmetry and in promise, if not in size, those other twins that had already captured his imagination, his heart, his lust-filled soul. She was the most beautiful woman he had ever seen. He had to have her.

It was strange how these things happen sometimes. At one moment, you find yourself wandering through life, hoping to meet someone you might be attracted to, fall in love with, and never ever want to be apart from again. And the next moment, *wham*! There she is. Standing right before you. Standing there and staring right into your eyes, all gooey with sappiness and tenderness and all that other stuff, just the way it says in the magazines and on TV. Standing there invitingly, hoping that you notice, that you feel the same way about her that she feels about you. Hoping against hope ... and more.

"So ..." the goddesses' voice chimed sweetly, dragging him back to reality. "What's your name?"

John swallowed hard and set the cup down. He cleared his throat. He had to be cool. He had to do this just right. Oh, he knew it wasn't a tough question. He knew he could handle it. He'd done so before many times. But now ... *Now*, his answer would have to be perfectly smooth, confident, relaxed, assured. He would need to be all of that and more if he was to capture this wanton beauty for his own forever. He knew his chances in life of ever meeting anyone again even half so desirable rested on the far side of slim. He was not about to waste his best shot. She was just too good to be true, his fantasy dream walking. If this was John's one-in-a-million shot, he was going to sink it.

"John," he replied. "John ..." He paused. He felt his knuckles tighten, his palms begin to melt. His feet grew suddenly to twice their normal size. His head began to throb. Fear washed over him like a condemned man on Death Row taking those last few desperate steps.

Wait a minute. Wait! Something's wrong, here. Something's very wrong! a little voice in the back of John's head screamed. Did he remember? Could he remember? Back a year ago or more. Back to the very first trip he'd taken with his parents to Las Vegas. It had been a high-school graduation present. He'd wandered down to the bar late one night, 1:30 or 2, long after his parents had turned in, and he fought his way past wall-to-wall bodies, a sea of sweating torsos, smoking cigarettes, waving cigars, beaded handbags, stacks of chips, plastic cups filled with silver quarters, until finally he spotted a solitary stool.

Sliding quickly through the crowd, he settled onto the perch and motioned to the bartender for a beer. As he slowly raised it to his lips, the woman seated next to him turned around. "Well, *helloooo*," she said seductively. She was dark-haired, dark-lipped, with plenty of eye make-up, but clean, not greasy looking, and when John's eyes swept across her, he couldn't help but notice that her peek-a-boo blouse was, indeed, peeking. "What's your name?" she asked.

"John," he replied, surprised that anyone so sophisticated would express an interest in someone as young as he. He sat up on the stool, trying to make himself look taller, older. After all, she was 23, 24 maybe. He couldn't tell. "John ... *uhh*, just John. You know."

"Well, nice to meet you, John Just John. My name is Marie ... Marie Amore," she said, holding out her hand for John to squeeze. He hoped she hadn't noticed the sweat on his palm and wondered how it had gotten there. "Are you here on business or pleasure, John?"

"Oh," John replied, reaching nonchalantly for his beer. "Pleasure. Strictly pleasure. I always come to Vegas when I want to have some fun. I love it here. Always something going on. You know? Always some action."

She smiled. "I know what you mean. I'm here for some action, too." She stared at John as he sipped from the glass. "Are you staying at the casino?" she asked.

Suddenly a bell went off within the distant recesses of his mind. *Ohmahgawd* ... she wouldn't be ... I mean, she couldn't be ...

"*Uhh*, yeah," John said. "Yeah, I am. And you?"

She smiled, ran her long nails gently across his forearm, and looked up at him. "I could be ... if you're *really* looking for some fun."

Suddenly, the bell not only rang, it went hurdling from the tower. John flinched. "*Ohh*, gee. Yeah, well, I mean ... sure. Who isn't?"

Fun ... as in fifty dollars and a lifetime of herpes? Fun as in a hundred bucks and she throws in an autographed HIV test? This wasn't exactly John's idea of a good time. Not to mention the fact that, for his first ever, well, *paramour*, he had always pictured something, someone, a bit more ... *conventional*.

"I mean, no. I mean, not really. You see, I've got this business, *uhh*, engagement. In the morning. You know, early. In the morning. Tomorrow? So, you see, I really shouldn't, *uhh* ..."

The woman leaned forward, her ample breasts dangling invitingly, unrestrained, mere inches from John's nerve center. "Oh, *nooo*. You're not going to put business before pleasure, are you? Life is *so-o-o* short." She slid one hand, long-fingered and delicate, through his hair.

"*Ohh*, yeah. God. Yeah, that's saying a mouth ... I mean, yeah, you can say that again. But you know the old adage. All work and no ... I mean, no rest for the ..." He felt his hands begin to tremble and his arm sink back down to the bar where the glass clinked softly against the damp marble. Slowly he pushed himself backward until he slipped off the back of the stool. "Look, I mean, I really appreciate the offer and all. I really do. That's ... that's just ... swell of you. Really, it is. But I think, under the circumstances and all, well ..."

The woman raised her brows and pursed her lips into a tight, inviting pout, all the while her eyes never wavering.

"*So-o-o*," John said. "I guess I'll be, you know, turning in."

She smiled. "Well, that's too bad, John Aiello. Are you sure you don't want some company?"

"*Ohh*, gee. I mean, yeah, that would really be, you know, swell. But, I really can't. I've got this ... meeting ... in the morning ... you know? And—" he spread his arms out to his sides, looking for all the world like a Mallard coming in for a landing, and forced a loud yawn—"I'm really tired, as you can plainly see." As he spoke, he backed slowly away from her and, lowering his arms, said, "No, I'm just going to ... hit the old hay and get some shut-eye. You know. Just me. Alone. All night long. Asleep."

"Well, then, maybe we can get together tomorrow night ... if you don't have any more business meetings, and if you're not so tired."

Oh, my God! I told her I'm staying here at the casino. I told her my name! I'm dead fucking meat! Jesus Christ, what if she looks me up? What if she comes knocking on my door in the middle of the night, stoned out of her head on drugs or something ... or drunk as a sailor? Or what if her pimp gets mad at her and beats her up and she comes to my room looking for help? Or, Jesus Christ! What if she goes to my parents' *room by mistake!*

"Hi, my name is Marie, and I'm a hooker. Is John in? He's expecting me." *Oh, my God, that'd be it. That'd do it.*

"John what?"

"What?" John said.

"I said, John what? What's your last name?" the goddess asked, staring over the counter past his mug of steaming coffee and out across a big, inviting smile that reminded him of that other smile he'd seen so long ago, a smile that had him so terrified of its potential for disaster that it ruined his entire trip.

"Oh," he said, fear suddenly coursing through him like a thoroughbred trailing at the wire. "John ... *uhh* ... John ... John ..."

John John John? John John John? Oh, that's a great name! What fun. You are so-o-o smooth, John John John! Anything else you'd like to tell her? Like maybe where you're from from from? Maybe like Walla-Walla-Walla?

"John John John! That's so cute. And unusual. You must get kidded a lot."

"*Uhh*, no. I mean, not that much. Not really. Some. You know, with a name like John ... *uhh,* you know. Some, but not a lot." He shrugged, praying for divine intervention. "But some. You know."

She smiled, her lips opening to reveal those same jewel-like pearls that had first lured him to her. He wondered how anybody could actually chew anything with teeth that small.

"My name's Mary Lou," she said, holding out her hand. "Mary Lou Feeney."

John shook hands with her, amazed at how soft her skin was, how warm, how delicate her touch.

Feeney!

"You mean, Mary Lou *Feeney*? As in ... *Feeney*? I didn't know old-man Feeney had any kids. I didn't even know he was married! I mean ..."

She giggled. "I'm not his daughter. I'm his ... well, I guess his niece."

John raised his brows, his eyes washing over her ample assets, and then he took a deep breath. That was close. John couldn't begin to imagine what kind of a girl could spring forth from the loins of a fruit cup such as Old Man Feeney. He breathed out again. He should have known. No one that shapely, that gorgeous, that stacked could be the progeny of a loon. He was ashamed of himself even for thinking it. For thinking *lots* of things.

And, better yet, he thought, *she's no hooker, for Chrissake. She's just a nice, warm, friendly waitress looking for a nice, warm, friendly friend. Just because she's stacked doesn't mean she's a hooker, for God's sake.*

On the other hand, John thought, he hadn't seen it coming in Vegas, either. He hadn't been able to tell. At least not until she had come right out and practically propositioned him. Could it be the same thing here? With Mary Lou Feeney? Could Old Man Feeney's niece be a goddam whore in sheep's clothing? That would certainly fit. That would certainly explain her being so ... warm and friendly toward him all of a sudden.

He shook his head. *Jesus, Christ, John. Can you pick 'em, or what!*

"I just work here whenever I need a little ... extra money," she said.

"You work here for extra money."

"Yeah. You know, to help out with school and things like that. I'm in college. At the University of Minnesota. Home of the Golden Gophers?"

She took one step back and threw her arms out to one side. "Hit 'em high, hit 'em low, come on Gophers, go-go-go!"

At the end of the cheer, she thrust her boobs so far forward, he half expected them to explode.

"*Ohmahgawd*," he whispered.

She looked at him. "What?"

"Oh. Oh, nothing. I was just thinking about ... something. I mean some *things*. Some ... *one*."

She glanced at him mischievously and reached up to tug at her top still straining to pop free. "These things can be a pain in the ass sometimes. You know?" She winked.

Winked!

"How about you?"

"*Huh*?"

"I said, how about you? Do you live here? In Chicago?"

"*Ohh ...*" John John John's mind raced around for an answer. If she were a hooker, he wasn't about to share his life story with her. And run the risk of her come knocking on his door in the middle of the night. On the other hand, even if she was, he didn't want to come off looking like a complete idiot. "Oh, no. No. I'm from ... *uhh*, South Dakota. Yeah. That's right. I'm just here helping my uncle work his nets."

"Oh," she said. "Then your uncle lives here."

"*Huh*? Oh, no. No. None of us lives here. We're all from ... we all live somewhere else. Far away, I mean. All over. All over the place." He hoped that she was buying it.

"What do you do in South Dakota? Go to school?"

"Yeah. Yep. That's what I do all right ... go to school. There. In South Dakota. You know, far away."

"Oh. At the University?"

"Yeah, that's right. In Fargo."

"Oh." She smiled again before pausing, the smile fading from her face. "Wait a minute. Isn't Fargo in North Dakota?"

John stirred uneasily. "Oh, yeah. Of course. But, I, *uhh* ... commute."

"Oh, well, that's fine ..." She squinted at him, picked up a glass, and wiped it dry. "I guess."

"*So-o-o*," John said awkwardly. "What's your size? I mean *sign. Major*. I meant to say, what's your major? What are you studying? You know. In college. In Minnesota."

"Nothing, really. I mean, I haven't really made up my mind."

Nothing. She's studying at the University and doesn't have a major.

"You?" she asked.

He shifted on his stool. "Oh ... same."

Her lips turned up into an impish grin. "You're cute, you know that? And kinda shy. I like that in a guy."

Holy God, she thinks I'm cute. And shy. And me? I think ... I've done it once again.

"Just for that, I'm going to give you another cup of coffee, John John John. On the house. For being so adorable."

As she reached for the pot, John could picture his father opening the morning paper to the scream of the headline: "Local Boy Arrested for Solicitation!" It went on to read: "'I didn't know she was an undercover cop,' young pervert insists. 'I thought she was just a really nice hooker!'"

She filled his cup, and John John John jumped back sharply.

"Oh, I'm sorry!" she said. "Is that hot? I'm so clumsy. Here, let me get you ..."

"No, no, that's all right. Really. Besides, I've gotta go. I've just gotta ... help my uncle ... pull in that net. He's waiting for me. Right now. Right down ... over somewhere, *uhh* ... somewhere else. Thanks, anyway. Really."

"Well ..." the goddess looked confused. "Okay, but at least let me give you a go-cup."

Oh, my God. Did she say D-cup?

"It'll help keep you warm."

I'll buy that!

"Here," she said, filling up a plastic cup and handing it to him.

"*Ohh*. Oh, okay, thanks. Thanks a lot. Really. Sorry I've gotta run and all, but, well, you know."

"If you get cold later, come on back, John John John. It gets lonely in here sometimes. Especially when my uncle's off somewhere getting supplies."

Your uncle. Right. Sure.

"Yeah. Yeah, I'll do that. If I can. I'll definitely do that."

John slipped off the stool and slid out the door, failing to notice the sun breaking over the lake. He scurried back to the rocks where his uncle was waiting, watching, tugging at the net to see if he could feel any action of the Piscesian kind.

Jesus Christ, John! What the fuck is the matter with you? Two women in two years, and they're both fucking hookers? What the fuck is the matter with you? You have a sign on your back? Twenty bucks, No waiting! What the goddam fuck is the goddam matter with you?

John worked quickly, quietly, helping his uncle pull up the net before letting it slide back down into the frigid abyss after they'd removed the handful or two of fish they brought up, wriggling like crazy to get free—or, perhaps, warm. He wiped his hands and wrapped them around the go-cup, and he took a sip as he watched the fish swirling around inside a bucket.

"You were gone for quite a while," John's uncle said matter-of-factly. "Must have been one helluva pee."

Pee! Ohmawgahd. *I forgot to pee!*

John looked again at the wriggling fish and instinctively crossed one leg over the other.

"Say, how long do you think we'll be out here? I mean, the fishing seems a bit slow. Maybe we should ..."

His uncle waved him off. "*Nah*. It always starts out this way. Usually, they don't begin running until after the sun's been up an hour or two. So far it's been only—" he hesitated as he checked his watch—"ten minutes. Let's give it another couple hours, anyway."

A couple more hours! John knew he couldn't wait that long. He was straining now. A couple more hours and he'd explode!

"I thought maybe Old Man Feeney's niece come down to work in her uncle's shop. She does that sometimes in the fall. Likes to make a little money before the start of school, although I can't picture the old coot paying her enough to make it worth her while. The old tightwad."

John paused. "His niece?"

"Yeah." John's uncle pulled an orange from a sack he'd brought along with him and began carving into it with a small pocket knife. "Goes to school at the University of Minnesota or someplace like that. Straight-A student, I understand. You know, Dean's List and all that kinda crap. She's studying to be a doctor or a lawyer or something, I forget. Old Man Feeney near as talked my head off about her last time I come out. Saying how proud everyone in the family was of her. I can't see how anyone related to that old buzzard could be worth a damn, but people say she's pretty smart ... and quite a looker."

John's ears shot up. "Did you say *hooker*?"

"What? What are you talking about? I said she's studying to be a doctor or something."

John's mind raced. *A doctor. A woman who looks like that and a doctor, too?*

His uncle nodded. "Doctor or lawyer. I forget which." He popped a slice of orange into his mouth and held a piece out to John. John shook his head.

"You know what?"

His uncle craned his head and peered up at him. "What?"

"All this coffee I've been drinking, I'll be damned if I don't have to take another pee."

His uncle shook his head. "Kids. I swear, when I was your age, I didn't pee but once a ...."

"Yeah, well, I won't be long. Then we'll check the net again, huh? See if they're running."

John peered back over his shoulder. The sun had begun warming the early morning air. The wind had died down, too—as much as you could expect this time of year right off the lake. As he thought about his uncle's words, he felt his legs involuntarily pick up their pace. He felt, too, the sudden release he would know, felt the easing strain on his bladder as he pictured himself before the porcelain god, listening to the stream working its way up and down against the back wall of the urinal, down across the oversized mint in the bottom, up the side again. He quickened his pace some more, knowing that if he was lucky, he'd make it just in time. And then have that second cup of coffee.

He bounded up the steps to the shop, pausing just long enough to push his hands through his hair. He took one last look in the glass and reached for the knob. He had some heavy-duty peeing to do. And some pretty serious schmoozing, too. He couldn't believe he'd been so dumb. He couldn't believe he'd let his imagination run away with him like that. That whole Vegas thing, that whole episode.

What's past is past, he thought. *You've got to quit worrying about every little thing and get hold of your senses.*

John opened the door to the shop and glanced around for Old Man Feeney's niece, but she was nowhere in sight. Must be in back. He angled his way across the floor and stopped before the doorway leading to the men's room. *Just in time*, he thought as he grabbed for the knob.

Suddenly the door flew open, and standing before him was Old Man Feeney, himself. The old geezer took one long, squinting look at him, and John at him, at the broom in his hands, at the stubble on the old man's face and the queer look in his eyes.

"Excuse me," John said.

The old man's eyes exploded. "Excuse you? Excuse you? Ain't you the son-of-a-bitch what's been putting the make on my niece? Ain't you the good-for-nothing two-timing little bastard what's got the hots for my younger brother's daughter, Sweet Mary Lou?"

John shook his head. "I ..."

The old man suddenly threw the broom into the air, swinging it around him like a palace guard wielding a scimitar.

"Go on, don't lie to me, you Goddam little punk! Why, I'll teach you to go creatin' trouble around here. I'll teach you to go bothering innocent young girls when all they want is a little peace and quiet. Go on, now, Mister Punk! Go on, now, and get your skinny ass the hell outa my place. *Now!* Before I do something I'm gonna regret. Like call shove this broom up your scrawny little ass!"

"Hey!" John cried as the broom caught him flush on the hip. Another blow struck him on the arm, and a third missed his head by inches.

"Jesus Christ, are you nuts?"

"Go on, I'll show you who's nuts and who's not. Git the hell outa here, now. Git the hell outa my shop, before I really lose my temper!"

John grabbed the door knob and rushed over the threshold just as he felt the old man's boot skim his ass. As he emerged in the sunlight, the door slammed shut so hard, one of the panes of glass shattered.

"*Somabitch*! Goddam little sneak! You keep your dirty little ass away from my Sweet Mary Lou, you hear? You keep clear of my niece, you know what's good for you!"

John glanced back inside the shop where Old Man Feeney was still swinging the broom around his head like a lariat and shouting at no one in particular.

"The guy's a loon," he said softly. For a moment, he couldn't believe what had just happened. He couldn't believe the old man had mistaken him for someone else. He couldn't believe ... Shit! He couldn't believe he'd ever see Mary Lou Feeney again.

Shit! Double shit! And she's gonna be a doctor!

John took one last look over his shoulder as he walked down the steps to the pavement, and then he stopped to look out over the lake. The waves were rolling in gently, now, their early morning thunder all but quashed. They lapped lightly at the shore, sheeting up and over the rocks and moving the sand and small pebbles first in and then out, again, as they receded back into the lake, only to be replaced by a new ebb and flow.

"Feel better, now?" John's uncle asked when his nephew arrived. John could only nod his head and stare blankly out at the waves. His uncle squinted up at him. "Say, what's the matter? Something wrong?"

John shook his head and scowled. "*Ahh*, it's just that I've still gotta pee."

"You just went, for God's sake!"

"No. I forgot."

"Forgot? How could you forget? I thought that's what you ..."

"Well, you know, I got me another cup of coffee, and the next thing you know, I'm heading back out here. Just slipped my mind."

"Well, you couldn't have had to go very ..." He stopped, grinned, and craned his head. "Say, is Old Man Feeney's niece working here today? Is she back in town?"

I shrugged.

"*Uh-huh*. I thought so. I figured there was something a little strange going on from the look on your face the first time you got back. So, go on, tell me. Is she ..."

He stopped mid-sentence, his eyes bulging, his mouth opened wider than the fish we'd caught that morning. I turned to see what he was staring at and suddenly understood why.

"Hi!" she called, lifting up her hand with a white paper bag glued to her fingertips. "I brought you something."

I felt myself smile instinctively. She was even more radiant, her skin more translucent in daylight. Her hair shone like the fjords in Norway in mid-summer. She oozed life.

As she approached, she lowered the bag to her waist and opened it, pulling a go-cup of coffee from inside. And a couple containers of cream and a pack of sugar. "I'm not sure how you take it, so I brought you some of this, too."

"Wow," I said, instinctively regretting that she hadn't dragged along a port-a-potty, too. "That's really ... you know. Terrific. Very thoughtful."

I introduced her to my uncle, who knew enough to grunt and busy himself rummaging through his fishing gear so we could have some privacy. I guessed that was the reason, anyhow.

"I just wanted to apologize for the way my uncle treated you earlier. I don't know what's gotten into him lately."

"He was a little, *umm*, terse. She laughed; I smiled. "I thought for a minute or two that he just hated fishermen."

She shook her head. "No, he's been like that for a while. Ever since he got this notion in his head that someone has been embezzling funds from him."

Embezzling? From where, the cash register? How much business does he do in that shop, anyway, twenty, thirty dollars a day? How much could anyone embezzle?

"That's good to know. I mean, not about the embezzling. I mean, for a while, I thought he had a special gripe against me. Even though I'd never met him before. I guess we just sort of got off on the wrong foot."

"Well, that's another thing I wanted to tell you."

"What's that?"

"How much I enjoyed having you stop by. Meeting you. Getting to know a little about you, John John John."

"You know that's not my real name."

She laughed, loud and raspy, a smoker's laugh. Deep and mysterious and sexy as hell. "I sorta guessed." She reached into her jacket pocket and pulled out a pack of cigarettes, holding one out to me. I waved it off and watched as she took it out and placed the business end between those two ethereal lips. What I wouldn't have given for a shot at them!

"Here," I said, fumbling through my own pants pocket before pulling out a Zippo. "Let me ..."

She leaned forward—her stunning architecture evident even beneath forty pounds of compacted goose feathers—breathed in once, twice before exhaling. Slowly, the smoke rose in a thin, steady plume into the sky. She raised her head slightly and closed her eyes as if in the midst of an orgasm.

"I'm going to quit one of these days," she said. "Maybe when I get back home. You know, for school."

I nodded. "Good idea. That can't be doing you any good."

"That's another reason I stopped by."

"What's that?"

"Just to see if maybe you wanted to ride with me to the train station. I have a ticket for the 10:35 to Minneapolis."

"Oh, wow," I said, glancing at my watch and then looking over at my uncle, trying not to look over at us. At least not so that we'd notice.

"I ... I'd love to. Really. But I'm here with my uncle. You know. Maybe I could take a rain check. You know? Maybe next time you come to town, we can get together for lunch or dinner or something, and then I can drive you to the station when you have to return home."

She looked down. Her eyes rubbed against the jagged rocks beneath our feet. "That's just it. I don't think I'll be coming back."

I took the empty sack from her, crinkled it up, and stuffed it into my pocket. "What do you mean? Why not? I thought you liked working here during the summers. You know, to get extra money for school and all."

"I guess ... Well, I just don't think I'll be coming back, that's all. But it would be great to have someone to talk to on the ride to the station, instead of looking at the back of some cab driver's head the entire way. I could use someone to talk to. I just hate the thought of driving all that way alone."

The offer was tempting, I had to admit. But I couldn't see how I'd explain it to my uncle. We'd come out there together to fish, not to chase women. Besides, I figured the only *real* reason she wanted me along was to pick up the fare once we got to the station. After seeing the bait shop and her uncle and all, it was a cinch that, if she wasn't dead-ass broke, she was close to it. That's why it just didn't make sense for her to up and quit like that. It just didn't make any sense at all.

And then she played her ace. Stepping closer to me, she unzipped my coat, pulled open hers, and pressed her body against mine. She put the cigarette to her mouth, inhaled, and held the smoke in as she opened her lips enough to throw them across mine. I heard my uncle cough involuntarily as we probed one another with our tongues before I felt a sudden warm surge sweep over me. And a sudden urge to cough, which I did, as smoke lunged out from between my lips.

"It's called French smoking," she whispered, "and it's the most intimate thing a woman can do to a man." She paused before whispering again, "Practically."

I breathed out in shock. "Wow."

She looked down at my pants, at the obvious bulge, peeked over to where my uncle was pretending not to be pretending not to see us, and looked back up into my eyes. "Yeah, wow." She stepped back enough so she could run her hands up the lapels of my shirt, stop at the collar, and slowly wrap both arms around my neck. "Did I tell you I have a train ticket for Minneapolis?"

I tried to say something, but the words never came out. I nodded.

"Well," she said, leaning in to kiss me again, long and lingering this time, before breaking away. "I lied. I have two."

Two? Two tickets all the way to Minneapolis?

Well, it was the most difficult thing I'd ever done in my life, I'll tell you that—even tougher than walking away from that hooker in Vegas—but I clasped her hand and squeezed it gently as I gave her a kiss on the cheek. Not to be anticlimactic, but I simply wasn't sure my lips could survive another round. And, as she walked up the embankment to the parking lot and the cab stand just a few dozen yards beyond, I stared after her, half expecting her to turn around and wave or motion for me to follow or give me the finger or something. *Anything.*

But she didn't. She just walked on. And I stood there, watching. And wondering. Until my uncle came up beside me. He hesitated before clearing his throat, and I finally turned to face him.

"Did you see that?" I asked.

"See what?"

I turned back toward where I had seen her last, seen the apparition slowly fade into the early morning mist clearing itself from the lake, seen her disappear from my life probably forever.

"Nothing," I said. "Nothing, really."

That evening, while I stood fanning the coals in my grill, trying to keep the hotdogs and buns from scorching, the phone rang. I pushed the food off to one side and closed the lid before answering.

"Did you hear the news?"

It was my uncle, sounding more excited than I'd heard since we'd stumbled across a mob hit at a small lagoon years earlier. "No," I said. What news?"

"It's all over the television and radio and everywhere. Old Man Feeney."

"Yeah, what about him? He become a born-again Christian or something?"

"Worse. He was killed earlier today. Cut right in two with a meat cleaver. Right down the center of the skull."

"*What?*"

"Honest to God. The police said his place was locked up until one p.m. or something like that, and they got a couple complaints from a few of the fishermen wanting to know what was up. I guess not long after we left. That's when they went down to investigate and found the place all closed and locked. They forced their way in and found him on the floor behind the counter in a pool of blood, dead as a doornail."

"*Wow*. I can't believe it. And I saw him only this morning."

"Say, that's right. You were down there a couple of times, weren't you? And you saw him, and he was alive and well."

"Absolutely. Too much so. He threatened to kick my ass out of there if I didn't leave his ..." I stopped short.

"Kid? Kid?" My uncle's voice rang hollow on the line. "You still there?"

"Yeah, yeah, I'm still here. Just a little in shock, that's all. Yeah, I saw him this morning. For a couple of minutes. He must have locked the place up right after I left. Someone must have broken in."

"Wow, amazing. Alive one minute and dead as a doornail the next."

"Did they say anything about who might have killed him?"

"What I heard, they haven't got a clue. All they know is that the cash-register drawer was open, and all the money from inside was gone."

I stopped again. Frozen for all time. And when I heard my uncle's voice on the line again, I snapped out of my stupor.

"Yeah," I said. "Yeah, Unc. Thanks for calling. Thanks for telling me. It's pretty remarkable. Yeah. But I've gotta go. I've got dinner on the grill, and I'd better get back to it before it's burned to a crisp."

After I hung up, I thought about the grill and I thought about Old Man Feeney and what he had said to me before he kicked me out of his place. And how I didn't quite understand what had gotten him so riled up all of a sudden.

And I thought, too, about Old Man Feeney's niece, and how she went out of her way to bring me a cup of coffee afterwards, just before heading back ..."

I rubbed my chin, my eyes glancing around the apartment on their quest for the Holy Grail. And, when they failed to find it, I felt my feet begin to move. Slowly. Ever so slowly. Toward the front hallway. The entranceway. Toward the clothes tree on which I usually hang my coats and sweaters and things such as that when I come in from the cold.

I grabbed the coat I had worn that morning and reached inside one pocket. I came up empty. I reached into the opposite one, my fingers instantly brushing something and grasping it. And when I pulled it out, I was clutching a crinkled-up white-paper bag. When I unwadded it and took a closer look, I saw it.

I saw Old Man Feeney's niece's blood-red lipstick along the top edge of the sack where she must have accidentally gotten some when she placed my coffee and creamer and sugar inside.

Except that, as I recalled both times I had seen her, she wasn't wearing blood-red lipstick. In fact, she wasn't wearing any lipstick at all.

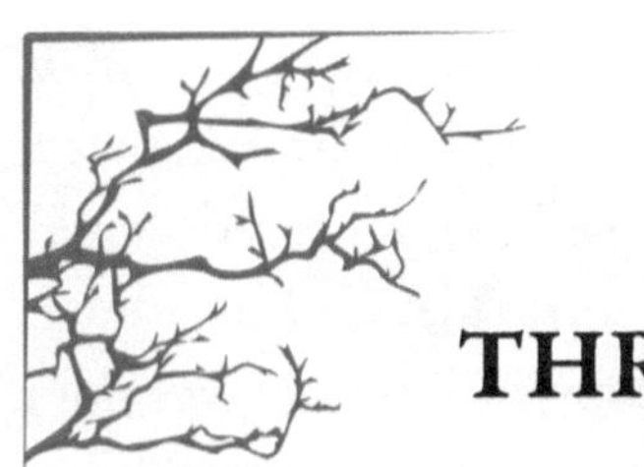

THREE: Greatness

THEY ALWAYS CALLED my grandfather a great man. But I knew better. There is something about great men that they cannot hide and something about un-great men that they could never feign.

But they persisted with their tales of greatness. So, what's a young boy to do?

It's important, I realize now, for a kid growing up into manhood on the Great South Side of Chicago to think of his grandfather as a noble fellow—or at least not as a schmuck. Your father can be an idiot; your mother can be a loon. That doesn't matter. You have to love them, anyway. It's in the rules. But a grandfather? Well, he pretty much has to earn your respect, deserve your admiration. And for that, I had to give the old boy credit. He worked hard at it. But *great*?

He was not big and hulking like the great men I knew from my Saturday morning marathons in front of the TV. I would curl up at one end of a tattered and smoke-scarred sofa and gaze in awe at the truly great men I saw there. The greatest of the great, of course, was *Cochise, Apache Chieftain* or something like that. He was the purveyor of all that is good and noble in the blood of men, especially *Red Men*. He was portrayed by an actor named Michael Ansara, who later married *I Dream of Jeannie's* Barbara Eden. *Damn*, you wanna talk about greatness? I rest my case.

How it is that for years I watched this truly great man grow in greatness as an Indian warrior and never once stopped to question why such greatness failed to aid the Native Americans in their plight against the greedy paleface is beyond me. I mean, if Cochise had been even *half* the man he was portrayed to be on film, the entire state of Nebraska and half of Oklahoma would still be owned by the Apaches today. *Minimum*. But then again, young stumps of boys rooted to the sofa before the glowing embers of the tube are not supposed to question the validity of such mini-screened heroes. So, true to form, I let it pass.

Perhaps that's how I came to know that my grandfather was not a great man. He had neither the huge, barrel chest of Cochise nor the indomitable will or unflagging courage. He wasn't as tall, either (a sure giveaway), although I never realized it as a young boy but only when I grew older and saw him towered over in snapshots by my father, who stands 5 feet 7.

My grandfather's face was sharp; his cheeks, pouches filled with angles that sank into deep, blue-black eyes. In his mouth were teeth—some cracked, the rest still cracking—that always seemed to smile even when his lips were sober.

There goes Jim Blasdell, the neighbors would say as his wagon rolled slowly down the street, milk bottles jingling. And I wondered if they were saying, too, *There goes a great man*. That, too, was a dead giveaway of my grandfather's overall lack of greatness in my own eyes. I mean, can you imagine a television show named *Mighty Cochise—Apache Milkman*.

I *did* regret never having gotten to ride with Jim Blasdell as he made his appointed rounds. Perhaps because it was rumored that his house stops were sometimes something *more* than mere house stops, if you know what I mean. I'm not really sure, never having heard the rumors until years after he'd expired, which is how my grandmother always phrased it when somebody croaked. Needless to say, a five-year-old boy could not expect to sit on the wagon for hours on end while his grandfather "made the rounds." And inviting the boy in wouldn't do at all. So, I simply never did get asked to go along; and maybe that, too, contributed to my understanding of the distinction between the great and the not so great.

To make matters worse, Jim Blasdell was not what one would call a successful businessman. After just a couple of years of working for himself, he sold his horse and wagon, his bottles and his business, and settled into a sort of quasi-retirement, all of this by the age of 45. It wasn't that there couldn't be money made from the milk business in those days right on the heels of World War II. And it certainly wasn't that being in business for oneself lacked prestige, dignity, and honor. Quite the contrary. More often I think it was simply that Jim Blasdell grew tired of the work, of *all* work, and decided to settle into a position more closely aligned to the lifestyle he'd etched out for himself in his head.

I was at my grandparents' home the day he consummated the deal to sell the business. I sat with my grandmother at the kitchen table, off to one side of the house, rolling dice and marking points in a Bohemian game of *Bunko*, while Jim Blasdell and Mr. Cabot talked finances in the parlor. I enjoyed playing *Bunko* with my grandmother. She was a slight, smiling woman with eyes like great blue plums that always shone with the gleam of the sun, inside or out. Every throw of the dice she filled with exuberant energy, so that one would suspect she was rolling at Monte Carlo to break the bank or very possibly the house, itself, instead of at 4531 South Hoyne Avenue to gain the love of a five-year-old boy ... and perhaps cookies and a glass of milk later.

But in the parlor! There lay my secret-most thoughts. I envisioned Jim Blasdell, primly attired in a natty gray pinstripe over a starched white shirt with a collar that jutted out nearly at right angles to his chin. He sat stiffly, nervously, enfolded in a massive, pink-cushioned easy chair with white lace doilies stretched meticulously over each padded arm. Across from him, Mr. Cabot, a portly, balding cherub with waxy cheeks slung out from his face and sagging far beneath his chin, tottered precariously on a thin-legged, straight-backed chair brought from the kitchen at his own request, all so that he might appear to the casual observer to be slimmer by far than he actually was.

From time to time, such words as *equity* and *district*, *down payment* and *balance forward* exploded from the visitor's lips and rattled through the house, settling finally on my naive ears. I was proud of my grandfather, for he was about to make a great deal of money. More money than anyone else in our family had ever made in a single day before—or even in a year. But I was sad, too, because it meant saying goodbye to Chestnut, the only real, live horse I'd ever known. I had hoped one day that my grandfather would will him to me, knowing of my love for such things. Though, in thinking back, it's hard to imagine sharing a three-room, third-floor walkup with a fully grown mare.

After what seemed an eternity, I heard the voices in the parlor rise in intensity and move to the hallway leading to the front door where they paused, lowered, rose again, and then they broke into several short, staccato bursts of laughter. Finally, there was silence. A few moments more brought Jim Blasdell, grinning like the little child he was at heart, to the kitchen door.

"Jim, did he ... did he buy the business?" Anna Blasdell clutched the dice tightly between her two palms as Jim walked slowly toward us.

"He bought the business," he said. "He bought the business. For eight thousand dollars, *he bought the business!* He put it in my very palm. Here it is, he says to me. I'm a busy man. I'm not going to quibble about trifles. And he pays me for it, lock, stock, and barrel!"

"Eight thousand ..." Her hands dropped suddenly to the table, the dice skittering across the floor. "Eight thousand dollars! All that money!"

"And there's more. He wants to pay me another thousand if I'll stay on with him the first month, show him the route, introduce him to my customers."

"Another thousand. That's *nine thousand dollars*! Oh, Jim!" she cried leaping to her feet and grabbing him, tears skating down her cheeks, settling on the back of his gray pinstripe. "It's so much money. Think of all the things we can do ... Oh, God bless us," she sobbed, yanking me up suddenly and flinging her arms around me. "Oh, God bless us all, sweet, merciful Jesus!"

Then Jim Blasdell grabbed hold of me, kissed me openly with those rotten/rotting teeth, and threw me so high in the air I nearly banged my head off the chandelier. He caught me and squeezed me and mussed my hair, and I laughed at him laughing like I'd never seen him laugh before.

"Quick, Jim. Let me see the money. Let me see what it's like to hold all that money in my hands at one time."

Jim Blasdell looked at her sheepishly before lowering me to the ground. "Well, I don't have the ... money exactly. Not here." He held out a gray slip of paper, grayer than his suit. "It's a check. For eight thousand dollars. His own personal check from his own personal bank. The First National Drover's Savings and Loan."

My grandmother's eyes stopped leaking, and her face turned white. "A check?"

"Certainly, a check. It's every bit as good as money. It *is* money. All we have to do is go down to the bank in the morning and hand them this, and they'll give us eight thousand dollars. It's as simple as that. You don't think a wealthy man like George Cabot is going to carry around eight thousand dollars in cash, do you? Why, he'd just be *asking* for trouble. With all the crime there is today, thieves and robbers on every street corner. He'd be insane."

"But, couldn't he have given you at least *some* of the money in cash so we could see it?"

"Anna, listen to me. That's the way big businessmen operate. Here, where it says certified and insured, see? He explained it to me. That means the bank guarantees the money to us anytime we decide to go get it. You just don't understand big business, that's all. You'll see. We'll take the streetcar to the bank first thing in the morning and cash it in. You'll see."

The next morning, Anna and Jim Blasdell slipped their check for eight thousand dollars through the slot in front of Teller Number 7. The man on the other side of the bars squinted at the paper, first front, and then back, squinted at Anna and Jim Blasdell, and then he rang for the vice-president.

Mr. Carpenter, neatly attired in a dark blue suit with darker blue veins dissecting it, squinted at the check, squinted at Anna and Jim Blasdell, and then, apparently satisfied, he opened the gate to his office and directed them to come inside.

It took some while for the words to strike home. Yes, he was positive. The check wasn't theirs. No, George Cabot never owned an account at the Drover's. It was all one gigantic hoax, a counterfeit check printed on poor stock and bearing a bogus signature. Furthermore, the police would have to be called in and an official report filed with the State. It was not right for a man like Mr. Cabot to go about, passing bogus checks on the Drover's. It could only hurt the Drover's reputation. Furthermore, it was illegal.

I did not see my grandmother and grandfather as often as I had before. My parents moved us from our third-story walkup to a brand new frame house in the suburbs. But I pieced together in my mind tiny bits of information from conversations around, above, and behind me—as young boys often do—and came to know that Jim Blasdell had taken a job as a custodian at the Gage Park Fieldhouse. What it was exactly that a custodian at the Gage Park Fieldhouse did was beyond me. But, sometimes, when we'd visit my grandparents' apartment, Anna Blasdell would pull from the bureau drawer a huge ring laden with dozens of keys of all shapes, sizes, colors—hundreds or even *thousands* of them—and I'd amuse myself for hours by pretending to fit them to the locks around the house. I imagined that only a great man would have possession of so many keys to unlock so many locks to reveal so many hidden secrets, and that *I* was that man.

On one visit, I found myself alone with Jim Blasdell, a rare occurrence, when my mother and grandmother and aunt went shopping for draperies or some such thing on South Halsted Street, where, I was told, could be found some of the best buys in town.

Before leaving, my grandmother turned to my grandfather and, wagging a stern finger in his face, admonished him: "Now, Jim. Don't you take this child to the bar!" At which Jim Blasdell, feigning mortal injury at such an accusation, retorted, "Oh, *no-o-o*, Ann."

After they'd gone, he asked me if I wanted to play checkers. I told him I didn't know how.

"Sticks?"

I shrugged.

"Well, then, what? Would you like to watch TV?"

I just couldn't get into it.

And then his eyes lit up as he asked, "Where's your coat?"

I pointed to the bedroom, and in two minutes flat, I found myself bundled up, down the stairs, out the door, and tracing Jim Blasdell's footprints down the street. I don't know how far we walked, exactly, not too far, until we turned into a dark building where the smell of sour air and thick smoke and noise—I could actually *smell* the noise, it was so heavy—swept over me, like the stale water from some diseased and dying lake, swept over me and threatened to pull me under. My grandfather hoisted me up onto a stool and took a seat next to me.

"Now, you just sit here, and Pete will bring you a soda."

My grandfather gulped some amber-colored liquid from a glass, said something to the bartender, and squirmed his way off the stool and past a roomful of people while I looked after him.

"Here you are, son," a man with a green shirt and a complexion to match told me as he set a glass of cola before me. "So, what's your name?"

The man wore thick glasses with wire frames, squinting to see. Someone nearby exhaled suddenly, and a plume of white smoke washed over us. "Davey," I coughed.

"Davey. Oh, you must be Jim's grandson." He held out his hand, and I took it, and I quickly let it go. "Nice to meet you, Davey. Just drink up, and if you want another, you just let me know. Nothing's too good for old Jim Blasdell's grandson!"

Someone shouted out to him, and Pete disappeared somewhere behind a wall of bobbing heads and clinking glasses, thick choking cigars and slender gagging cigarettes. I sipped from my glass, watching the lights that shone alternately red and green in the alcove above the bar. The sudden strong smell of whiskey settled over me, from the bar or from one of the men standing behind me, I didn't know. But it made me realize just how alone I was, how alone and small ... and *frightened*.

Somebody laid a nickel in a metal slot, and the room burst to life, the rat-a-tat-tat of a great mechanical monster piercing the stale air. It was terrifying, with its vibrating lights and innards, with bubbles that seemed to rise from nowhere to snake their way up inside a large hollow tube, all lighted in a swirl of gaudy colors. Yet, I couldn't draw my eyes from it, from the flicker of the lights, from the dancing figures along each side of a giant headpiece pushed up tightly against the wall. Another whiff of whiskey, stronger than the first, a drunken elbow to the side of my head, more rat-a-tat-tat, the monster belching out, beckoning me closer, to walk up to it, touch it ... so that it could grab me, suck me swiftly into its screaming bowels, and spit me out, again ... a million tiny shards of shattered glass.

From the back room, where my grandfather had disappeared, came the sound of more music, faster and more inviting than the first. Dancing music, hauntingly disguised by the din of a thousand laughing voices, yet unmistakable. Another hit to the head, the other side this time, and a huge man with glassy rolling eyes draped himself over me, spilling ice in my lap, and cried out for another drink.

I quickly slid down from the stool, determined to find my grandfather, and struggled toward the back room, slipping through narrow openings in the human wall of flesh before me, weaving in and out as Jim Blasdell had done before he had disappeared.

"*The fuck you did!*" someone cried out, and a handful of people laughed as I wormed my way along, determined to escape to ... to *where*? Past person after person, past one man pressing his hand hard up against a woman's breast. Her hair was bright copper, and two gold teeth glistened in her mouth. The man buried his head against her thick, sweaty neck as she fumbled with his private parts through his neatly creased and permanently stained pants.

"He ain't no good for you, for God's sake," the man's voice cried out, coal black eyes staring down at me.

"I ain't never felt no little boy's cock before," Gold Teeth gloated, grabbing for my arm. "Hey, kid, come on over here a minute, why don-sha?"

But I was gone, past ever more bodies shoving me forward and back. Tears welled in my eyes, and I fought hard, shoving my way through, to hold them back. It wouldn't do to have Jim Blasdell think I'd been crying. It wouldn't do at all to have my grandfather think I'd been afraid.

I pushed with all my might against someone from behind and finally burst past him, through the archway leading to the back room, where I saw, against the back wall, another blue-and-red glass box pouring its musical heart out. To one side of the monster learned two silver spikes, crossed with brown leather straps—the kind of chrome and wood and leather you see on the March of Dimes posters only larger, their soft mahogany bindings leaping and jumping with each beat of the box. Three chairs to the right of the spikes sat Jim Blasdell.

"Grandpa!" I shouted, the word instantly gobbled up and lost to the wind. I stopped. Jim Blasdell had his legs wrapped around a beautiful, young woman, perhaps 22 or 24, maybe a little older, with long, golden, silky hair. All around them men and women were dancing, stumbling, sitting, leaning, laughing, propping themselves up against the tables, the chairs, each other.

The Poster Girl beneath Jim Blasdell opened her mouth, and I imagined that I heard her moan—a long, low, throaty sound. Her head fell back, revealing the most beautiful face I had ever seen. Full, wet lips pursed together before parting ... all the while those deep, guttural groans rising from her throat, rising up and disappearing into the night, rising from her very soul, as her eyelids opened and closed to the sound of the music.

Jim Blasdell pulled himself up upon her suddenly, covering her face with his own. The chair tipped forward, and the two slumped to the floor in a single loud *thump*. A giant hand grabbed the flesh of one thigh, kneading its way higher and higher, until it paused at the very entrance to nirvana before retreating slowly, ever so slowly, a pair of silken white panties clasped firmly in its talons.

"Oh, my God, Jim," she cried. "Oh, my God, give it to me. *Give* it to me ... *hard*." She grabbed for his crotch, the way that Gold Teeth had done with me, all the while her skirt rising higher, the deep, guttural sounds snaking their way from her ivory throat. "Oh, my God, shoot me your load. Give it to me right here, Jim. *Give it to me* now!"

Jim Blasdell died in abject poverty on the day following my sixth birthday. I had seen him five, maybe six times in all the years that had passed. I could have seen him more, but I would make excuses to avoid him.

Not that I didn't love my grandfather. Not at all. In fact, I loved him dearly, his wit, his tact, has coyness when it suited him, his gruffness when it didn't. Still, each time that I saw him, I smelled the foul smell of whiskey, heard the laughter, felt the terror in my heart. Whether real or imaginary, it didn't matter. It was there. And it made me want to cry.

He died finally of cancer, complicated by pneumonia. Or maybe it was the other way around, I'm not sure. But even though I couldn't bring myself to forget that horrifying day at the bar, I couldn't bring myself to hate him, either.

Perhaps it was his suffering that made people recall him as a great man—those last few months were agonizingly painful. Or perhaps to them he really *was* a great man. He would give a person the shirt off his back or his last five dollars if it would endear him to somebody's heart. He needed love just that badly. No, not needed ... *craved!* Not simply the love of a faithful wife but of everyone. In that way, I suppose, I'm just a little like him. But that is another story, and it will keep.

In the year of my 21st birthday, I left home for good in order to pursue a career in journalism. I went to school days and spent most of my evenings covering city council sessions, school-board meetings, and other crap that everyone, particularly my editor, told me would help turn me into a bona fide reporter. It wasn't very glamorous, but it wasn't bad, either, as my work often ended before ten, giving me a chance to write my story, slip it under the *Journal's* door on my way home, and still catch a couple hours for myself.

One Friday night I covered a particularly interesting school-board meeting in the 17th District. It was interesting because of this fantastically attractive woman seated next to the speaker's podium on stage. After the meeting, I worked particularly hard at getting an interview with her, which I did, purely in the line of duty. Still, some types of duty, not coincidentally, turn out to be more pleasurable than others, and so, it happens, did this.

We adjourned to a nearby pub, where I discovered her name was Christina Faulkner. She was a bit older than I, unmarried, with no children and a 38-inch chest. The latter I discovered for myself at her apartment later that evening. We were alone and had grown very well acquainted with one another over our mutual admiration for Hemingway and gin.

"David," she purred, sinking softly into the plush foam of the sofa, "I think it's time we ... laid our cards on the table."

"Okay," I said. "I like cards. What did you have in mind?"

She pulled herself forward and very slowly began unbuttoning her blouse, interrupted momentarily by a long, languid kiss, her silvery tongue darting in and out of my mouth. "I don't want you to think I'm a sex-crazed woman," she said, reaching behind to unsnap her halter, "but I knew before our first drink that I'd just *have* to have you."

"What a coincidence," I said as I helped her out of her bra. "I was thinking the very same thing."

She folded her hands across her chest as the garment fell to the floor and turned away from me as I settled back against the cushion. It wouldn't do to appear too anxious. After all, she was a woman of the world, traveled, refined ... and I was twenty-one and in my prime but still willing to take my time, to let things develop slowly, to show the tender, sensitive, *feminine* side of my nature. My eyes followed hers. Her eyes devoured mine. She wriggled her way closer to me, kissed me lightly on the lips, and looked deeply into my soul. I could see the delicacy in her, feel the hesitation she felt in the situation. I could respect that. I would take my time and be certain to move gently over her body, softly, caringly, stopping to kiss her on the lips and whisper sweet something into her ear. I would ...

Suddenly, she dropped her arms to her sides.

"*Ohmahgawd*!" I said softly before hurling myself savagely against her, my mouth ravaging first one cherry-red nipple and then its animated twin. "*Ohmahgawd*, you're ... *fantastic*!"

I pushed forward again, my lips raging, realizing that it had been so very long since I'd known a woman in the biblical sense. As in *never!* I pulled my head back, took in the beauty of her heaving bosom, looked up at her face—angelic and wanton at the same time, flushed and fired with heat, her breath coming in short, quick pants—and then fell forward on her again when she let out a groan, slipped off the sofa, and while I clung to her tits, we fell over backwards onto the floor with a *thump*.

"Oh, my God!" she cried. "Oh, yes. Oh, my God, don't stop. David, don't stop!"

Well, I know the value of being compliant, but I also know the value of breathing; so, I *did* stop—long enough to rip off my shirt and wiggle out of my pants and down to my shorts, ready for Round Two. Before I could mount my next offensive, she struggled to her feet, removed the last of her clothes, and took me by the hands. "Let's go to bed."

My kind of woman, I thought, saying instead, "I'm ready."

She smiled at the bulge in my boxers. "So I see."

She led me up the stairs to the second floor, her ass wiggling seductively, her long thighs and soft scent guiding my every step. I sank deep into the satiny coolness of the bed and watched in the mirror as she fondled first one mammoth breast and then the other. Her head rolled back, and her long, golden hair hung nearly to her waist. She smiled an open-mouthed smile, all the while her tongue flitting in impatient little circles, a deep, throaty, gurgling sound spilling from her lips.

My mind flashed. Gurgling sounds. Long, light swirls of golden-blonde hair. Another flash, like the flickering cries of some cavernous monster.

"You're so deep in thought," she said, crossing the floor and climbing into bed next to me. Her breasts swung seductively as she leaned forward to kiss me. "I hope it's something good."

I sat upright and looked down at her legs. "You're ... *limping*."

She flushed suddenly, as though I'd unlocked some magic Pandora's Box in the very ill-timed ignorance of youth. "Most people don't notice."

"It's my job," I replied in my best, most casual journalese. I hoped I hadn't offended her. *Prayed* I hadn't offended her.

"It's just a little stiffness. It'll go away. Whenever the weather turns suddenly, my left leg gives me a little trouble."

"Kind of like arthritis or something?"

"I'm not *that* old," she quipped, poking me in the ribs. "No, it's from my childhood. A type of paralysis I had as a kid. In fact, I might have been confined to a wheelchair for life if it hadn't been for a friend helping me out. He gave me the money I needed for an operation and corrective braces."

"Nice friend."

"Well, actually, he was more than a friend. If you know what I mean."

I thought I knew what she meant. "And is he still ... *more* than a friend?"

She shook her head. "He died several years ago. Besides," she said, smiling faintly, "he was married."

My mind whirred. The music box, the long, golden hair, the Poster-Girl braces leering out at me from the dark. Could it be? All the while the steady rat-a-tat-tat crying out louder, calling me closer.

Can it possibly be? Was there any conceivable way?

"David? What's the matter?"

"It *can't* be," I said, the words slipping out past unwilling lips. My heart beat wildly as I leaped up from the bed and quickly slipped back into my shorts. Christina's full, wet lips parted questioningly. Her eyes peered deep into my soul. Could I find the strength to ask her? It all fit. It *had* to be. It *had* to. Yet, it *couldn't* be. "Oh, my God."

"What is it? What's the matter?"

"It's just ... something ... I was thinking of asking you."

"What?"

"How old are you?"

She laughed. "How old am ... are you *kidding*? Why?"

"Please. It's important."

Her face faded to chalk. "My age is that important?"

"Please."

She hesitated before reaching for a cigarette, slipping it between two provocative lips, and setting it off. "Okay, then, how old do I look?"

I felt myself blush. "Sorry."

She paused, shaking her head. "No, I mean, it's okay. A little weird, but okay." She hesitated before adding, "Let's just say I'm old enough to be your ... older sister."

"And your mother? What's her name?"

She paused, furrowing her brow. "Susan. Faulkner. Why?"

"Did she have ... did she wear braces, too?"

"Yes. She had polio as a child and never quite grew out of it. Medicine wasn't as far advanced back then as it is today. Why? Why do you ask? Did you know her?"

I felt my palms growing clammy. "I think ... I saw her a time or two."

"Oh? That must have been a long time ago. You must have been just a child."

I nodded. "And this ... former lover ... the one who paid for your operation ..."

Her nose crinkled up, and she let out a sudden laugh. "He wasn't *my* lover, silly. He was my mother's."

"Your mother's ..."

"Mom passed when I was six, and I went to live with my aunt. She was a spinster who never had any children, so she raised me like her own daughter. Jim used to stop by occasionally to visit."

"Jim?"

"*Uh-huh.* That was my mom's friend's name. He always brought us something whenever he stopped by. Candy usually. Occasionally flowers or some little trinkets he picked up somewhere along the way. And then, one day, he said he had come into some money and wanted to hire a doctor to operate on my legs. And that's what he did. I went in to Mercy Hospital for an operation, and after that, I was fitted for crutches for six months. I'll never forget when I could walk for the first time on my own. Without limping. Without falling."

"What was Jim's last name? Do you remember?"

"Of course I do. He was like a father to me. The only one I ever knew. Jim Blasdell."

My eyes popped open.

"Oh, come on. You mean you knew *him*, too? How? Where?"

I sighed. "Chicago, remember? The great South Side? Everyone knows everybody on the great South Side."

She laughed. "I guess so. Small world, though, you have to admit."

"Except for one thing that still puzzles me. The Jim Blasdell I knew was always broke. He lost his savings on some bad investment, and he took to drinking. I can't recall a time when I'd seen him sober or at least not smelling like booze. I wonder how it was that he managed to come up with enough money for your operation."

"Oh, I can answer that. He stole it."

"*What?*"

"He used to work for the Chicago Parks Division, Gage Park I think. Anyway, they had an audit one day, and the department came up four thousand dollars short. They traced the theft back to some guy in accounting who said he'd taken the money and given it to Jim. After the guy was found out, he claimed he didn't know what happened to the money. Jim died before they could investigate. My aunt told me the story."

"So, he was never charged."

She took a quick breath and exhaled before shaking her head.

Oh, my God. What if? What if? Oh, Lord, I have to ask. I have to know.

"This Jim ... He wasn't your ... I mean, biologically, he wasn't ... What I mean to say is ... I mean, was he ..."

"My biological father? No. My real father was a sailor. Mom met him at the canteen one evening, and they just hit it off. He went off to sea on active duty shortly after I was born. We never heard from him again. Mom thinks he might have been killed in action and his body never found. I'm not so sure."

I let out a breath.

"Why all the questions? What's this all about?"

I sat down on the edge of the bed, embarrassed that I'd let the moment slip away. She looked down at my shorts and shook her head before patting the bed by her side. I wiggled up next to her, and she took one hand and ran it over her full, swollen breasts. "Lover," she purred, pulling me slowly back down to her side, "let's talk later. Let's make love now."

And, as she pulled my lips to hers, forced my mouth down her chin to her throat, smothered first one breast and then the other against my face—I felt all the passion building all over again as my shorts swelled with life once more.

"Take them off," she whispered, "and do me." She rubbed my erection firmly, kneading me, *needing* me. I quickly slipped out of my boxers and tossed them to the floor as she smiled. "That's more like it, don't you think?"

Suddenly, that was *exactly* what I thought. And as my mind raced quickly past the last twenty years of my life and the fortuitous turn of events, I couldn't help thinking one more thing.

Jim Blasdell was a great man.

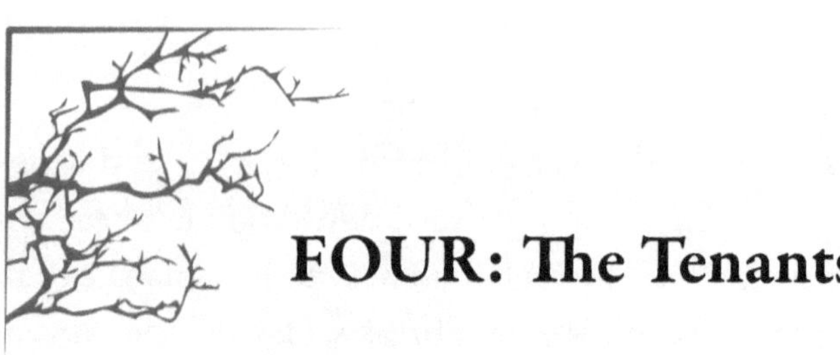

FOUR: The Tenants

CARTEL SQUINTED AT the paper before him. Was it East 67th Street ... or East 76th? He crushed out a cigarette in the cup on his desk and closed his eyes. The butt hissed, spit a puff of dying smoke skyward, and expired.

Shit. I hate growing old.

"Tell Mrs. Rasci," he spoke absently into the report, "there's no sign of her three skips yet. We'll call her when we get something."

"That's just it," the gray-haired man standing behind the papers said. "Now, there's four."

Cartel's eyes popped open, and his hands dropped to his desk. He peered up over his glasses. "What?"

"She just called in to report another one."

He lay his pencil down and slowly squeezed his 200-pound frame as far back into the chair as it would go. "When?"

Meyers sighed. "I just got off the phone with her. She found out last night. Thought you'd wanna know."

Cartel paused. "Don't tell me. He owes her back rent."

"Same as the others."

"How much?"

"She says four hundred."

He shook his head. "Four hundred dollars. That's a hundred more than the last one."

Meyers turned toward the door, stopped, and peered back over his shoulder. "You want me to send someone over to take the report?"

He thought for a second, looked down at the cup he was swirling in his hands, the butt swooshing softly from one side to the other. "No.

No, this time, I'll do it myself. Something's not right here. Nobody rents an apartment to four different people, and they all skip out owing money. Nobody would be *that* unlucky. Or *dumb*."

"I don't know," Meyers said. "The way she sounds on the phone ..." He made a whirling motion with his finger. "A little ditzy, you know?"

Cartel grabbed his coat from the chair. "If the captain asks, tell him I'll be back in an hour. But don't tell him where I've gone, understand? I don't want him to know where I'm headed. I just wanna check this out for myself. This just can't happen. Not to *anybody*."

Meyers turned back toward the door before stopping and peering back over his shoulder. "Okay, but if he finds out, he ain't gonna like it." He thought for several seconds. "You know the address?"

"Yeah," Cartel said. "Better than I know my own."

The lieutenant groaned as he goaded first one leg and then the other out from behind the wheel. He ached all over. *Fuckin' flu.* When he'd finally pulled himself from the car, he looked up the side of the weathered, three-story brownstone on East Chestnut. The chiseled bricks, once painted gleaming white, radiated an eerie gray-green beneath a gloomy Chicago sky. He wondered if it might rain. That would solve one of his problems. He wouldn't have to go over to his ex-wife's house, *his* house, to dig up some stinking strawberry plants she had so generously consented to donate to him.

He mounted the concrete steps slowly, pausing at the aging wooden door standing guard to the palace. Ornately carved and fitted with beveled glass, its mossy green jacket showed the wear of too many years, too many battles waged and lost. The knob, once shimmering brass, had been painted and worn clean, painted and worn clean again until it glistened like the domed head of a dozing eunuch. No hint of its original finish remained.

Cartel huddled against the wind slicing down Chestnut, the icy blasts sweeping in across the city on the back of Lake Michigan, rolling in and funneling down the concrete canyons of the Near North Side.

He thought for a moment that it was starting to snow. He looked up at the paint peeling off the side of the building, the wind stripping it like bark from some ancient white birch, settling to the ground in layers around the structure's roots. The building even smelled like an old birch—dank and musky. The smell of age. The smell, he thought, of death.

The wind reared up again, sending leaves and dust swirling down the center of the street and slicing through his slicker. *When the hell am I going to start wearing a fucking hat?* He lifted his fist to strike again against the thin, wrinkled skin of the door. *When the hell am I going to* buy *a fucking hat?*

He hunched his back against the fury of the wind until the lock on the door jiggled. The knob turned. The lock jiggled again. *Come on, come on!* Cartel danced from one leg to the other, staring anxiously at the knob.

Slowly the worn, weathered door opened to a worn, weathered face. The face exposed itself slowly. "Oh, it's you, Mr. Cartel, darlink. I'm so sorry I kept you waiting, no? But I tell you, I'm so surprised to see you are here, and not that other dumbbell who came last time."

Cartel stared into her dancing eyes. Set in a face nearly indistinguishable from the stone, they looked strangely out of place, the lively baby blues of someone a quarter her age, still filled with the passions of life, the exuberance of youth.

"Come in, come in to my little place. It's so cold outside. You know, I was cleaning my little flat on the third floor and it takes me a little time to walk down all those steps."

"That's okay, Mrs. Rasci. I understand."

"Come in and I'll make some coffee to warm you."

"No, please. Don't go to any trouble. Besides, I don't have the time." He pulled the door shut against the wind, surprised at the weight bearing down on the sagging brass hinges. "I got the report you called into the precinct, and I came right over."

She turned and stood before him, motionless. She had a way of standing so close to him that it made him uneasy. A way of invading his personal space, as if she were after something from him and not about to leave until she got it. He shifted one foot awkwardly back.

"Now, what do you think of that. Did you ever hear of such a thing? This makes the fourth one who just ran off owing me money. Can you imagine, Mr. Cartel, darlink? The fourth one!"

"Can you give me his name, Mrs. Rasci, and tell me a little about him, what he looks like, maybe his age, things like that?"

"Back in the Old Country, you never saw a thing like this. People was careful with their money, and when they made a word with you, you could depend on them to keep it. This little fellow here," she motioned toward the basement flat where he guessed the tenant had been staying, "I should never have rented to him. You know, Mr. Cartel, darlink, I have nice people living here. Two nice girls on the first floor and Mrs. Fougherty on the second floor in a little flat. So nice. You never hear a peep out of them. But *that* dumbhead!"

"Mrs. Rasci?"

She looked up into his large, round face. "Yes, darlink?"

"What's his name?"

She waved her hand. "Oh, Walter something or other. I have his name written down somewhere on a little piece of paper. You know, I always ask my tenants to pay me cash. I don't believe in all this other stuff, this checks and debit cards and stuff. I know his name is Walter something. I have it written down on a piece of paper."

"Do you have a lease?"

She looked at him blankly, and she suddenly slapped her hand against the side of her head. "Of course. All my tenants sign a lease. You know, I don't want no troubles. I don't want nobody saying, 'Oh, no, Mrs. Rasci, you said I could have the apartment for fifty dollars a month!' or nothing like that. You wait here, and I'll go get it for you. You wait here, and I'll be right back."

"That's not necessary," Cartel said. "I'll have one of my men stop by later to pick it up. But can you at least give me some idea of what this Walter looks like? Where he works, what he does. Does he have any relatives, any ... any friends that you know of? Anyone who might know where he is now?"

"I tell you something funny. You know that little fellow before this Walter? I can't remember his name. But he was *so-o-o* good looking. Such a good-looking little fellow. But I tell you something, Mr. Cartel, darlink. He used to bring his girlfriends home with him ... these tramps! You know something, I don't understand about this country. All the beautiful things the people have here, and this feeling all the time for the sex and the tramps. I tell you something, it's a sin, a good-looking little fellow like that fooling around with these ... these *things* with their short skirts and their ratty hair and ..."

"Mrs. Rasci—" Cartel twisted his face to one side—"what about Walter?"

"Well, Mr. Cartel, darlink, I am coming to that. I think after this one good-looking young fellow gave me all the trouble with these women and then ran off owing me three months' rent, I think all right, Velchenka, the next time you rent out this little flat, you will rent it to some ugly fellow. Then there won't be no fooling around. Well ..." her mouth turned up in a sly smile, "this middle-aged man rings my doorbell and asks to see the apartment I got for rent. Well, I tell you, I nearly have to laugh. Mr. Cartel, he is ugly as sin! As *sin*! Forgive me to say it, but he looks like some kind of a little fish or something."

"Can you describe him for me, Mrs. Rasci?"

"So, he looks at the apartment," she continued, ignoring his question or possibly not hearing it at all, "and he tells me he has a good job at a factory somewhere and that he would like to give me the rent. I ask him if he has a little girlie friend or something, and he says no. He was married, but now he's divorced. Isn't that a shame? But I think no girl in her right mind would ever go for such a ugly man, so he gives me a hundred dollars cash, and he rents the apartment."

"Can you show me the apartment, Mrs. Rasci?"

She paused. "You haven't seen it before?"

"I just want to take another look."

"Well, I don't know. I'm not sure how clean it is. I just found out he was missing yesterday. I haven't ... "

"Please. Just a quick look, Mrs. Rasci, that's all."

"Oh, sure, sure," she said, fumbling in her apron for a key. Cartel followed her out the front door and down the steps, one agonizingly slow step after another, to the basement entrance. For the life of him, he didn't know why she hadn't slipped, fallen, and broken her neck years ago. "So, when the second month comes around, he says to me, *Oh, Mrs. Rasci, I lose my job and have to owe you the rent for a couple of days.* Then he says, *Oh, Mrs. Rasci, my ex-wife is sick and I have to pay her hospital bills.* Then he says, *Oh, Mrs. Rasci, I'm expecting a check from the government for my taxes and I will pay you everything when I get it next Tuesday.*"

Cartel followed her through a dimly lit corridor lined with old chests smelling of cedar and old cardboard boxes, smelling of mold and old broken floor lamps not smelling of anything in particular. They shimmied past disheveled, discarded furniture that looked as if it had been salvaged from a junk bin centuries ago. And several more that were still waiting their turn. The last few rays of daylight filtered through a single window at the far end of the hall, its faltering beam spilling across the floor and into the two-room flat. A few second-hand chairs lined one kitchen wall, and as Cartel moved across the floor toward the stove, a handful of roaches dashed madly across the yellowing enamel, disappearing *en masse* through the gas grates.

"And then one evening when I come down to bring him his little supper, what do you think I find? He is drunk. He starts crying on my shoulder and telling me how bad things is for him. And I tell him to get away, to go get sober! Now, how do you like that? Such a young man, and he was drinking his money away. I tell myself, Velchenka, you are such a dumbhead. You believe all these lies. Such a dumbhead you are!"

"And how long ago was that? How long between then and when you discovered he'd skipped?"

"Well, it is maybe two weeks, maybe less. Last night I go to bring him some food, and I say to myself, now, Velchenka, you must ask him to pay you the money what he owes you and to move out. It's no good to have drunks around everywhere you go. They are dirty, and they lie, and they could start a fire and burn your house down. So when I knock on the door and come in, what do you think? He's gone! All his stuff is gone. Everything is gone."

Cartel turned the knob on the old Roper range.

"Oh, that old stove don't work no more. I had it disconnected."

Cartel ran his finger over the top and sniffed; a hint of cleanser, nothing more. Mrs. Rasci stood near the kitchen sink, chattering on, while Cartel opened some cabinets, checked the solitary closet off the bedroom, opened the bureau drawers. All empty. Spotless. Picked as clean as a Thanksgiving turkey in a household of twelve.

"I don't seem to find anything of Walter's here, Mrs. Rasci. No papers, pencils, ashes, food, nothing. Not even a speck of dust in the trash can, here."

"*Ohh*," she said, waving her hand. "He didn't have much. A couple little things. Some dirty clothes and a couple little things like that. I threw them all in the trash, such filthy dirty things."

"*Uh-huh*. And how about the other three skips? I don't remember. Did any of them leave anything behind?"

"Oh, they didn't have much. None of them had much. They all wasted their money on women and liquor and that one little fellow, he smoked the dope. You know, Mr. Cartel, darlink, I rent a furnished place here. None of these crazy people are like you or me who got some things and who save their money. You know, you are smart, Mr. Cartel, darlink. You are so smart. I know you are. That's why I like talking to you. You're not like these other dumbbells who come to see me. That's why I like you. Such a gentleman, and so smart."

Cartel walked back into the bedroom for another look. "I was just wondering about that sofa, there. It's new, isn't it?" The sofa sat next to a makeshift cot and mattress between the bureau and a floor lamp, neither of which had seen a showroom floor since America elected Roosevelt to be president—the *first* one.

"Oh, the old sofa was no good no more. I give it to the Salvation Army. They come and take it away and resell it. That's how they make their money, and I get inside a good feeling helping the poor unfortunates like some people we know."

"*Uh-huh.*" Cartel pushed his fist into the cushions—soft, overstuffed, inviting. They could easily consume a man his size. Well, not *easily*. "Nice," he said.

"Mr. Cartel, darlink, I have to go back upstairs now. It's getting close to five o'clock, yes? Poor Mrs. Fougherty, she has trouble with her eyes and can't cook so good no more. I have to make her supper and bring it to her, or else she has nothing to eat. She is a good woman, kind. She worries all the time about Velchenka. You would please lock the outside door when you leave, no? Just pull on it hard until it clicks."

"Sure. And if we hear any news about Walter, we'll phone you."

"Oh, no," she said, ambling toward the door. "He is nothing to bother about, Mr. Cartel, darlink. He is not good enough to waste your time and worry about. I don't care that much about the money he owes me. I got plenty of money. My grandmother used to say in the Old Country, 'Velchenka, you have only one thing nobody can take away from you. Your mind.' You know, Mr. Cartel, darlink? That woman, she was so smart. Like you. She used to run her own seamstress shop and sold flowers and took in laundry, and people would come to her and ask her to do their work for them. She tell me, 'Velchenka, you see how some people are so dumb? They got two good hands, yet they willing to pay someone else to do their work for them.' I tell you something, Mr. Cartel, darlink, that when my mother died, it was the best thing that ever happened to me when my grandmother took me in and raised me up. I tell you, you're so young. Like a baby, so young and so smart. That is why I don't like to see you worry about such a dumbhead like this one who live in a flat like this without nothing to their name. They won't ever amount to nothing, believe me. They wouldn't even know they have a brain in their head, they are such dumbheads. That's why I can't feel sorry for them when they cry on my shoulder, *Oh, Mrs. Rasci this*, and *Oh, Mrs. Rasci that*. No, they not like you, so smart and nice to talk to. I like it when you come to talk to me. But you don't got to worry about them, those dumbheads."

"Well, that's my job, Mrs. Rasci., worrying about dumbheads." Cartel's mind drifted as the old lady wandered off down the corridor. If her grandmother had been anything like her, it was no wonder Mrs. Rasci was so well off. She probably had the first dollar she ever earned. *And probably will have until the day she dies.*

Cartel stepped out into the hallway and pulled the door to the small apartment closed behind him before taking one last look down the corridor toward the back of the building. He spotted an open doorway a few feet farther down the hall and picked his way past some junk piled high until he reached the light switch. The yellow glare spilled softly over a giant behemoth, an old converted coal burner, chugging and sputtering away in a vain attempt to match wits with the coming chill of winter. Cartel spotted a stack of old clothes and rummaged through them. Men's clothes. Underwear. Socks. Pants. Shirts.

Strange. She said she'd been widowed for more than ten years. Yet, these can't be but a couple years old, judging from their condition. I wonder. ...

He stacked the clothes back in a pile and walked over to a wall lined with empty cardboard boxes. Behind him, a crate suddenly tumbled from its perch. Cartel leaped to one side, grabbing for his revolver, when a small, gray rat skittered along the baseboard and disappeared into a hole between two bricks. Cartel breathed out deeply. Against the wall, the shadows bobbed and weaved like a roomful of dancers on hot coals as the furnace belched rhythmically. He holstered the gun and kicked aside some more boxes. There, two feet above the floor, he discovered a cast-iron pipe poking its aged head up from the concrete. A handle extended from the center of the pipe. He examined it closely, following it back as far as his eyes could see. He turned the handle halfway, then full, and listened. Silence. Finally, he turned it back to its original position and shifted the boxes back to where they had been.

Strange.

Cartel turned back down the hall and opened the hulking door to the building, pulling the monster closed behind him and stepping back into the chill of the waning sun. The wind had stopped blowing, the calm betraying a pleasantness that existed only in his mind. To make matters worse, he wasn't any closer to solving the case of the missing skips than he'd been an hour earlier. And, yet, somehow, something in the back recesses of his mind told him that he was.

Meyers fingered a small memo pad as he spoke. He was a funny looking man with a long forehead and straight, thin hair that slunk down and across his face to one side where it seemed to reattach itself to his scalp as if by magic, like a barnacle clinging to the hull of an aging ship. His nose was long and thick at the end, a full Roman nose, while his eyes were small and bird-like—always darting, always searching, seeking to take in everything about their surroundings. He was a good enough investigator, although Cartel wished he showed more motivation. He was one of those people who did enough to get by, enough to keep out of hot water, no more. Cartel, on the other hand ...

"What'd you find out?" Cartel asked.

"The stake you asked for at the Rasci place? He just called in."

"And?"

"And he reported the usual. The two girls left the apartment this morning at 7:45, just like always. One returned at lunch and went back out half an hour later. Mrs. Rasci swept down the front steps and threw some breadcrumbs to the pigeons around ten. The two girls returned to their apartment around 4:45."

"No sign of the other one—that ... Mrs. Fougherty?"

Meyers shook his head. "Nothing. Although the lights in her apartment go on each evening around 4:30 and off, again, a little before ten."

"Anyone else enter or leave the building? Any strangers? *Anyone?*"

"The gas reader showed up this morning around 11, and Mrs. Rasci let him into the basement. He was there for three or four minutes and left."

Cartel hesitated, rummaging through the scant information Meyers had given him, searching for something unusual. *Anything* unusual. "What time is it now?"

Meyers squinted at his watch. "Quarter past five."

"Well, have our stake stick with it 'til everything's quiet, then reel him back in."

"Right." the man said, stopping suddenly. "Oh, and one other thing."

Cartel looked up.

"About 2:30 this afternoon, two men from the Salvation Army pulled up and went inside. A short while later, they came out carrying a couch."

"A couch?"

"Yeah. You know, a sofa."

"A sofa?"

"From the basement. Mrs. Rasci let them in, and a few minutes later, they carried it out to the truck and took off."

Cartel rubbed his chin. *The only sofa I saw yesterday was brand new. Why would anyone donate a brand-new sofa to charity?* "Who's our stake?"

"Tony Barducci. Why? You want him?"

"Yeah. Get him on the horn. I just got an idea."

Cartel slipped back into his chair and crossed his arms. *This is it. You did it once too often. You're gonna play with fire, you're gonna get burned, old lady. No doubt about it. You're gonna get burned.*

Through the doorway, Cartel saw Meyers motioning him to pick up the phone. And then ...

"Cartel! Cartel, you get your fuckin' ass in here. *Now*! You hear me?"

Cartel jumped like his ass was on fire. Whenever the captain shouted like that, it spelled trouble. And Cartel had a good idea just what that trouble was. He hurried past an armada of metal desks leading to the captain's flagship. He glanced down at Meyers, holding out the receiver. "Barducci," he whispered.

"Tell him I'll get back to him later. I *hope*."

Cartel peeked into the captain's doorway. "You wanna see me, Cap'n?"

Lombardi scribbled furiously across a sheet of paper before him, his hand moving faster than the cop's eyes could follow until he finally jammed the pencil down so hard, it snapped in two. Lombardi blinked, took a deep breath, and slowly looked up. "Get in here and close the door!"

Cartel turned and reached for the knob.

"No. No, wait. On second thought, leave it open. Leave it open so that everyone in this fucking office can hear what I'm going to say to you."

Cartel turned back around and folded his hands behind him. He stood straight and tall, eyes focused on a spot on the wall just beyond the captain's head ... just the way he'd learned to do in the Academy. It was a posture he hadn't used for fourteen years.

"Is the captain displeased with something I've done?"

Lombardi rose slowly from his chair and walked around the corner of his desk. He approached Cartel cautiously, warily, like a hungry ferret might stalk a clueless mouse. That's how Cartel had always looked at him. Like a ferret. With his long, thin nose, his swollen, darting eyes, his bushy brows and scraggily mustache. He even moved like a ferret, on short, stubby legs that couldn't outrun a lamppost. Most of all, though, it was the way the guy thought; it was his thought process. His brain was always working, always scheming, always planning. His mind never stopped. Cartel once bet a fellow officer that the guy's brain was still racing even after he went to sleep, but neither of the cops could figure out a way to find out for sure, so they called the bet off.

"I got a call a short while ago from some woman over on Chestnut Street," he said slowly, deliberately, exaggerating every other word.

Oh, shit.

"She was concerned because she'd seen a car, a dark four-door sedan parked across the street from her apartment building for the past three days. It never leaves, she told me. And there's always someone inside it. A man or a woman, she couldn't tell, but would I mind coming over to check it out?"

Oh, fuck.

"So I told Scaliaggi and DeCico to check up on it. I told them to be careful. I told them someone might be casing the place, planning a robbery or a kidnapping or maybe even a murder, you never know, do you, Cartel?"

Cartel raised his eyebrows and shrugged. He opened his mouth to speak before quickly slamming it shut again.

"Well, Scaliaggi and DeCico got there and, sure enough, they found the car that the woman had called in about. And, sure enough, they found someone in the car that the woman had called in about. And, do you know who that someone was that the woman had called in about?"

Cartel cleared his throat. "It was ... probably Tony Barducci. I imagine. Sir."

The captain circled Cartel until he stood just inches from his junior officer's nose. He rocked back on his heels, then forward onto the balls of his feet. He rolled back and forth for what seemed to Cartel like hours until he finally broke the silence.

"*No-o-o*," he said slowly, deliberately. "*No-o-o*, it was probably *not* Tony Barducci, you imagine!"

Cartel's eyes shifted quickly down to Lombardi's, then back to the same spot on the wall behind the desk.

"It was *definitely* Tony Barducci. And you don't *imagine*, goddam it. You fucking *know* it was." He paused "Goddam it!"

"Yessir!" Cartel snapped.

"It seems that someone who used to be a lieutenant in this precinct decided to place a stake on the woman's house because the woman has had some tenants move out, owing her money. Can you imagine that, Cartel? Can you imagine anyone being so dumb as to waste official department manpower and money that way? Can you imagine anyone in his right mind doing such a thing with police resources being as low as they are in these tough times? Can you just imagine? All because of a couple of skips that that very same lieutenant has been unable to locate!"

"Sir, I, *uhh* ... it was me. Sir."

Lombardi cranked his head to one side. He learned his ear so close to the cop that Cartel thought for an instant he was going to kiss him. The captain rolled his eyes slowly around to look straight into Cartel's face. "What ... was ... you? *Sir?*"

Cartel paused. "Sir?"

"I said, what was you, Cartel?"

"It was me who ordered the stake on the Rasci place. *Sir!*"

Lombardi shifted slowly away from his officer, turned his back, and took two trembling steps toward his desk. "It ... was ... *I*," he said softly.

Cartel looked at the back of the man's head, at the bald spot forming there. "Sir?"

"It was *I*, you fucking moron!" He whirled around so suddenly that Cartel nearly tipped over backward. "Subjective complement of the verb 'to be' is *I*, not *me*! And if it *were* you, then you disobeyed a direct order about not wasting precinct time on a fuckin' hunch you had about some old lady and her skips. If you hadn't, then you wouldn't have wasted precinct time, and you wouldn't have wasted precinct money. Not only did you have a stake sitting out there for the past three days, but by not telling me, I had to send two of my best men out after him, which means that, at least for a couple of hours today, I was without three of the eight men in my entire fucking department!"

"Yessir. I'm sorry, sir. It won't happen again, sir. I just ... wasn't thinking. I ... I had a hunch ..."

"You had a *what*?"

"A hunch, sir."

He shook his head in disbelief. "Listen, here. You don't have hunches, Cartel. Do you hear me? You don't have hunches. Not today, not tomorrow, not *ever*. You don't have hunches, and that's an order!"

"Yessir."

"You don't have hunches, *period*! You have *evidence*. You have *proof*. You have some poor fucking bastard nailed to the wall before you ever even *think* about wasting my manpower on a stakeout because of your fuckin' hunch. Do you understand? We don't do things around here because of hunches."

Cartel nodded.

"Do ... you ... understand?"

"Yessir."

"Good. Now get your ass back to your office, get on that fuckin' phone, and call Barducci in. *Fast!* And don't ever—*ever*—place a stakeout in the field without clearing it with me first, is that understood?"

Cartel nodded. "Yessir. Perfectly, sir."

Lombardi slipped back into his chair and snapped his head toward the door. "*Now* you can close it," he said as Cartel walked out of the room. When the lieutenant reached Meyers' desk, he motioned for the uniform to follow Cartel to his office.

"Jesus," Meyers said, closing the office door behind them. "What the hell got up the old man's ass?"

"How do I know? Maybe he's on the rag."

"You want me to call Barducci in?"

Cartel paused.

"I say, do you want me to ..."

"*Huh*? Oh, yeah. Later. First, I want you to run a check on someone for me. Velchenka Rasci."

Meyers craned his neck to one side and squinted. "*Huh*? What about Barducci? Shouldn't we at least ..."

"Just do it. I want a full check, from the time she left Hungary until twenty minutes ago, understand? And check up on her husband, too. He's supposed to have been dead for ten years now. Run a full report on him, too. You'll have to dig around for his first name. Got it?"

Meyers shrugged. "You're the boss."

Damn straight I'm the boss. And I'll be goddamned if I'm gonna let some bubble-eyed weasel too afraid of his own shadow throw me off this one. She did it, and she knows she did it. She knows she did it, and she knows I know she did it. She just doesn't know that I know how she did it.

"Oh, and while you're at it, call over to legal and have them work up a warrant for Rasci's arrest."

"A warrant? *What*? For what?"

Cartel thought for a moment. "What the hell, might as well go for broke. Let's make it for murder one."

"Mr. Cartel, darlink, what a surprise! I didn't expect to see you again so soon. I was just talking with Mrs. Fougherty, you know she lives on the second ..."

"Mrs. Rasci, I wish this were a routine visit so that we could chat. But I'm afraid I'm going to have to place you under arrest for suspicion of the murder of your four tenants. Sergeant Meyers, here, has the warrant. He also has a warrant to search the building. Sergeant," he said, turning to his aide, "you and Rossi start with the third floor, Mrs. Rasci's apartment, and work your way down."

"I ... I don't understand what is happening. Is this some little joke, or what, darlink? Tell Velchenka ... what it is you want?"

"It was really very clever, Mrs. Rasci. Very clever. But the sofas gave you away."

"The sofas?"

"No one grows up an orphan in Europe, lives through two World Wars and a major depression, and comes to America and buys a new sofa every three months. It's just not in character, you know what I mean?"

"I don't understand, Mr. Cartel, darlink. Could you say it so an old dumbhead like me could understand?"

"You really don't like the men who rent your basement apartment, do you, Mrs. Rasci? I mean, you really *hate* what they stand for."

"I don't like dumbheads. I don't like the sex and the drinking and ..."

"So you set out on your own little crusade to get rid of them ... or at least as many of them as you could without drawing too much attention to your activities."

She shook her head, her eyes for the first time displaying a hint of fear, a look of confusion. It was an expression Cartel imagined she had worn back in Europe, in Hungary, after her mother's death and before her grandmother had taken her in.

"You killed your tenants one by one in cold blood, Mrs. Rasci, didn't you? You killed all four of them."

She shook her head again. "I kill no one, Mr. Cartel. Velchenka Rasci is a woman of life and of love, not a killer of people. She is God-fearing woman of peace and love."

Cartel nodded absently. "At first, I couldn't figure out how you disposed of the bodies. That's always the hardest part. I had my men sift your trash for any signs of human remains or blood. I had a stake watching your every move. But you were too smart for that. Then I got the bright idea that you were stuffing your victims' corpses inside the sofas. That would explain why you bought a new sofa after each tenant disappeared. So I called the Salvation Army and asked a few questions. Naturally, the sofas would have been quite a bit heavier than usual with a man's body inside. But when I asked the pickup guys about the last sofa, they told me just the opposite. Oh, they said it was big and bulky but that it was actually lighter than you'd expect for a sofa of that size. That really stumped me. Maybe she's not guilty of murder after all, I thought. Maybe I'm barkin' up the wrong tree."

She smiled. "Mr. Cartel, darlink. You know I could not do such a thing like that. I am a poor old lady with nothing to live for but my tenants. My two girls, and Mrs. Fougherty. They rely on me. I help them, I cook for them, I visit with them. I am not some criminal. I am not some murderer. You know that now, yes? And so I will go upstairs and tell your Sergeant there is no need for ..."

"Wait. Hold on a minute. I'm not done, yet, Mrs. Rasci. Do you see what I'm getting at? Just about the time I was thinking I had it figured all wrong, that's when I decided to run a background check."

"And what is that, darlink?" She shifted on two stumpy legs. "What is *background check*?"

"That's when I look into your life's history, going all the way back to Hungary."

"*My* life's history?"

Cartel nodded. "And that of your husband. Poor guy. Seems he died more than ten years ago. A *lot* more. In fact, it seems as if he died closer to ... oh, thirty-five years ago or longer."

She smiled. "I am an old woman, Mr. Cartel. For an old woman, time passes quickly, or time stands still. Time races ahead, or time dies. But time is never on your side."

"It seems that, in your case, it *was*, Mrs. Rasci. It appears that your husband died just a year or so after the two of you were married. He died of, what was it again? Oh, yes. Asphyxiation. Gas poisoning, wasn't it?"

"Yes." Her mouth turned down at the corners, and her eyes seemed suddenly sullen. "Yes, that is right." Cartel could see even after all these years that she had once been very beautiful. Stunning. The kind of woman that any man might have fallen in love with. Especially an older man, a jeweler, worth hundreds of thousands of dollars, possibly more. "It was ... an accident. It was very sad. I cried. Just a little girl, such a small, innocent little girl. I cried so much ..."

"I'm sure you did, because you loved your grandmother dearly."

She nodded. "Yes, I did. She was so good to me. She taught me everything. She taught Velchenka how to read and how to write and how to be a lady, and she taught me ..."

"How to kill?"

Her eyes rolled suddenly in her head, her pupils swelling to twice their normal size. "Mr. Cartel, I ..."

"She did do it, didn't she? Your grandmother. The courts found her guilty. The Hungarian justice system. And they sent her away to prison, where she died the same year you came to America, the year after your husband died. And left you his fortune."

She shook her head, lightly at first, then harder. "No, she could not have done such a thing. My husband was a good man. She would not have harmed ..."

"Didn't she call him something at the trial in Budapest? Didn't she say, in her own defense, that she killed him because your husband had been a drunkard and a liar and a ... *dumbhead*?"

"No. No, he was not a drunkard. He was not a dumbhead. He loved me. And I loved him. I mean ..." she looked down, the wheels of her memory spinning freely, grinding out the traces from the past—"as much as any young girl of 18 or 19 could love someone."

"At first, they couldn't find his body, isn't that so? And because of that, your grandmother very nearly went free."

"Yes. Yes, they could not find him ..."

"But then, when the authorities began snooping around the cellar of your grandmother's home, they discovered something."

She looked up at him blankly, and he thought he noticed a small damp spot growing in the corner of one eye.

"Lieutenant Cartel? Lieutenant!"

Cartel turned toward the stairway.

"Lieutenant," Meyers said, skipping down the steps leading to the foyer. "We're not quite through with the third floor, but I thought you'd want to see this." He held out a clear plastic bag. Cartel took hold of it and lifted it toward the light. Slowly he lowered it to his side where Mrs. Rasci's gaze remained fixed.

"Thanks, Meyers. I think you can stop searching now. And call for a van. Mrs. Rasci is going for a ride."

"Got it," he said, reaching for the door.

"In fact," Cartel added. "Make that call to Captain Lombardi, personally. Tell him I hereby request that he get his skinny ass out here, and tell him to make it fast."

Meyers grinned before ducking through the doorway and disappearing down the steps.

Cartel turned back toward the old woman standing before him, looking for all the world like a helpless child, like an orphan of war, like a small doll that some equally small child would someday cherish for her very own and then abandon.

"You know what this is, don't you, Mrs. Rasci?" He jiggled the bag.

She shook her head, paused, and nodded.

"It's your embalming kit, isn't it? Your needles, your scalpels, some kind of fluid ... formaldehyde, is it?"

She looked up into his eyes and nodded again.

"That's why those sofas were lighter than they should have been, isn't it? Because you opened them up, removed some of the padding, and placed a sealed body bag with your victim's remains inside before closing the sofa up again. Isn't that right? A few pounds of bones, a few pounds of desiccated organs, and some human tissue shrunk down to practically nothing. The padding you removed weighed more than the victims' remains you sewed inside, didn't it, Mrs. Rasci?"

She thought for several moments. "They are nothing. They are not worth bothering with, Mr. Cartel, darlink. You know that. These ... these ... *dumbheads* and drinkers and dope smokers and these ... these ... *things* that crave the sex. These things ... like animals. You can see that. You are a smart man, Mr. Cartel. Very smart. Like me, you don't like these people, these crazy people who got no job and who don't work and just drink and have the sex and steal and lie and ... you don't like these people. I don't like these people. These are not people, Mr. Cartel, darlink. You and Velchenka, *we* are people. *We* are alive. We know the value of life. We know how to work hard and how to keep away from these others. We are not like them, we are not some ... *bums*. It doesn't matter what happens to them. They are not worth worrying about. The world is better place without them. All they cause is pain for others. The world is better place without them."

Cartel heard the crunch of the tires in the street. Meyers came up the steps, peeked in, and motioned over his shoulder. Cartel pulled the cuffs from behind his back and slipped them over the old lady's wrists.

"Mr. Cartel ..." she said, "I like you. You are not like the others. I like talking to you. You are so smart, and such a gentleman. But tell me, nobody could find my husband. Nobody knew that my grandmother had told a confession to protect me. So, she did, and now she is gone. How did you find this out?"

"Well, you had me stumped for a while, I admit. And I was just about to give up on the case. Except for two things."

"What two things, Mr. Cartel, darlink. Tell Velchenka. Tell an old dumb lady, so that she know." A sparkle had suddenly come back into her eyes.

"Well, the last time I was here, I took a look around your basement."

"It's so dirty there, Mr. Cartel, darlink, you should not have ..."

"I found the men's clothing, and I thought that was the smoking gun I needed to tie you to the murders. But when I looked more closely, I noticed the sizes were all large or extra large, and the descriptions you gave us of your tenants were all of smaller men."

She smiled. "Such little fellows."

"Then I noticed the gas pipe ... with the shut-off valve? I wasn't sure at first where it led, until the second thing came along. And then I knew the pipe led to the basement flat where your tenants were all murdered."

"But, all old buildings have gas pipes in them, darlink. What is so unusual about that?"

"Yes, but this gas pipe had a shutoff valve that was clean of dust and dirt as if it had been handled recently ... maybe several times. Or, more precisely ... *four?*"

She looked suddenly childlike—caught with her hand in the cookie jar, an impish grin crossing her face.

"So smart. And such a good-looking man, too." She shook her head. "If Velchenka was thirty years younger!"

He smiled. "Then I remembered that you said you had disconnected the stove in your tenants' apartment, so you had no reason to fiddle with that valve handle ... ever."

"You are so smart, darlink. I am proud to know a person so smart like you."

He sighed. "So, putting two and two together, I figured that's how you killed them, because that's how your grandmother killed your husband in Hungary—by turning the gas on in the house as he slept. That was in the confession she gave to the police just before *you* were to be arrested for the murder. From that and the information I got from the Salvation Army, I was able to figure out the rest."

"Look out. Step aside!" The captain's burly voice rang from the steps leading to the front entry. "Where is he? *Cartel*! *Cartel*! Where the ... oh, here you are!"

Cartel turned, glancing over his shoulder as the captain snaked his way past several uniforms to reach them.

"There you are! Just what the hell do you mean, draggin' my ass—what did you call it again? My 'skinny ass'?—out of a warm fuckin' office out here in the cold? You've got some explaining to do. And you'd better make it Goddam fuckin' good!" Lombardi pushed his way into the foyer, caught sight of the woman, and froze. "Oh. Oh, I'm sorry, ma'am," he said, his tone suddenly softening. "I didn't realize anyone else was..."

Cartel turned back to the old lady, who had curled her lips in disgust. He continued: "You see, Mrs. Rasci, when that background check came in on you, it had your entire family history on it. I doubt that so detailed an account would ever have existed except for the fact that your grandmother had confessed to the murder of your husband in court, and the court stenographer's job was to take down what your grandmother said ... *everything* she said ... right on down to the revelation that your grandmother had a couple of occupations that you had never thought to mention to me. You neglected to tell me that she had been a pretty fair upholsterer in her day ... as well as one of Budapest's most respected embalmers. She helped her husband, your grandfather, run a mortuary there for years, didn't she?"

The old lady smiled. "She run a little mortuary there, yes ... until my grandfather die."

"Of natural causes, I assume."

Another twinkle lit her eye.

Lombardi wormed his way around Cartel's heft and spied the cuffs on the old woman. "What's going on here? Why is this woman in cuffs? What's this all about?" he asked his lieutenant.

"I sent the coroner out to the Salvation Army warehouse. The four missing stiffs are at County now, thanks to Mrs. Rasci. Or, three of them, anyway. We're still running down the fourth sofa."

"Sofa? What the... what are you talking about, sofa?"

"It'll all be in my report closing the case."

Lombardi looked from Cartel to Mrs. Rasci and back again before drawing closer to the cop. "You'd better be right, Cartel." He turned to the old lady. "All right, Mrs. Rasci," he said finally. "You'd better come along with me. Looks like you've got a date with destiny." He motioned toward the door and signaled one of the uniforms to take her out to the van.

Cartel grabbed Lombardi's arm. "Oh, and Captain? Make sure you head right back to the station with her, you hear? No side trips to the coffee shop. We don't want any misuse of official department resources."

Lombardi glared. "*You*. You'd better watch your step, Cartel. You could *still* end up pounding a beat."

Cartel smiled. "Might not be so bad. I could use the exercise."

As the cop turned away, the old lady stopped and peered back over her shoulder. "But what about my two girls? What about Mrs. Fougherty? I have to bring for them the dinner. I have to ..."

"Don't worry," Cartel said. "I'll make sure they're looked after."

"Until I come back?"

He smiled. "Until you come back."

"Can I call them? Can I talk to them? They will worry about Velchenka." A tear formed in her eye.

Cartel shook his head. "I'm afraid not, Mrs. Rasci. At least not for some time. But I'll tell you what. *I'll* call them. I'll call them for you. And I'll come to see them from time to time, too, just to make sure everything is all right. And I'll pass along any information you want."

She turned and reached out her hands, placed them—two dainty, wrinkled, fading white lilies—inside his. "I like you, Mr. Cartel, darlink. You are such a gentleman. And so smart."

Cartel smiled and held her hands for several moments before finally releasing them. As she turned to accompany the uniform down the steps, she stopped to look up at Lombardi, a frown suddenly creasing her face.

"*You?* You, I *don't* like!"

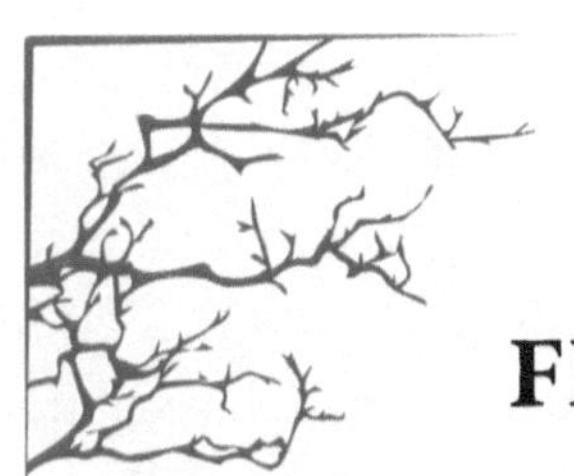

FIVE: The Union

TO THOSE WHO GO THERE, it's the Union, and its hallowed halls have stood forever. It was there before Bronco Nagurski. It was there before George Halas. In fact, it was there before *football*, for Chrissake. Some undergrads insist its foundations run back to He, Himself, the Creator of A.T.F. (All Things Football). And that He, too, had once been a tackle majoring in history at the University of Illinois-Chicago.

Scarier, still, some people believe He's *still* there. Which, if you ask me, is a damned long time to spend in pursuit of a basic B.A. Still, it is not impossible for me to believe. After all, He can do anything, if I am to accept the approximately 647 thousand hours of religious training crammed into my skull by the good nuns of St. Simon and pushed through my brain until the excess seeps out of my ears like processed pork out of the business end of a grinder. So why wouldn't He attend UIC? Sit in the Union, sucking on a Carling's Black Label? Or anything else He wants to do? You don't believe me, ask Sister Francine.

So I, too, sit in the Union, thinking of things to write. Although at the moment, I find myself seriously distracted by a white-bloused, yellow-skirted honey of a woman of obvious Norwegian ancestry. Her hair is the color of yellow birch, gathered at the base of the neck, flowing down the shoulders, and spilling down to the small of the back. Her eyes are pure azure—the hue of the Scandinavian seas in the summer. What else *would* they be? Her lips are berries growing wild by the hillsides overlooking the sea and discovered by accident, stumbled upon, plucked, and devoured wantonly.

But it is those azure eyes that I find fascinating as they watch me while I write, search me for the answer to some unknown, long-lost question, search long and hard above a small, straight nose and gently parted lips. Yet, it's not the azure eyes nor is it the rosebud-and-cream complexion that distracts me most nor her legs, which swell into long, full thighs, opening and closing like the gently parting lips of a giant gaping clam, at once peaceful and inviting and then monstrous and foreboding. Nor is it, as incongruous as it may sound, her two mountainous breasts which she thrusts suddenly toward me by leaning back into her wood-spindled librarians' chair and running her hands through thoughtfully disheveled mounds of thick, billowy hair.

None of these things distract me from my writing as I watch her watching me but, instead, her fingers. Or, to be more precise, her *finger*. One finger. *The* finger. *That* finger. Long and thin, nicely shaped, perfect for her stature. And, most importantly of all, free from such oft-encountered encumbrances as pear cuts, teardrops, marquise, and other such appropriately named slices of glass. I find myself wondering how so perfectly formed a creature as this cannot be married. Nor engaged. Nor, at the very least, indulged. I mean, is there a God in heaven or isn't there? And, if so, why has He created no world-renowned heart surgeon, no semi-infamous criminal lawyer, no bank trustee, corporate vice-president, Mafioso chieftain, or university humanities-department chairman who has noticed this golden treasure, this full-blown woman who makes all others pale before her? Not only noticed her but also betrothed to her his everlasting loyalty? His fortune? A lousy villa in Cannes, for Chrissake?

She closes the book in her lap and says a few silent words to a pale and fragile brownette seated across the table from her, drinking beer. I wonder briefly about both women, neither of whom looks studious enough to be enrolled in the university. And then I dismiss the thought, assuming that maybe they met there simply for a quick brew and the stimulating atmosphere. Glancing around the *Rathskeller*, I see the goddess say in tones growing increasingly louder for my benefit that she is tempted to grab an hour that afternoon and spend it dangling her feet in the bubbling cool waters of the Memorial Fountain.

Before I have time to comprehend what that means, she rises like the Phoenix from the ashes, turns her magnificent profile toward me, and disappears behind a mammoth frieze-adorned pillar before she reappears from behind another, disappears, reappears, and finally disappears again for good no matter how hard my 20-30 eyes strain to discern otherwise.

I look down at the blank piece of paper on the table and look up to where the image had been, her aura lingering for a second like the mist over Lake Michigan, and I mutter to myself, *Oh, shit. You've done it again. Blown the goddam chance of a lifetime.*

My eyes scan the perimeter, furtively seeking a replacement goddess on whom to feast, someone for me to worship from afar. Beyond the Gothic glass panes, my vision falls upon a braless redhead on the patio. She is dressed in shorts and a gauze top, her sudden movements sending delightful ripples across her blouse, stern tracings of erect nipples made firmer, still, by the filmy material and highlighted by the playful light beyond. Still, she is no goddess.

Back inside, my vision strays toward the very darkest abyss of the room, its cavernous bowels where a thin young girl with no chin and mousey-brown hair leans forward, exposing a portion of one very small breast and none of the other, which I suppose is equally small. Her eyes catch mine. She looks surprised, appalled. Could any man tall, slim, and athletic find her appealing? She glances to the side and back, a peculiar *Who Me?* look in her eyes, before leaning even farther forward and exposing even more of her to my lean and hungry gaze. By rights, I should be ecstatic. *Thank you, oh, Lord, for sending me this golden opportunity. You are, indeed, all-loving, all-understanding, all-caring.* But in place of ecstasy, I feel disappointment.

Slowly I maneuver a mechanical pencil across the page, forming very carefully, very methodically, the letters, *s-h-i-t*. I stab the page, breaking the point on the pencil and drawing condescending glances from a million pairs of glowering, beady eyes unsympathetic with my plight and ready to burn me, via some communal telepathic process, to a lifeless, dreamless, *spermless* cinder.

Not this time, I tell myself. *Not again. I will not lose her. I* cannot *lose her*! I stuff the paper and my mechanical pencil into a brown case and burrow my way toward the exit, bumping students with full food trays and empty beer pitchers ("I'm sorry, I'm sorry, so sorry, excuse me, please"). I muscle my way to my destiny to where I expect to see my golden-trussed goddess dangling her shoeless feet—dainty, I'm sure—in the cool, bubbling water. I can picture her clearly. She has shed her clothes—for she's just that spontaneous a Child of Nature—and her creamy white breasts spill their 38 glorious inches out and across her chest. As she laughs, they shake gently, firmly, her large, taut nipples swelling in eager anticipation even as I imagine coming upon her.

"Pardon me," I picture myself saying, "but I couldn't help but notice you in the Union."

She looks up at me quizzically, the slightest hint of a smile dancing in the deep blue pools of her eyes.

"You are without a doubt the most beautiful woman I have ever seen," I continue, "and I would very much like to make love to you."

It is my fantasy, but it turns out to be short-lived.

"Watch out, for Chrissake," a gravelly voice growls as I swing the heavy wood-and-glass door of the Union open as if made of cardboard. "What the hell's a-matter with you, anyway?"

"Sorry," I respond blankly, reality finally settling back in. "Really. I'm sorry." I bend over, making a gesture to help pick up his books before the fantasy returns, and instead I dart past him in my search for my golden goddess.

"Crazy Goddam son-of-a-bitch!" the voice calls after me. But I am already vaulting down the steps, rushing toward the street, dashing like a crazed halfback through an opening between a Toyota and a Volkswagen. Suddenly, I slow to a walk. It will not do to appear too anxious. I have lost the battle with more than one foe by falling into *that* trap before—by appearing too anxious, too flustered, too anxious—or did I already say that? Regardless, I will be sure not to visit *that* bottomless pit again soon.

As I approach the memorial pool, my eyes dart from one person to the next, settling for a moment on an overweight sausage of a woman stuffed obscenely into an orange-and-green bikini and sunning herself at the edge of the water. To a young toddler splashing bare-assed in the shallows while his mother chats on her phone. To a pair of young lovers wrapped oblivious in each other's arms. But nowhere do I see my dream woman, my mystery goddess, my fantasy of fertility. Not shoeless. Not clothesless. Not topless. *Not at all!*

"I might have guessed," a voice behind me says.

I whirl around and stop, frozen, an ignitable stone on a bed of hot lava. Somewhere, there *is* a God.

"What?

"I said I might have guessed ... you know, that you're a writer. I was watching you in the Rathskeller."

"Oh, yeah. *Yeah*?"

"You are, aren't you? I mean a writer?"

I glance at her neck, at a slim strand of gold running down to the top of her cleavage and then back up over her shoulder. I follow my eyes farther up to her cheek, which bears the golden glow of ripe nectarines in late summer. She wears no makeup, and yet her complexion is flawless. I long to reach out, to stroke her skin just to see if it's real, if it feels warm or cool or what. But I don't dare. I tremble at the very thought, struggling to control my fears, my anxieties, my curiosity, my lust.

"What makes you say that?" I ask at last.

"I saw you looking around the room and then writing something down. You know, watching the people around you. Just like a writer would do. Besides, you just seem the type. Strong, silent, masculine."

"Really." *Damn! All this, and she's brilliant, too.*

"Sure," she says. "In fact, you remind me of someone. Someone I used to know. Someone ... kinda special."

"Oh?" I respond cavalierly. "Another writer?"

"Actually, he was a plumber."

I crane my head and squint. *Did she say,* It was in summer?

"I'm sorry. What was that, again?"

"I said he was a plumber." She giggles coquettishly. "Oh, don't get me wrong. He was a wonderful person. Strong, silent, very macho ... kind of like you. A real man of the world, you know? Sort of an ... intellectual."

She reaches out suddenly and touches me on the arm, her hand delicately poised just above my elbow. I can hear my heart beating, feel the warm tenderness of her lips against mine. *My God, could this be it? Is she actually touching me? Is this the moment? Is it all up to me now? Am I supposed to make the next move? Reach out suddenly and sweep her body tightly up against mine, feel the warm, full firmness of her breasts against my chest, her thighs against my thighs, her soul against my soul?*

"In fact," she continues, "I was in love with him."

"Oh, *really*?" I reply, gulping hard. My arm where she clutches me begins to tingle.

"Really," she says. "We went together last summer for more than three months. It was fantastic."

"Fantastic," I reply. *Great. I remind her of someone she finds fantastic. Any more good news in store for me today?* "But," I continue, "you're not...I mean, you and he ... Are you ..."

"Still seeing each other? No." She removes her hand and giggles once more. "We broke up last fall."

I wonder briefly about a woman who finds such things amusing.

"How come?" I ask, not realizing the words are mine.

She shrugs. "I don't know. I guess he just wasn't ... concerned enough about me, you know? He didn't really care about satisfying *my* needs."

I gulp hard as she smiles at me again, her eyes searching mine for the road to eternal happiness. *Here I am*, my heart screams out. *Right here. Right in front of you. I have the key to the lock. And I'm willing to give it to you.* Free. *No strings attached.*

"I once wanted to be a plumber," I lie.

"No," she says.

"Sure. I really considered it for a long time once. In my younger days. You know, when I was a kid."

Christ, that does it. See the beautiful young maiden pack up her bags and move to another continent. Watch the gorgeous princess vanish in a puff of smoke, leaving an old warty frog in her place. Witness the transformation of 112 pounds of sultry sex-goddess into a pillar of icy salt. Why the hell do I do it? How *do I do it? How do I manage to keep saying such stupid things? How could I make it through twenty-five years of life, twenty six, practically, without ever having learned to talk intelligently?*

"That's super," she says.

Super? The woman is a student in college and still says *super*? And I'm worried about how *I* talk? I suddenly realize there may be hope for me yet.

Her eyes glaze over slightly, and her head tips to one side as she stares deeply into me. This, I realize, just may be the real thing. I imagine myself being a rich and famous writer one day, attending parties like Truman Capote, F. Scott Fitzgerald and Zelda, or even someone still alive, maybe someone like J. K. Rowling for God's sake, I don't know. And I waltz into the room with this vision of loveliness on my arm as all voices stop, all eyes turn to us. Every woman there instinctively hates her, and every man there wants to fuck her. But she only has eyes for me. *Me!* That, I realize, is the answer to a lifetime of prayers.

"It's amazing how you remind me of Fritz."

"The cat? I remind you of a *cat*?"

"No, silly. You know. My old boyfriend."

"Oh, the plumber."

She nods. "I'll bet you're every bit as virile as he was. A real man's man."

I think she already said that, but what the hell. "Well," I say, feeling the blood rush into my cheeks again, "I don't like to brag, but I have been told that, you know, well ... that I'm pretty much on the overtly virile side."

"Like Hemingway."

I shrug. "Sure. Okay."

"I'll just bet you have lots of women friends, too."

"Me? Oh, sure," I lie. "Plenty of them. Too many, actually. Sometimes I wonder just why the hell I can't be satisfied with, oh, say, forty or fifty." I wait for her to laugh. And wait. And wait some more. And the meaning of the word, *awkward*, pops glaringly into mind.

"*Really!*" Her eyes nearly burst as she contemplates the complexity of the concept.

Yes! Jesus Christ, I scream to myself, *the kid comes through at last.* High fives all around the table! *Thank you, God. Thank you, thank you, thank you, thank you, thank you. Wittiness doth finally prevail.*

I shrug coyly.

"I knew it," she says. "I had you pegged for a ladies' man the moment I saw you."

Keep it up, Lord, and I'll do anything you ask. I'll go to church on Sunday. I'll go to church on Tuesday. Hell, I'll build a church on Tuesday, if that's what it takes. Just say the word.

"Well," I say, "I don't like to brag ..." Which, of course, is only marginally stretching the truth.

She laughs suddenly, bending low and sending her hair cascading down in front of her. Slowly, she straightens her back, pulling her mane up again, giving me a spectacular view of the canyon in slow motion. Suddenly I understand what it was that kept our forefathers plodding steadily west. The spirit of the Great Rocky Mountains. Adventure and discovery around every bend. I feel my mouth getting dry, my tongue sticking to the back of my teeth.

"Just like Fritz," she says finally, and then she stops laughing as she draws herself very, *very* close to me. My palms drip with anticipation. I can smell her perfume. Not the cheap, bottled, dime-store stuff. This is the real thing, the delicate bouquet of a beautiful woman. That singular, indescribable sweetness that comes from deep within. And I am ready. All my dreams, all my hopes, my anticipations, my desires, my goals in life are about to be fulfilled. With her at my side, walking hand-in-hand through life, how could I miss?

"You want to know something?" she asks, her voice so soft, the words slipping from her mouth so gently that I can barely see the movement of her thick, inviting lips. "Something I've never told a single solitary soul before? The *real* reason Fritz and I broke up?"

I gulp loudly, realizing for the first time that I have never seen lips that full and inviting before in my life. I gulp again at the thought, hoping she can't hear. I attempt to reply, but only a soft, sickly, rasping sound comes out.

"Well," she continues, the words barely audible against the bubbling of the nearby fountain. "The real reason was ... a social disease."

My addled mind balks. *What was that? What was it she said? Did she say, I mostly eat peas?* I frown, look into her eyes long and hard, before finally realizing what words she had actually uttered. But what did she mean, a social disease? Did she mean she had trouble relating to others? Did she have difficulty getting along in large groups? Appearing in public? *Is that it? Is that what she means?*

I feel instinctively that I should not under any circumstances ask my next question, but nonetheless I hear the words squeak out of trembling lips: "What kind of social disease?"

"You know. That thing that people who aren't ... *careful* ... can contract? I mean, no matter how particular a guy and girl might be, sometimes it just ... happens. You understand."

Understand? Understand? Of course, I understand. But understand what? That the girl of my dreams, that my very own goddess, the one to whom I am ready to dedicate my life, my soul, and my dreams got the clap? From some guy named after some fucking cat? From some goddam plumber?

"*Uhh*, I'm not sure," I say.

"Well, I mean, you can't blame *me*. We were going to be married. I'd saved myself for just the right man. Just the right one, you know? Or at least I thought I had. And I probably would have married him, too, and had a wonderful life with him. A little home in the country. A couple of beautiful children. I always wanted a couple of beautiful kids. And maybe some kind of mutt. But after that, after he contracted that, that *disease*, well, it was just out of the question. I mean, I couldn't even look him in the eye anymore. Not like I can *you*."

I nod, still too dumbfounded to speak. And then it strikes me. *Did she say* he *got the disease or* they *got the disease? God, is this really happening to me? Why, Lord? Can you give me a hint?*

"So ..." she sighs, sending her swollen, perky, and possibly diseased tits heaving. "That was that. Pitiful, isn't it?"

I nod my head again. "Awful." The consequences are simply too devastating to fathom. There he was, the lucky son-of-a-bitch, diddling the most stunning creature ever known to humanity, practically, on the very eve of tying the indelible knot to her for all time—because what moron in his right mind would ever even *think* about leaving her. *Ever*? Or even *dying* on her, for God's sake? There he was, Fritz the Cat, tottering on the brink of nirvana, when suddenly he shows up with a big dose of the creeping crud. *Jesus, what an idiot!*

"Just think. If only he'd been more discreet," she says. "But, then, of course, you know how men are." She smiles at me, as though suddenly able to read my mind. As though she'd been *born* to read my mind. All at once, I feel uncomfortable, as if I want to crawl into a hole or something.

"Oh, no," I say, shaking my head. "Not all men ... I mean, I'm not really ..."

"And that's alright," she adds quickly, taking hold once more of my arm. I wait for the tingle, but it fails to reappear. "I understand that a man has ... well, certain needs. That those needs are different from a woman's. And that's why our little talk here is so important. You understand, don't you?"

"Important," I repeat.

"Exactly," she says. "That's why I'm glad I met you today. People like you and me, we understand one another."

"We do?"

"We know what we have to do."

"Yeah, sure." I say. I feel a little like a right fielder in a game of right-handed hitters. Something is going on here, that's for sure. I'm just not certain it involves *me*.

"Absolutely," she says.

"Why?" I ask, not particularly sure of my motivation. I mean, as far as I could tell, it was *Game, Set, Match* from the moment she mentioned that little "problem" her fiancé may have visited upon her. I don't care how beautiful a woman is, I'm not sticking my pen into a dry inkwell. If you know what I mean.

"Because, silly, I can tell you're a very macho, very virile man. And I know you want to be protected. And you don't want to have a relationship with anyone unless you're careful."

I nod. "Sure. Of course. That's me, alright. That's for *damn* sure."

"I know you're a lot more considerate than Fritz was. I mean, I was lucky when you really stop to think about it. I never came down with anything, thank heaven."

What? Are you serious? Is she *serious? Did I really hear her right? Did she really escape the Jaws of Death unscathed? Oh, yes, my God! Oh, thank you, Lord Jesus!*

I felt like high-fiving myself, but I figured that would look a little peculiar, so, instead, I nodded knowingly.

"But all those tests and things," she continued, "and all those embarrassing trips to the doctor. I could have died, you know?"

Do we really have to go into all the details now?

"But I know you're different. I know you're concerned about your relationships. After all, if a woman is worth having ... *sexually*, well, you just want to be safe. Especially someone as experienced with the opposite sex as you are."

"Of course," I reply, wondering just what the hell she was talking about. And why.

"That's the reason I wanted to show you these."

I watch as she reaches into her purse and pulls out a small handful of colorful cellophane wrappers.

"What are they?" I ask. "Bennies?"

She laughs. "No, silly. They're condoms. You know, for protection. Like I said. I could tell from the moment I first saw you that you're different. You're resourceful. You're concerned and caring. I knew right away that you understand."

I do not understand.

"After Fritz and I broke up, I was so disillusioned with men, so disappointed that one human being could do that kind of thing to another that I joined the Sexual Protection League—the SPL. Have you heard of it?"

The NFL? Sure. Who hasn't?

"Well," she continues, "the SPL is just about the most wonderful group of people I ever met, you know? They started up on the north side of Chicago a few years ago, and now they're national practically.

Their motto is, 'A happy relationship is a disease-free relationship.' Cute, huh?"

"Disease-free," I say, absently. "Yeah. Adorable."

"And so, of course, I offered to help out by doing anything I could. That's when I began selling some of their products. For the good of humanity. And to make a little money to help pay my tuition. But mostly for the good of humanity."

"Humanity." I wonder just how on earth pimping for free sex benefits humankind.

"What color do you like?"

"*Hmm*? Color?" I ask.

"I think mauve would be just perfect for you. Or maybe teal. Yes, that's it. To go with your eyes. But, then again, a lady likes to have a selection to choose from, doesn't she? So, why don't we just choose three each from the seventeen different color groups represented in the collection?"

I nod. "Three each. From the seventeen ..."

"That should be enough to hold even a stud like you for a few days!" She throws her head back again and laughs before returning her attention to her purse. "Where is that ..."

"Seventeen. Sure," I say finally. "Why not. What the hell." *I mean, how much could they cost? A quarter apiece? Three for a dollar? Besides, she was right. It was just good sense to play it safe. You never could tell. And if things worked out the way I planned, I could put them in a drawer somewhere and will them to our kids when I died.*

"Textured, ribbed, or plain?" she asks.

I shrug. "Hell's bells, I'm stumped. Surprise me."

She laughs. "You are just so *precious*. I can see you really *are* a considerate partner. Let's give you one of each. If you want more later, you can always reorder."

"One."

"*Uh-huh.*"

"Of each."

"That's right," she says. "And three of each of the different colors. You know, three red textured, three red ribbed, three red plain ..."

"Three red ..."

I watch as she pulls out her cell phone, opens up her calculator, and begins punching in numbers, her cute little Scandinavian nose bobbing up and down, her sexy red tongue dancing across her lips. "You know something? I was right. You're *exactly* the kind of man I thought you were, exactly the kind I admire. The kind of man I always hoped Fritz would turn out to be."

"Really?" I say. *By God, I think I'm gaining here. I think I'm I gathering some steam. And if my dream girl is a little* eccentric, *so what? Since when the hell has eccentric been against the law?*

"There," she says, totaling the order and holding it out for me to see. "That's three times three times seventeen. That comes to $676.57, including sales tax."

I gulp again, this time harder than before and not caring at all whether or not she hears.

"Six hundred seventy-six dollars ..." I repeat.

"And fifty-seven cents. Including sales tax." She holds up a bagful of goods and waves it before me, like a farmer tempting an old nag with a sack of oats.

"I ... I don't think I have that much cash with me."

"Oh, that's alright," she says, stuffing the bag into her purse. "I take PayPal and personal checks."

I stare at her blankly for a moment, and then I begin making motions as if searching for a non-existent checkbook.

"By God," I say finally, after peering into every nook and cranny on my body. "Say, you're going to think I'm a real scatterbrain, but I'm afraid I ..." I look up at her, at her outstretched hand, at the shiny black leather case she's holding out to me.

"Honestly," she says. "You men are all alike. You're lucky to have us women around. Fortunately, I have this banking software installed on my phone." She waves it in front of me like a matador flashing a cape before a belligerent bull. "Just tell me the name of your bank and give me your account number. The software will fill in the routing information. Then just type your e-mail address into the little box here—see?—and sign at the bottom, and the rest will be handled automatically."

"The name of my bank."

"Yes, that's right."

"And my account number."

"*Uh-huh*. And your e-mail addy. And you'll get your receipt instantly. Now, which bank is it?"

"*Uhh ...*" I hesitate for only a moment or two, only long enough for me to question seriously whether or not I should go through with this whole thing. I mean, was she interested in me or wasn't she? Or was this nothing more than a sales pitch? If that were it, if it really were only a sales pitch, I had to admit it was a damned good one.

No, I decide. *No, she's on the level. She's simply concerned about my being concerned about all the women roaring through my life and trying to help me out.* I wonder if my chances of riding off with her into the sunset will somehow improve if I have a shitload of condoms in my saddlebag.

"It's the First National Securities of Chicago," I blurt out finally, hoping against hope that she doesn't realize there is no such facility anywhere within the entire bowels of the City of Chicago. For a moment, I toy with the notion of saying that it's a subsidiary of the Amalgamated Bank of Syria and that the transaction will probably take an extra day or two to complete, but it dawns on me that my chances of scoring with my fantasy woman will go right down the tubes with that one. As will I, if she finds out the truth and decides to prosecute me for passing a bum check. But that's another matter entirely.

"Fine. Your checking account number?"

"That would be … *uhh, one*, one, seven …"

"One, one, seven …"

"Three, one, seven …"

"Three, one, seven …"

"*Uhh*, fifty-two eighty-four."

"Fifty-two …" Her voice drifts off as I watch her manipulate her Asanti 4373K for several seconds before she taps a button and holds out the screen for my inspection. There, sure enough, right below the words, *First National Securities of Chicago* and the bogus account number I just gave her, is the sum total of $676.57 spelled out in good old U.S. of A. dollars. "Just put your John Hancock on the bottom line, next to the X," she adds, and for a brief moment, I wonder just where the hell I am going to come up with $676.57 anyway once she finds out there really is no First National Securities of Chicago, and I have to devise a Plan B to produce the funds to keep me out of jail. My only hope is that, by the time the order is submitted and rejected and submitted and rejected a second time and possibly a third, my fantasy woman and I will have moved on to bigger and better things, such as mind-blowing sex and lifelong mutual commitments, and she'll be mine. And we can have a good, long laugh about it together years later.

"There," I say, motioning with the stylus across the solid black line at the bottom of the screen and handing the phone back to her.

"Jack M. Blakely. *Super*," she gushes, pressing another button. She waits, watching, as I sweat bullets while taking in the remarkable sight of the twins struggling to free themselves even in the presence of such unbridled mendacity. Do they *ever* rest?

"This is embarrassing," she says, shaking her head.

Oh, crap. I should have used that Syria thing!

"I'm afraid I just lost my Wi-Fi connection. I'm going to have to finish running this off when I get back to the office. I'll e-mail you a copy for your records and send you your order." She shoves the phone back into her purse and pulls the latch closed. "If you don't mind my getting in touch with you tomorrow."

I feel my lips purse and my head shake involuntarily.

"Good, because I just know you're going to love them. And get *so-o-o* much use out of them. They're just a super investment."

Suddenly, a little birdie lands on my shoulder. It weighs roughly twenty-three pounds and has the wingspan of a Douglas F4 Phantom Fighter. And I realize at last that, for better or worse, I am not a creative writer for nothing.

Goddamit, I curse to myself. *Shit. It's all a hoax. One great big, gigantic, unmitigated hoax.* I watch her fiddling with her phone as my chin drops to my chest. *She's a con. Nothing but a fucking con. A scammer. She's pulling a grift on me! She's setting me up for the slaughter! She had this planned all along. I was nothing more to her than a mark from the very start! And a dumb one! What a jerk.*

Suddenly I feel as if I'm the lowest, most ignorant, most gullible person on earth. How ridiculously foolish I am. How fucking gullible!

And then it dawns on me. It *couldn't* be a scam. Not in a million years. *All you have to do is open your eyes and take a look at her. She is honey and molasses, maple syrup and cherry jam spread out on a slice of freshly baked sourdough bread. She is goodness personified. What am I thinking?*

Besides, I remember, I'm the one who said I have an account at the First National Securities of Chicago, so when she *does* go to place the order, *I'll* be the one running the scam.

What the hell am I doing? What's wrong with my brain? I just committed a crime. Or at least I think I did. Why did I do that? I could end up in prison!

I am tempted for a moment to spill the beans about my own inherent dishonesty and throw myself on the mercy of the court, but I somehow manage to fight off the urge when I look deeply into her two eyes—and elsewhere—and realize I have to have her, no matter what, and hear my own words slipping from two very willing lips: "Which reminds me. I have these two tickets for Saturday's big game. You know, against Ohio State? And I was thinking ... wouldn't it be great to go to the game, then maybe out to dinner afterward? A little wine, a little dancing. And, who knows, maybe a relaxing evening at my apartment afterward."

This will tell the tale. This will wrap things up. This is where we separate the wheat from the chaff. Where the rubber really meets the road.

She smiles, takes my hand, and squeezes it gently. "I'm sorry," she says, "but I don't think so. You see, as much as I'd like to, I have this strict personal policy of never dating my customers."

"Well ... I'm not a customer. I mean, not *technically*."

She lifts her shoulders and raises her brows. She holds up her phone with my signature still etched on the bottom and waves it gently from side to side. "Sorry. Afraid this says you are."

"But ... but ..." I frantically search for another way off the hook. Something to tell her I'm not who she thinks I am without telling her I'm not who she thinks I am. Instead, I find myself saying simply, "That order? It's not ... really an order. I mean, not until I pay."

"It's good as gold to me," she says.

"But ... well, it's not any good. I mean, not really. Not technically."

She pauses, her eyes searching mine. If only I can convince her to cancel the contract. Negate our deal. That's my one hope for not blowing everything. Tear the thing up, marry her, and move to the suburbs. Buy a Mercedes, settle down to two-point-four kids, and live life happily ever after.

But first things first.

"And why do you say that?" she asks.

I hesitate, preparing to bite the bullet. All my life, it seems, has come down to this one singular moment. All the days I spent manipulating my way through school, all the times I'd invested conning my way through various summer jobs, all the women I'd snowed. They all came down to this.

"Because ... I made up the bank."

She raises her brows again.

"And I gave you a phony checking account number."

She looks down at her phone.

"And ... and ... and ... the name is fake, too," I say. "It's really Jake Striker."

She looks at me incredulously, as if I'd sprouted another head or at least a second set of ears. For a moment, I think she is going to cry. And then I see her lips curl down and her eyes narrow.

"That wasn't a very nice thing to do, Jake Striker."

I shrug. "What can I say? You caught me flat-footed. I'm between paychecks. I just didn't want you to leave. You know, without having a chance to get to know you better."

"So, you lied to me."

I moved about uncomfortably. "Well, not lied, actually. More like ... failed to tell you the truth."

"Well, now I'll tell *you* some truth. Here's what we're going to do. We're going to go down to the bank together, your *real* bank, so you can draw out the cash and give it to me directly. In that way, we'll both be living up to our agreement, and you won't be guilty, you know? Of writing a bad check."

This time I feel *my* eyes turn to slits, wondering if I'd heard her cor-rectly. *Did she say,* Of fighting a fat chick? I shake my head, my mind whirring as the reality of her words finally sinks in.

"I don't think that's a good idea at all."

"Well, then, how about if we go down to the Third Precinct and have a little heart-to-heart talk with my uncle, instead."

"Your uncle?" My mind races back through every good cop/bad cop film I've ever seen. What the hell would Dirty Harry do at a time like this? I wracked my mystery-writing brain for a solution. Nothing popped into view.

"Yes. He's a sergeant with the police department, in Vice. I think he'd be very interested to know how you stopped me on the street and tried to pick me up. Or whatever it is you really had in mind. And then set me up for a check-kiting scam."

"A sergeant?"

"Third Precinct."

"Well," I tell her, the wheels beginning to pick up a bit of speed. I recall a story I wrote once that had a chick like this in it, a story I sold to *Ellery Queen's Mystery Magazine* or somewhere. Something about a sexy, beautiful skirt who tries to scam a widower out of his bank account, only to have the old man catch on and turn the tables on her. In the end, he was forced to shoot her, and she died in his arms.

I hoped this wouldn't come to that.

"I'll tell you what," I said, talking slowly to give my mind a chance to catch up. "I think we can go one better than that. Let's say you and I … you know, let's do like you say and the two of us go down to my bank, and I'll withdraw the cash from my account and give it to you. Then you give me a receipt for it, and we'll stop by the precinct where your uncle works, and you can explain to *my* uncle, who just also happens to be a cop at the Third Precinct as well, just what you're trying to pull. Now, isn't *that* a coincidence? I mean that both of our uncles work for the exact same precinct? I mean, what are the odds?"

Turn the story topsy-turvy and dump it back in the Perp's lap. That's the way the last one went.

"Are you kidding me?" she asked.

"He's in Bunco and Vice. I'll introduce you, and you can explain to him how it is that you approached *me* and … and …"

Come on, Brainiac, don't let me down now!

"—and how you struck up a conversation with me out of the clear blue sky. And why it is that you're pretending to be a college student when I'm just betting the closest you ever came to a classroom was probably diddling some professor who works there. And how there really isn't any Sexual Protection League or whatever you called it. And how you never had any plans whatsoever on delivering those overpriced condoms to me once you got my money."

"I don't understand. What are you talking about?"

"And, while you're at it, you can tell him why it is that you're so damned anxious to get hold of my personal banking information."

Bingo! That does it. I see her smile crack harder than a soft-boiled egg against a picture window on Halloween. For the first time since I laid eyes on her, I see her lips begin to quiver and her eyes dart back and forth as if seeking an avenue of escape. And finding none.

"Your ... uncle? Seriously? At the Third Precinct?"

"Uncle Frank? Yes. He works undercover in the Bunco and Vice Division. He's a captain, and his department investigated fraud and white-collar crime." I pause. "Little scams a lot like this. You know."

She issues a weak denial through slightly parted lips and dancing eyes. "Well ... I mean, why do we have to start proffering charges against one another? Why can't we just resolve this between ourselves? No need to get anyone else ..." She hesitates as she pulls out her phone, holds it up for my inspection, and deletes the order she had just placed for me. "There." She lets out a deep sigh. "All gone. Just as if it never took place." She hesitates again. "Okay?"

I look at her, rub my chin as if I'm thinking, and finally shrug.

"Okay. I guess it was just a big misunderstanding. No harm to anyone."

She takes my hand, shakes it, and draws closer to me, kissing me slowly, lightly on one cheek.

"What's that for?" I ask, hoping for the answer of all answers. I mean, sure, she may be a con, but she's still drop-dead gorgeous. And a good man can always straighten out a woman gone astray. At least, that's the story I tell myself, and I'm sticking to it. So I wait to hear the magic words: *Oh, darling, I just couldn't go through with it. I could never have done it to you. Not to the man I love! Can you ever forgive me? I'll make it up to you. I promise. Whatever it takes, I'll make it up to you.*

Instead, she says, "Let's just say it's for being such an understanding man. I meant what I said earlier, about how I can see that you're different. I saw that in you right from the start."

I feel my brow rise instinctively.

"Besides," she adds, "you can't blame a girl for trying to pick up a few bucks here and there, can you?"

I shake my head and make a low clucking sound with my tongue. "What would your uncle say?"

She giggles. "I don't have an uncle. Both of my parents were only children." She shrugs. "And neither of them ever worked for the Third Precinct." She pauses. "You?"

I look at her, more angelic than before. Purer. More God-like. I am fading fast. I know it. I can't hold out much longer. I want her; I need her. And soon! "Me?"

"Come on. Fess up. It's just a little too coincidental for you to have an uncle working at the same precinct as mine, wouldn't you say? I mean, how likely would that be?"

"Well, I ... I guess." I think about it for several seconds. I smile. "I mean since we're both confessing here. Okay, you're right. About that part. But I *do* have an uncle. In fact, I have several of them. It's just that none of them works for the Chicago P.D. In fact, the only uncle I ever see is Uncle Jed, and that's once a year at Christmas time. He's a dermatologist."

She laughs, deep and loud and throaty. "Maybe when I get old and gray, I can call on him to see if he can help."

As if that *will ever happen!*

And then it dawns on me. *What do I have to lose? The afternoon isn't a complete wash. Not yet, anyway.*

"You know," I say, reaching my hands out for hers. "Now that we've both come clean, why don't we just start out all over?"

"You mean like two normal people just interested in getting to know one another, no strings attached?"

Before I can respond, I feel a hand on my shoulder and, seeing both of her dainty mitts still clinging to mine, I sense instinctively that it spells trouble.

"How's it goin'?" a deep, gravelly voice spills out the words like curdled milk from a three-week-old carton. I look behind me and up. Up. *Way* up at a monster of a man, possibly thirty to forty feet tall. And, even though it is well over 90 degrees in the shade, there are snow clouds swirling around his head. And around his big, sagging jaw. And when that jaw lowers so that the monster can smile, a formidable hunk of steel catches the light and nearly blinds me. I am just about ready to yank myself from the monster's grasp, dash wildly across the patio, and dive into the pool when suddenly my dream woman comes to my rescue.

"Oh, just super. I've been waiting for you!" she chirps. " I'd like you to meet a good customer of mine. He just bought the Super Stud package."

"Hi," I say, playing along and smiling with all my might. He holds out a hand the size of a sirloin steak, and I take it tentatively. He can squeeze as hard as he wishes. There is no way I am going to object. Not even frown. Nor do anything else that might in any way be construed as an even remotely unfriendly act. Hostility is no way to placate a monster. I learned that in the fourth grade.

"Moose plays tight end for the Illini," she says. "And he also runs errands for a couple of ... *businessmen* on the lower South Side. Isn't that a *stitch*?"

I turn to my goddess and feel the smile slipping away. "Yeah," I say softly. "A stitch."

"Seems we're not going to get a chance for that do-over after all, are we?"

I shrug, wondering suddenly how anyone so drop-dead gorgeous can be so inscrutably evil. How could I have misread her so? How did I fail to see her coming?

"Seems not."

"We better get goin,'" Moose says. "Nice tah meet youse."

I nod, my heart sinking as he starts down the street and she turns after him. "Yeah. Likewise, I'm sure," I lie, and I turn dejectedly away. Even the best mystery writers in the world sometimes come up a buck or two short.

Suddenly I feel the softness of honey-blonde hair spilling across the back of my neck and whirl around.

"By the way, your Saturday plan sounds just great," she says , adding softly, "And after you get back to your apartment ..." She turns her back to Moose.

"Yes?" I say, my heart feeling a sudden swell of blood pulsing through it. *Can it be? Is it really going to happen? Is there hope for us yet?*

She clutches my hand, slipping something cool into my palm. "Try the red ribbed one. It drives them crazy."

"*Uhh*, just a minute," I say, glancing down before moving closer. I whisper barely loud enough for *me* to hear. "How about *you*? Do I get a chance to find out if the red ribbed ones drive *you* crazy, too?"

She straightens up suddenly and breaks into a schoolgirl grin. "Oh, I'm afraid not. I absolutely *hate* red. Besides, I'm on the pill."

My heart spills once more across the pavement, and I am just about to concede failure when she stops, turns back to face me, and smiles once more. "But I wouldn't mind dinner. Italian? Around seven? I'll call you with my address."

My eyes pop open. "Wait a minute. You can't call me. You don't have my number. You erased the order, remember?"

"I undid the erase right afterward."

I freeze for several seconds. "You ... you undid ..."

"The order," she says, and she throws back her head and laughs, deep and throaty. She stops and stares directly into my eyes. "Do you love me?"

I love her with all my heart and soul and the rest of me, too—whatever remains after our encounter. I can't help but wonder if Moose, some ten feet down the street, feels the same. He stops and looks back at us over his shoulder. She turns to him. "Go on ahead, Moose. I'll catch up with you in a couple."

I watch stunned as he nods and does as he's told, and before he's out of sight, she throws her arms around my neck and pulls herself so close to me, I can feel the warmth of her breath on my lips.

"Do you find me irresistible?"

I struggle to speak, my words turning to air and drifting away on the afternoon breeze. I finally nod and manage to whisper, "Devastating."

She giggles. "Do you want to make love to me?"

I exhale, breathe in, and pause. "Oh, God, yes. You'll never know how much."

She pulls herself closer, still, until her lips, wet from her tongue, slide up against mine, her mouth opening slightly as she explores the very depths of my passion. After what seems a lifetime, she slowly backs away, her eyes never once leaving mine.

"Until tomorrow evening, then," she says, turning to leave. "Oh, and one more thing."

I let out a sigh and feel my brows instinctively rise.

"Make sure you're hungry. I have a feeling I'm going to be *ravenous*!"

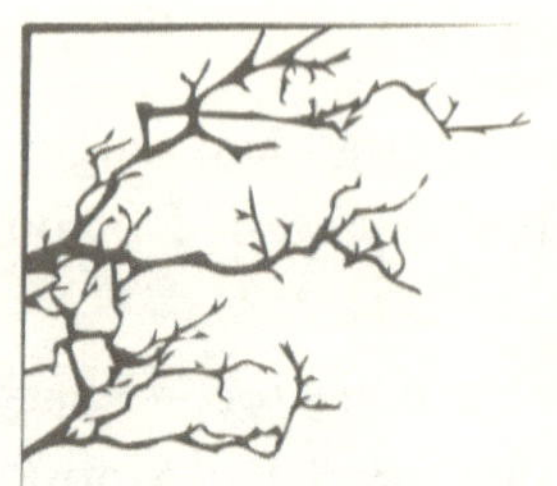

SIX: Trapped!

HIGHTOWER EYED THE investigator casually. There was something about his appearance—his potbelly, the thin, greasy gray hair, the bulbous nose and fragile, fading lips—that made him look more comical than compelling. His shirt was a bilious affair sewn up years ago in hues of red and green and brown. His pants were khaki, cut off at the knees and predictably wrinkled and thread-worn at the pockets, something you might expect to find on a ten-year-old schoolboy with a penchant for keeping way-too-large treasures in way-too-small pockets. He wore thin black socks, a ribbed polyester-and-nylon blend, inside scruffy Jesus sandals that had been begging for retirement since 1943.

His face was sallow—that same Dick Nixon look that helped Kennedy gain the White House after the former Veep saw the debates go south on him back in '59—and pocked with scars from some long-ago battle with acne.

But his eyes were what caught the contractor's attention the most. Not his eyes so much as the way he used them. He periodically focused them on his target, where they seared their way deep into the unsuspecting victim before skirting away as if frightened of seeing too much, of being discovered attempting to unmask whatever it was they might turn up on the fellow. Not dancing, as though carefully choreographed and planned movements, graceful and willowy like those of a gifted ballerina, but rather bolting from the arena, stumbling over one another in an awkward attempt to escape with their lives intact. Like a meadow filled with whitetail deer freezing as the headlights from a speeding car bearing down on them before the beasts shoot off in every direction imaginable ... and some that aren't. All in all, those eyes made him seem quite humorous, extraordinarily strange, and more than a little harm-less. Or so they lent one to believe.

"So, you got this heating contractor working for you," the investigator said, those eyes flitting nervously from a bowl of spinach dip that he'd been hoarding between two stubby knees and a buxom blonde laughing languidly with a group of people at the far end of the room, "and you gave him twelve grand, and he didn't do anything for the money and then ended up closing his doors and taking off. Is that about it?"

Hightower waited for the eyes to return to him. "Yep. Exactly. He took the money under false pretenses and then just vanished. His wife, or his ex-wife now, I guess—although I think they were still living together until he split—his ex said she had no idea of where he was but told me he'd taken a bunch of her stuff with him, too, including a brand new red pickup truck with all the trimmings. She said she'd bought it for him because she had good credit, and he had none, and he'd been paying her back a little at a time each month."

"Why would she do a stupid thing like that?"

"Because he'd cut her in on a share of his heating-and-cooling business, and he promised her she'd make a ton of money off him."

"And he didn't have the money to buy the truck himself, and he didn't have the credit," the investigator mused. "Classic."

"She called him every name in the book, plus a few I'd never heard of before. I mean, she was *pissed*."

Peeps leaned forward, the bowl of dip tottering precariously on the edge of the sofa before he reached down, grabbed it, and set it on the floor between his feet. "You call the police?"

Hightower shook his head. "This just happened a week ago, and we weren't sure he was actually gone until I talked to his wife. We were going to take it to the D.A. first thing Monday morning. Drop it in his lap. I've heard some talk about this guy being a con, running similar scams in the past. Although you'd never know it to talk to him. He always seemed willing to help out on short notice, always really seemed to care, you know?"

"Most cons are like that. That's how they make their marks. Build up their confidence, and then they nail 'em when they're not looking."

"Yeah. I guess. Kicker is, this isn't the first theft we've had."

Peeps raised his brows.

"Hell, no. We had somebody break into our shop and steal nearly 15 thousand worth of tools and equipment. We had one of our own foremen buy nearly six thousand dollars' worth of roofing supplies when he only needed two grand to finish the job. The rest just sort of *disappeared*. Then Trinidale Builders Supply shipped twenty-two thousand dollars' worth of finish materials to a home we were building for an older couple out in the sticks. It wasn't even under roof. The sheetrock wasn't up, doors and windows weren't in. But they dumped more than twenty grand worth of toilets and faucets and Jacuzzi tubs and ceramic tile and carpeting and lighting fixtures in an open garage, and then they billed us for it."

Peeps looked puzzled. "Well, hey, at least you *got* the stuff. Coulda been worse, right? No big loss."

"Yeah, we got it, all right. But the kicker is, we never even *ordered* it. I'd never even *discussed* ordering it with them. Why would I? We were six months away—at *least*—from getting to the point where we could use it. That's six months of tripping over it every time one of our framers or sheet rockers came or went. When I asked Scott Sandalman to show me an order form or a signature on an invoice or anything, he couldn't."

"I don't understand," Peeps said. "How could they just do that and get away with it? Didn't you report it?"

"Not yet. That's another one I was getting ready to lay on the D.A. According to Sandalman, he's still looking into the matter and will get back to me. He says their interior designer, Kelli Powell, swore that I gave her the go-ahead. In the meantime, we were working on a renovation for her—that old, three-story stucco disaster across from the courthouse, you know? But when we finished and it was time for her to close on her loan and pay us off, she refused."

"What do you mean? She refused to pay you off?"

"Pay us off, hell. She refused to *close*!"

"*What*?" Hightower threw his arms out to his side. "Why would she do a thing like that? She must have been paying through the nose for a construction loan. Why wouldn't she want to convert that into a long-term mortgage as soon as possible?"

"I don't know, but I talked to her mortgage broker myself. *Several* times. He told me all he needed was her signature, and the money was hers. It was all pre-approved, just waiting for her to come and get it. He begged me to help get her to sign. Once they paid us off, we'd sign a release, and we'd be done."

"I just don't understand why she wouldn't close on her new mortgage if she was that close to finishing."

"My guess is that Sandalman paid her not to. He knew she owed us more than sixty grand. And he knew that, so long as she didn't pay us, we were going to have a *helluva* time making up for that loss of revenue in this town. I think he wanted us out of business. We were a threat to him. Same thing with his dad. The Old Man is on the loan committee at First National Bank. We called the bank president and asked for a short-term loan to see us through. He told me that, with our solid reputation and our strong collateral, it was a cinch. But after the loan committee met the following week, the guy called to tell me he was turning us down. When I asked why, he said that certain members of the loan committee had heard about some bad business deals we'd made recently and decided we'd be a poor risk."

Peeps shook his head.

"He stopped short of admitting that those 'bad business deals' had been engineered by Sandalman's own son to drive us out of business. And, of course, the Old Man was all too anxious to help sonny out."

"Yeah, I see what you mean. That's pretty shabby, all right. But at least you still had that twenty grand of stuff they delivered. I assume you used it eventually."

Hightower shook his head.

"Didn't you?"

"That's the *real* kicker," the contractor said. "Before we could get there to close the place in and lock the stuff up, someone drove a truck out one night and stole everything. I mean *everything*. I think they left the carpeting. Probably didn't want to hassle with it because the rolls are so bulky, I don't know. But twenty grand out the window. Just like that." He snapped his fingers.

Peeps shook his head. "I hope you were insured."

"We were, and so were the owners of the home. But when we went to put in a claim, the Hartford agent handling it said that he'd made a mistake and that he had failed to sell them theft insurance, even though he had sworn to us all along—*and* to our clients—that we had the most complete coverage we could possibly get. Turns out he was related to Sandalman somehow. An uncle or something. Big surprise in this town."

"Man," Peeps said, staring down at the wine as he swirled it in his glass. Hightower thought the guy's eyes were beginning to glaze ... but, hey, after all, it *was* a party. Probably he shouldn't even have brought it up, anyhow. But meeting him that way seemed pre-ordained. After all, Peeps *was* the investigator for the D.A.'s office, the fellow he would have ended up talking to on Monday morning, anyway. And he *was* willing to listen. Hightower always said that, whenever fate turns your way, you'd damned well better not get caught napping.

"You've had a run of bad luck since you moved here, that's for sure," Peeps added. "When did you say that was? I mean that you came to town and hung out your shingle?"

"Two years ago. And I doubt that luck has anything to do with it. This town ... the people ..." He shook his head. "I've never seen a more immoral, a more corrupt bunch of clowns in my life. Even the police. When we reported the tools missing to that jackass detective they have down there, you know what he said? 'Don't count on getting any of them back.'"

Peeps shook his head and took a deep swig from his glass before shifting his weight back into the sofa.

Hightower continued: "Gives you a nice, warm, welcome feeling inside, you know? And when we reported that six-thousand-dollar roofing theft, the same cop said, 'Don't you think it's strange that you're the only business in town getting ripped off?' Can you believe it? I was so pissed, I could have strangled him."

Peeps raised his brows. "Now *that's* illegal."

Hightower smiled.

"One thing I don't understand," Peeps said. Why would Trinidale Builders Supply want you out of business? Seems to me like they'd make more money off you if you stuck around. After all, you're a contractor, and they sell construction materials to contractors."

Hightower popped a stuffed mushroom into his mouth, swallowed, and washed it down with a short swig of wine. "That's the deviousness of it all. He wanted us gone because we opened up a showroom on Main Street a few months ago. That upped the ante. All of a sudden, we're no longer just another builder in town. Now we're another builder *and* a materials' supplier, just like Trinidale Builders Supply. We handle everything from windows and doors to countertops, sinks and tubs, electrical fixtures, flooring, roofing. We sell wholesale to our clients. I couldn't believe when I saw Sandalman's prices how badly they were ripping this town off. Some markups more than a hundred percent. That's when I decided to step in and offer folks an alternative. We're biting into the profits of Builders Supply big time. And Sandalman, I'm sure, doesn't like that one bit."

Peeps shrugged. "I've seen him do some weird shit in this town, no doubt about it. He's one ballsy Mo-Fo."

"Yeah, well, weird isn't quite the word *I'd* use," Hightower said. "If this kind of thing keeps going on, we're going to be out of business. We're going to have to shut down. And I don't think that's something most of the people in this town want to see happen."

"No," Peeps said absently. "No, of course not."

Carrie stretched her arms slowly across the island countertop until she caught Hightower's eye. She was wearing a tight-fitting sundress, an impish smile, and little else. Hightower noticed that Peeps had gotten a good look, too, as the woman's breasts swung free beneath the thin cotton chintz, two mature pears dangling invitingly from the Tree of Life. Peeps cleared his throat.

"Hey, come on, you two," Carrie said. "I didn't invite you and Willie here to talk shop. This is a party, remember? Your glasses are empty. Saddle up to the bar, boys. What'll it be?"

Hightower smiled. He liked Carrie. Hell, why not? She had moved to the southern Chicago suburb of Trinidale from Denver with her husband, Dom. They rented a patio apartment right across the courtyard from his. They soon became good friends—although Dom was something of a jerk, always wearing a shit-eating grin designed to hide the fact that he was constantly running away from something, always self-conscious, the class nerd, yet all the while strutting around to make you believe he was the master of his every emotion. Hightower never really understood what Carrie saw in him, except that it was a second marriage for them both, and sometimes when you marry on the rebound, shit happens.

Other things, too, had happened once the Potashes moved to Trinidale. In the eight months that they'd lived there, Carrie, Dom, and Hightower had enjoyed dinner together several times, mostly on the patio but sometimes at their place, indoors, and they'd even done a little reckless, if harmless, imbibing from time to time. Carrie, especially, seemed to relish letting go, giving up her inhibitions—what few there were. Now, Hightower found himself remodeling an old, abandoned building for them, turning it into six condos—one for the Potashes, one for Carrie's buxom, 24-year-old daughter, and four more to rent out at a tidy little monthly profit down the road.

Hightower handed over his glass. "Sounds like a plan," he told the hostess. She quickly filled his glass with a toasty little Bordeaux she'd picked up at the market earlier.

"And, you, Willie," Carrie said to Peeps as he held out his glass for a topper, "quit monopolizing the best-looking man at the party ... *and* our general contractor. I want you both to mingle." She turned to Stan Omado. "Stan," she called, waving her hand in the air like a cowgirl about to lasso an errant steer, "come on over here, will you? Save this party. And Christie, you, too. I want you to meet our general contractor, Darryl Hightower."

Hightower liked Omado. He was crude, boorish, overweight, and in his seventies, although you'd never know it. He ran the other lumberyard in town, the one Hightower had given most of his business to since falling out with Sandalman's Builders Supply.

Omado ran his business the way the old man's father had done fifty years before him. Along with three of his brothers, a nephew, and a niece, it was a real family operation, with Omado heading the clan. Hightower had even heard that the guy was a made man. A Mafioso with ties going right back to Sicily, and he believed it. But Omado never tried to muscle him. In fact, the guy seemed to take to Hightower like a father to a son. The fact that Omado allegedly hated the Sandalmans and Builders Supply didn't hurt any, either.

"Hey, youngster," Omado said, holding out a thick, meaty paw. He clenched Hightower's hand, held it warmly, affectionately, squeezing his palm while grabbing his arm with his free hand. Whenever he spoke, he looked directly into Hightower's eyes, and Darryl could see in his every gesture, every glance, the posture of power. *Mafia*-style. "How ya been? Haven't seen you around for a few days. Are you keepin' busy?"

"You oughta know, you robber baron. We've been buying all of our lumber from you for the past six months. I think we've been keeping your whole damned family alive!"

"Yeah? That so? Why? You give up on Builders Supply? You on the outs with Sandalman?"

"Oh, no," Hightower winced. "Not me. Not with Sandalman."

Stan chuckled, made more small talk, settled his large Italian frame into a small teak bar chair and spilled out what was on his mind.

"Youngster, you're good for this town. I'm glad you moved here." Hightower raised his brows. "No, I mean it. I really am. We've needed new blood in this town for the past thirty years ... *talented* blood. Oh, I've seen some good people come and go. But none of them had what it takes. None of them was ready to, you know, stick it out." He grinned. "Invest in their futures here."

Hightower grinned back. "You're just happy to have someone else in town who likes opera. Don't give me that crap. I'm wise to you."

The Sicilians—they all had a love for opera. It was a real greaseball thing. They had it in their blood, their Sicilian heritage. In Italy, you go to the opera to show others how much breeding, how much taste you have—how much better, well rounded, and well trained you are than they. And Stan Omado ate it up. He had at first seemed surprised that someone so young would know the librettos from *Don Giovanni* and *Falstaff* by heart. Hightower played on that common bond. Darryl had grown up under the wing of an Italian family on the Great South Side of Chicago, after all, and knew what made a good Dago tick, another reason he got along so well with the head of Trinidale's Omado clan.

But it wasn't until Christie came over and introduced herself, took Hightower's hand, her massive swollen breasts straining beneath the light cotton blouse she wore over Bermuda shorts—her tanned, full legs and strong, firm thighs standing in marked contrast to the pure white of her face—it wasn't until then that Hightower felt himself spring to life. It was suddenly beginning to look like one helluva party.

"You know," Christie said after hearing Hightower's recount of his problems with the Sandalmans and Trinidale Builders Supply, "we ought to do something about it. It's just not fair that Darryl is being singled out, targeted like that by some low-lifes who just happen to have all the power in town."

Carrie shook her head. "Absolutely. It's abhora ... abhora ... you know that word."

"Abhorrent," Christie said.

Carrie nodded, convinced she'd never be able to repeat it. "That's the one!"

Carrie's husband sneaked in behind his wife, craning his neck over her outstretched back to see into the living area, his bulbous eyes glowing thicker by the moment. "*What's* the one?" He turned to his wife.

"I think it's time to get rid of the Sandalmans once and for all," Christie said. "Either that or make them reimburse Darryl for everything they've put him through. For all of his losses."

Hightower smiled, the faintest trace of a buzz unraveling inside his brain. "Hey, I appreciate it, believe me, but I'm going to talk to the D.A. on Monday. Or Peeps, here, will." He nodded to the investigator, who was still mesmerized by Christie's architecture. "Besides, I thought Stan had all the power in this town."

Carrie bowed down, extending her folded hands up and over her head. "You're right. Forgive us, Stan. Darryl's right. Compared to Stan the Man, here, the Sandalmans are rank amateurs."

"Very rank," Dom Potash added.

Omado stood up slowly and leaned his weight forward, his large gut swaggering before him. He started to speak, took a sip of wine instead, and then he sat back down.

Hightower laughed suddenly. "What was *that* all about?"

Omado's thick brows shot up, and his eyes widened. "What? Oh, that?" He looked to Carrie, then to her daughter, and then he returned his gaze to Hightower. "I was going to say something, but you don't need an old guy like me giving you advice."

"That's *exactly* what he needs," Carrie said. "If you have an idea, let's hear it." Hightower thought he detected a tinge of slurring unfolding in Carrie's words and looked from her to Peeps, whose head was drooping against his chest, his glass sandwiched between a bulbous belly and two thick, meaty hands.

"Hey, Stan. You know the Sandalmans better than I do. You grew up in this town with them. If you have some advice, I'm all ears," Hightower said. "Lay it out!"

Omado waved him off. Paused. Squinted. "Well, if you're sure ..."

Hightower nodded. "I'm sure. I want to hear it. It may be of some help."

Omado turned from him to Carrie, then to Potash and Christie before finally glancing down at his shoes—white buck leather slip-ons with ornate gold buckles. He shifted one foot slightly. Hightower hadn't seen shoes like those since *The Godfather.*

Part II!

"It's obvious that the Sandalmans want Darryl, here, out of business. Hell, I'd want him out of business, too, if I were as greedy as they are. I know. Old Man Sandalman and I go back a long ways. I've known him since grade school if you can believe it. And I disliked him as much then as I do now."

"Yeah, but it's his son who's calling the shots," Christie said. "He's running Builders Supply now. His dad is retired."

Omado cleared his throat. "That's true. But I guarantee you, the Old Man still has his hand in the business. And what this youngster here says is true. He didn't get his loan from the bank because of Old Man Sandalman. That was how all his problems started."

Hightower's ears perked up. "You know that for a fact? How?"

Omado held out his glass, and Carrie filled it nearly to the top, motioning for Hightower to pass his over. "Well, let's just say there's not much that goes on in this town that I don't know about. Let's just say a little birdie told me."

Carrie handed Hightower his wine and grabbed Peeps by the shoulder.

"What?" Peeps snapped. "Oh ... sorry. I must have ... it's been a long week, and the wine ..."

"Pay attention, Willie. Stan has a plan to help Darryl out with the Sandalmans. Listen."

"Well," Omado continued, "it's just what everyone says. You have to fight fire with fire. The Sandalmans are playing dirty. They're underhanded and mean. So you've got to get down to their level. Give them a dose of their own medicine. Make them realize you're not going to go away. Let them know they *can't* intimidate you."

Hightower shrugged. "I wouldn't call it intimidation. I'd call it ... desperation and being scared to death."

"What's your cash flow like?"

Hightower paused. Everybody paused. Even Peeps appeared to perk up suddenly, straining to hear.

"Well," the contractor said, his mind whirring, "I'll tell you one thing. As God is my witness, I'm not as rich as you."

The room burst into laughter.

"No one is as rich as Stan," Carrie said. "Rumor has it that whenever God runs short of cash, he looks up Omado. Of course, He doesn't like the interest rates ..."

Omado chuckled before sipping from his glass and continuing. "Okay, so let's just say you're strapped for cash."

Hightower nodded.

"Say, Stan," Potash said. "I've got an idea. Why don't *you* lend Darryl some money. After all, if he goes out of business, our condos go down with him. And *you* lose the lumber sales."

"Hey, Dom," Hightower said, "if Illinois Custom Design goes out of business, your condos will still get finished. Someone else will step in and take over. I'll see to that."

Dom held out his hand, relief washing his face.

Carrie grabbed his arm. "We don't *want* anyone else to take over. We want *you*. We want the best." She turned to Omado. "Come on, Stan. What's on your mind?"

"Well, I could always lend the youngster some money, that's true. But that wouldn't solve the problem here. The Sandalmans would continue hounding Darryl until he eventually had to call it quits. Believe me. I know these people. They're rotten. They're just bad folks."

"So?" Hightower asked.

"So," Omado continued, "here's the plan. You and Willie, here, work up a case. Go over everything the Sandalmans have pulled, every stunt. Write down all the financial damage they've caused you. Document the thefts, list the items stolen, everything. Then get together with the D.A. and bring the Sandalmans up for charges. File a complaint and get them in court."

"Court? What good would that do? They'd just deny it," Christie said. "They always just deny everything."

"That's right." Carrie drained her glass and set it on the counter for Dom to refill. "Besides, these people *own* the courts in this town. You know that. *Everybody* does."

"That may be true," Omado said. "But if we work up a strong enough case and file *criminal* charges—I'm not talking about some piddly little civil stuff, but actual *criminal* charges—there's not a jury in the world that wouldn't nail the coffin closed on the Sandalmans and their dirty business practices once and for all."

Peeps shook his head. "I don't know. This all sounds like a civil matter to me, and that means a quick trip before the judge and just as quick a dismissal."

"Wait a minute," Hightower said. "Isn't it criminal to conspire to put someone out of business?"

Peeps shook his head. "Sure. But we'd need proof."

"Well, what about that twenty-two grand worth of stuff Sandalman had delivered to the job site without me ordering it? What about their billing us for *that*?"

Peeps' eyes widened, and he cocked his head as he glanced at Omado. Hightower went on.

"And how about the insurance thing? Refusing to cover our losses? And the bank loan? And the heating contractor who ripped us off? He once told me that Scott Sandalman was his best friend. Don't tell me *that's* not collusion."

"Now you're talking," Omado said.

Peeps rubbed his stubbled chin. "We'd need a plan. We'd need to know exactly what to put into the complaint and then be able to back it up in court. We'd need documentation. And witnesses."

"Wait a minute," Potash said, his eyes suddenly sparkling with excitement.

Carrie squinted back over her shoulder. "What's going on in that devious little brain of yours, darling?"

"Wait just one minute. Hell, we've got the D.A.'s investigator right here. We've got Darryl. We've got Stan. He knows as much about the Sandalmans as anyone alive. And Christie's in law school; she could help us out from a legal angle. Why not do it? Why not go through a … a …" He paused, searching for just the right word. "A *rehearsal*? Yeah. Why don't we see right here and now whether or not we have enough evidence to build a criminal case against Sandalman? Why don't we lay it all out and see if it floats?"

"What you mean, '*we*,' white man?" Carrie asked, a childlike giggle creasing her lips. She took a gulp from her glass. "It's *your* plan."

"Well, the stolen money for the heating material *was* slated for *our* job. And we have just as much interest in keeping Darryl afloat as anyone in town. I'd say that's a definite '*we*.'"

Carrie poked him playfully. "All right, then, boys and girls. Let's break down into teams. One side plays devil's advocate, and the other side answers the questions."

Peeps stirred. "Say. I've got a better idea."

Hightower craned his neck.

"What say we lay this whole thing out like we were in court?"

Christie shrugged. "What do you mean?"

"You know." He twisted his back to Hightower. "A mock trial." He turned to Carrie. You could be ... well, you could be *you*."

She giggled. "That's a stretch."

"And Dom," he added, "you be ..."

Potash raised his hand. "I know, I know. I'll be the judge."

"Well ..."

"Yeah, come on. I have a very analytical mind. Besides, if the judge really *is* in Sandalman's hip pocket, I can do that, too. I can be had."

Carrie smirked. "Oh, yes. You can believe *that*."

"Well, okay, then," Peeps said. "But no horsing around. We want this to be real. You're the judge. You're also in Sandalman's hip pocket, but you have to maintain the absolute illusion of propriety. You can't be obvious about it."

"Illusion of propriety. That's my middle name." Potash smirked—Hightower caught it. *How appropriate*, he thought.

Peeps whirled around. "And Stan. You know the Sandalmans best of all. With what you know, you can be ... well, you can be the kid, Scott Sandalman, I guess."

Omado threw his hands into the air. "All my life, I get the shit parts."

Hightower leaned close to him as if about to reveal a great secret. "Yeah, but think about the power trip you'll be on—Stan Omado *and*

Scott Sandalman all rolled into one. Man, together, you could rule the world!"

Omado turned to the youngster and scowled. "I do that already."

Hightower leaned back, and he saw the grin form on the old man's lips. He laughed.

"Okay," Peeps said. "Christie, you could be ..."

"I could be the chaste, sweet young thing my mother and stepfather think I am, but instead I'd rather be Mrs. Darryl Hightower," she said, her eyes riveted to the contractor, her breathy voice barely audible, her lips opened invitingly.

Carrie bolted. "Now wait just one minute," she said, her voice rising above the din. "That's not right, you know that's not right." She walked around the bar and stopped before Hightower. "I saw him first!" She bent down to throw her arms around him, squeezed him, kissed him on the cheek. Hightower could have imagined it, but as she pulled back, he swore her tongue moved slowly back into her mouth.

Potash pounded an orange against the countertop. "Order, order in this court. There will be no more outward displays of wanton affection in this courtroom. Especially by my wife. Is that clear?"

Carrie winked at Hightower before turning seductively toward her husband. "Perfectly, your honor. *Purrr-fectly*!"

"All right," Peeps said, the wheels in his mind whirring. "Christie, with your vast knowledge of criminal law ..."

"I'm studying international business law," she said.

"With your vast knowledge of international business law, you will be Mr. Sandalman's attorney."

"Oh," she giggled. "Do I get to depose the plaintiff?" She rubbed her thigh up against Hightower, who felt himself blush, all eyes scouring his for some reaction.

"To tell you the truth, I never had much use for attorneys in the past," Hightower said, smiling. "But this one I think I'm going to *like*!"

Carrie pulled a handful of popcorn from a bowl on the counter and hurled it across the room. "Let's keep it clean. She's the daughter of the woman with the hots for the defendant!"

"Okay," Peeps said. "Good. We've got a judge, we've got Sandalman, we've got Hightower—I assume you won't object to playing yourself in our little courtroom melodrama—and we've got Sandalman's defense attorney. Now, who's left?"

"Who's left," Carrie cracked. "How about if I play the bereaved widow so I can strangle you all!"

"Careful," Potash said. "She's good at that."

"No, no, no," Peeps said. "Not right. Besides, there is no bereaved widow in this case. I have a better idea. We're going to need a cooperative witness. You can be that. You can be Mrs. Carrie Potash, majority owner of the ..."

"*Umm*," Carrie waved her arms wildly. "*Ohh, ohh*, I've got it ... the Illinois Arms Hotel!"

"Precisely," Peeps said. "The Illinois Arms Hotel. And, as such, you are concerned about protecting your investment in Mr. Hightower and his contracting firm, here—what is it, Illinois Custom ..."

"Design," Hightower and Christie said simultaneously before breaking into a laugh.

"That's it. You're concerned about your investment as well as in seeing your project through to completion."

"Oh, goodie, Darryl and I will be working closely together!" Carrie said.

Christie threw out her chest, more than twice the size of her mother's. "Careful, *Mrs.* Potash. As attorney for the defense, I cannot allow any *unnecessary* fraternization with horny witnesses. Horny *married* witnesses."

Carrie raised her brows, aiming them first at Christie and then at Hightower. "Well, who said it's unnecessary?"

The room burst into laughter as she downed her drink and motioned for her husband to give her a refill.

"What about *you*?" Hightower said, turning to Peeps, hoping for all the world that the heat the contractor felt rising to his face wasn't obvious. "What role are *you* going to play?"

Peeps rubbed his stubbled chin. "Well, let's see. We don't have a D.A., yet. I guess I'll play ... the prosecuting attorney!"

All his life, Hightower had enjoyed courtroom dramas. The tension, the intellect, the mental sparring and thrusting, the jabbing and counter-jabbing. To him, watching *Twelve Angry Men* and a dozen other courtroom classics was like watching a good prize fight. You knew going in who the better fighter was, who had the better record and the better stats. And you had a pretty good feel for who was going to win.

Yet, for one reason or another, when it boiled right down to it, the victory never came easy ... and the fight was never actually predictable.

That was why Hightower likened them. The fight was never over until the referee made the final call.

So, when Peeps asked him in all honesty to relay to the court the information relating to Scott Sandalman and the bogus sale of twenty-two thousand dollars' worth of finish materials, the theft of the materials from the jobsite shortly after, the $12 thousand theft of funds from the Illinois Arms Hotel by Sandalman's best friend, the failure of Sandalman's own interior designer to close on her remodeled property in order to pay off Illinois Custom Design for the funds due it, the return of $6 thousand worth of roofing supplies to Trinidale Building Supply for cash, and the other misdeeds perpetrated against the company and Darryl Hightower, president and C.E.O. of same, he had no difficult in doing so, despite the whiskey that had been consumed on the stand—the Potashes having run out of wine but not out of straight sour mash Kentucky bourbon—and presented the facts in a plausible and seemingly irrefutable manner.

The fight had mere seconds to go.

And then—after Carrie Potash relayed what amounted to the same facts about the financial difficulties she and her husband endured due to evidence pointing directly to Scott Sandalman and Trinidale Building Supply in their blatant attempt to force their competition out of business—the fight was all but over, and the D. A. rested.

It was only then, when it came time for the defense counselor to call Scott Sandalman, himself, to take the stand in an effort to refute the most damning of the charges leveled against him that Peeps looked around, paused, sipped from a wine glass filled to the brim with hard booze, and announced incredulously that the defense attorney was not present.

"Why is the defense attorneys ... the defense ... *attorney* ... not ... present?" the judge demanded, punctuating each word with a sip of liquor.

Peeps' arm swept the room. "Because, your honor, because we failed to appoint one." He paused, smiled, and raised his glass to an admiring gallery before taking a long sip and a deep breath. "A defensh attorney, I mean. Defensh attorney. *Attorney*. That's because why. Your justice-ship."

"What?" Potash demanded.

"We just ran out of people."

"Well," Potash said, his eyes rolling around his head in a vain attempt to focus attention on something, *anything*, "we can't have that. We can't have that at all. We'll jes have to ... appoint a new defensh attorney. *Attorney*." He took a swig from a bottle stashed beneath the counter and tottered precariously on his stool. "Who ... whosh going to be the defensh attorney now?"

Peeps lifted his finger and started to speak, and then he stopped.

"Your honor," Omado said. "If I may address the court."

Potash weaved to his left. "The court recognizes Stan Sandalman."

"Scott Sandalman."

"Scott Stan Sandalman," he added.

"Your honor," Omado said. "Although it may be highly irregular, considering the fact that we do not have enough persons present to play all of the principal roles in our little libretto, it seems only reasonable to ask the plaintiff, himself—Mr. Darryl Hightower—to act not only as the president of Illinois Custom Design and Construction, but also as the defense attorney for Scott Sandalman, of which I am one and the same."

Christie leaped up off her chair and waved her arm. "I object," she said.

Potash's eyes swelled to twice their size. "And on what grounds do you 'ject, young lady?"

"On grounds," she said, trying to stifle a laugh, "of that I was named defense attorney earlier this evening, that's on what grounds I 'ject." She sat back down. "That's on what grounds."

Potash turned to Peeps. "Mr. District Attorney, is thish true?" He took another swig from the bottle and barely whisked it out of reach as his wife swiped at it.

Peeps looked at Christie, scoured her chest, and then he turned back to the bench. "I don't remember."

"Your Honor," Omado said. "Your Honor, if I may approach the bench."

"You ..." Potash burped. "Oops. You may 'proach anything you wanna."

Omado rose, swayed on his feet, and then sat back down.

"Or ..." Potash said. "You may speak from there."

"Thank you, your Honor."

"Thash very welcome, I'm sure."

"Your Honor, whether or not Ms. Christie was appointed defense attorney for yours truly, I would suggest in all due interest of meting out justice that Mr. Hightower be allowed to defend me in this courtroom this even. I mean, evening."

Christie raised her hand again. "Then what am I gonna do?"

Omado smiled. "Why not be the District Attorney's investigator?"

She crinkled her brow. "Wait a minute. Wait jes a minute. We've got a vestigator here already. Willie Peeps. He'sa real-life vestigator for the District Torney."

Omado shook his head. "Oh, no, Ms. Christie. You forget. Mr. Peeps *is* the District Attorney. He's the one who's prosecuting this case against me—I mean Scott Sandalman, I mean *me*—and doing a very commendable job, if I might say."

"Well, then, whosh the vestigator?"

"You are."

She paused, a genuine look of confusion creasing her forehead. "Well, then, who am I working for?"

Omado replied, "For Mr. Hightower and the state. Your job is to work closely with the plaintiff and with District Attorney Peeps, here, in order to assure that this court finds me guilty of defrauding the plaintiff and conspiring to run him out of Dodge. I mean Scott Sandalman. Out of town, I mean."

She turned to Hightower and smiled. "Are you saying that I getta do what with him? I getta interview him? That what you mean?"

Omado nodded.

Christie licked her lips and turned to Hightower. "Why don't you think you should get the hell outa here wi' me so we can go someplace more private?"

"Your Honor," Carrie said, "I object."

"On what grounds?"

"Ona grounds that she's married."

"Getting divorced!" Christie cried.

"Ona grounds that she's getting divorced."

The judge clapped a wooden spoon against the Formica. "Overruled. The court hereby appoints Mr. Darryl Hightower defensh attorney. *Attorney*. In defensh ... defense ... of Mr. Scottie Stan Sandalman. Next question."

Christie raised her hand. "I move for a delay."

"A potty break," Carrie said.

"A recess!" Omado cried.

"Bring out the wine!" Peeps said.

"Scotch!" Potash called.

"Whatever."

Potash banged the spoon against the counter. "Thasha excellent idea. I need a potty break, too." He set the bottle of bourbon on the counter." Help yourself." He banged his gavel again. "Court journed for twenty minish. Or more. Whosh gotta Scotch?"

After several minutes of relative confusion and everyone had disappeared down the hall, the court began funneling back in to appear before the bench, the judge staggering in to call court back into session. Peeps asked to be heard.

"Thash a little irregular," Potash said, "but if no one has any jections, you can be okay by me."

"I have a jection, your honor, sweetie pie," Carrie said, leaning on the counter as her husband looked admiringly down her dress.

"I don' know why," he said, "cause you look good to me."

"Your honor!" Peeps cried out. "I object! The witness is leading the judge."

Carrie turned to face him. "You're damned right I am. I'm gonna lead him right into the sack in a few more minutes, you're not careful."

"I object again!" Peeps cried.

"On what grounds you jecting? Carrie asked."

"I can't remember anyone's role anymore. Who is Hightower's defense counsel?"

"Me!" Carrie called out, grasping Darryl by the arm and leaning against his shoulder. "I'll defend him anywhere he wansa go!"

Omado scooted forward from his perch on the sofa. "Look, everyone, we're making this whole thing entirely too complicated. Let's just have one guy, Darryl, here, be the plaintiff." He paused, turning to the bench. "That's the one who got his stuff stole from him, right?"

"Sounds gooda me."

"Good," Omado said, trying to stand and giving up after two attempts. "And what's his name, here, Peeps, he's the prosecutor."

"What am I sposed to be?" Christie asked.

"And how 'bout me?" Carrie said.

"You can all be drunks."

Potash picked up the orange and banged it once against the counter, sending a thin sliver of juice squiring halfway across the room to splash against Hightower's cheek.

"Look!" Carrie cried. "He's been shot!"

Christie staggered up to him, licking the fluid from his face. When he started to back away, she grabbed him around the neck and kissed him on the lips. The courtroom erupted in objections.

"I don' care," she said. "I know he's guilty."

"Guilty? He's not even on trial here. Sam is!" Potash said.

"I'm not Stan. I'm Scott Sandalman," Omado said, holding up his drink.

"Then I accuse you of stealing our stuff," Potash cried, "and tryin' to put poor Darryl here out of business before he could finish our job." He went to bang the orange on the counter again, but it split in two, both halves skittering off the counter in opposite directions. He looked surprised before turning to his wife. "Get me another gavel!"

"No need, your honor," Peeps said. "I move we adjourn this court til the cows come home." He chuckled softly to himself.

"There are no cows," Carrie said.

Christie let out a soft moo and turned again to cuddle against Hightower.

"Just a matter of speech. Thash a way of sayin' I think we should adjourn until tomorrow."

"On what grounds?" Potash demanded.

"On grounds that if we don't, I'm gonna pass out on my face, 'at's on what grounds."

"I can't so-order," Potash said, "on count of I don't have a gavel thingy."

"I seconda motion," Omado said. "Til tomorrow, then."

"Til tomorrow."

"Til tomorrow."

Hightower threw up his hands. "I'll bring the wine."

The following morning, Saturday, brought little wine but far too much daylight for Hightower's taste, and along with it came a football game in which the Sooners beat their traditional rival Longhorns, or the other way around. Hightower never missed the game, and the television set was on, but he was nowhere to be found. That is, until slightly before six, when he emerged from his shower with freshly nicked neck and cheeks and a mostly neatly trimmed beard. He wondered if he'd imagined the night before, Christie practically throwing herself at him. The thought brought a warm sensation to his loins. Not that he minded. He splashed some Polo onto his hands and rubbed it across his chest and belly before stepping into a pair of lightweight, white cotton pants tied off with a white drawstring. Throwing on a crisp, silk shirt and stepping into his docksides, he rolled a brush through his hair and, shaking his head and inhaling, headed out the back door.

Across the way, Potash had already fired up the grill and was preparing to sacrifice some raw meat to the virgin princess who, coincidentally enough, just happened to emerge from the back door with two wine coolers in her hands.

Catching Hightower from the corner of his eye, Potash waved. "Hey, Darryl. Hungry?"

Christie waved. "Thirsty?"

Actually, Hightower was neither, but he smiled and pretended to be ravenous, which, after getting a closer look at Christie, he was.

Dom shook his hand, grabbed a beer from a cooler, and disappeared back into the house while Christie settled in behind the patio table. She motioned for Hightower to take a seat next to her.

"I hope we didn't come across like a bunch of horses' asses last night. We were all pretty well lubricated." He waved her off as he watched the tautness of her lightweight top reveal two erect nipples. She caught him eyeing her and leaned forward.

"Do you approve?"

He shrugged. "Of what?"

She folded her arms beneath her chest and slowly lifted them up and out just as the back door opened. Dom reappeared, carrying a plate filled with potatoes ready for the skewer.

"I saw you last night," she said more softly, "trying to get a look down my top. So, I thought I'd beat mom to it today and wear something less ... confining."

He nodded, sipped his drink, and set it down. "So I see. And, yes, I approve."

"A little?" She grinned, her eyes narrowing as if she were a chameleon targeting a fly that had landed a heartbeat away.

"More like ... a lot."

When the food was ready and Hightower was already feeling little pain, the group sat down to dinner, during which Dom and Carrie talked about the case they had set up while their daughter contented herself with running her shoeless foot up along Hightower's leg, to his crotch, and back down again. Hightower smiled often and pretended it wasn't happening, his pleasant demeanor convincing Carrie that she had bought and served the perfect cut of steak.

After dinner, Darryl and Christie retired to the patio where, darkness cloaking them, he reached out, pulled her flush against him, and kissed her. She responded by rubbing hard against him.

Within several minutes, Carrie came out with a bottle of Pinot Noir, filled their glasses, and gave Hightower a seductive smile. "Looks like things are warming up out here," she said. Christie dabbed at her long, silken blonde hair with perfectly manicured nails. Hightower felt himself blush—either because Carrie was Christie's mother or because mom was damned near as hot as her daughter, even without the extraordinary scaffolding. "Sorry to break this up," Carrie continued, "but Stan and Willie are here. Stan said they've been kicking some things around, and he thinks they've come up with something. You'd better come in. You're going to want to hear this."

"We're not really going to play that silly game again, are we?" Christie asked.

Carrie took a sip from her glass. "I think we'll soon find out."

Inside, Stan Omado stood next to the counter, propping his belly up as Peeps walked around the room in tight little circles.

"What's going on?" Christie asked Dom.

"*Shh!*" Potash said. "He's thinking."

Peeps stopped suddenly and looked up, appearing surprised to see anyone else in the room. He froze for several seconds before his eyes exploded. "I've got it!" he announced, punctuating his thought with his index finger.

Dom looked from Carrie to Christie to Omado and back. "Got what?"

"How I can approach the D.A. on Monday to get him to file charges against Sandalman."

"Can't you just go to him and tell him what's happened to Darryl?" Dom asked. "And to us? Our job is held up for who knows how long because of those supplies."

"It's not that simple," Peeps said. "Before I can ask him to charge someone, especially a big fish like Sandalman in a small sea like Trinidale, I have to have some solid proof. And that's what we're going to give him."

"Proof? How? What kind of proof?"

Peeps reached into his pocket and pulled out his cell phone.

"Yeah? So?" Carrie asked. "I'll bite. Who are you planning to call?"

"No one. Not just yet, anyway. But we're going to get the D.A. all the proof he needs, and we're going to make sure Darryl has enough materials to finish your job, despite the thefts."

"How?"

"Well, Stan gave me the idea just this morning. He's going to advance Illinois Custom Design an extended line of credit, while we lay out Sandalman's entire scheme, step by step ... *on tape*." He said the words as if they were a magical incantation before he punched a few times on his phone and motioned to Omado. "Why don't you explain what I'm talking about, Stan."

"Well," he said, clearing his throat. "That's it in a nutshell. We'll front the materials for you, youngster, so you can finish your job and drive Sandalman out of business for good."

Darryl looked confused. "But how?"

Peeps held up his finger before punching his phone again. He waited a few moments and held it up as it belched out its magic:

Why don't you explain what I'm talking about, Stan?

Well, that's it in a nutshell. We'll front the materials for you, youngster, so you can finish your job and drive Sandalman out of business for good.

But how?

Peeps clicked the recorder off.

"That's a great parlor trick," Carrie said, "nice recorder." She turned to Omado. "And we want to thank Stan for making sure our job won't be shut down with that line of credit for Darryl. But I still don't see how any of this is going to provide the proof we need to take to the D.A."

"You will," Peeps said. He propped the phone up on the counter and turned to take in five sets of anxious eyes. "I've been thinking about this whole thing since yesterday, and I came to the conclusion that we started it all wrong."

"What do you mean?" Dom asked.

"Well, instead of Stan playing the role of Sandalman, we'll have Darryl here do Sandalman's talking for him. After all, who knows better what Sandalman did to shut down Illinois Custom Design than its president? So, I'll ask Darryl some questions, and he'll answer as if he were being interviewed by the *Sun-Times* or WBKB or someone."

Carrie's eyes lit up. "Or the D.A.!"

"Right," Peeps replied. "And we'll tape everything. Including the corroborating witnesses, Carrie and Dom Potash, here. That way, the D.A. will know *everything* that Sandalman did, he'll know *exactly* what damages Darryl and the Potashes suffered, and he'll know *precisely* how Sandalman sabotaged your jobs, all just to put Darryl and Illinois Custom Design out of business because he couldn't stand the competition."

Hightower looked at Potash, grinning from ear to ear, and then turned to Carrie, who sat with her drink in her lap, craning her head and nodding. He looked at Omado, who sat with folded arms, looking for all the world like the Cheshire cat who had just swallowed Alice. And then he turned to Christie, who had already turned to him.

"I like it," she said.

"I do, too," Carrie said, and Dom chimed in.

"Well," Hightower said, shrugging, "we'd might as well make it unanimous."

"Good. Let's get started."

"I could use a fresh drink," Omado said.

Carrie sat back in her chair. "Is that permissible in court?"

"We'll bend the rules," Peeps said, and Carrie grabbed the bottle and began making the rounds while the investigator turned on the recorder. He motioned so that everyone knew it was running, and he introduced the proceedings and all the participants, dated the recording, and explained how Darryl would be speaking on Sandalman's behalf in the man's absence. Then he introduced Hightower with a question:

"Illinois Custom Design and Construction filed a complaint with the Trinidale Police Department regarding a theft in excess of twenty thousand dollars of unordered goods that were ultimately removed from a remote jobsite for which Scott Sandalman was supplying materials, is that correct?"

"Yes," Hightower said, feeling giddy with power. It was the first time he'd ever felt such a rush—as if he were holding another man's life in his hands while being appointed judge and executioner.

"Did you know that Trinidale Builders Supply's owner, Scott Sandalman, authorized the shipment of those materials to your site?"

"I didn't at the time, no. And it was twenty-two thousand dollars' worth, actually."

"Did you later receive an invoice for those materials billed to your company account?"

"I did, yes. It was about a month later."

"Did you at the time realize that you neither ordered those materials nor authorized anyone else working for you to do so?"

"Yes, I knew that. You see, at the time, Trinidale Builders Supply had a woman working for them by the name of Kelli Powell. She was an interior designer and decorator whose job was to ..."

Peeps held up his hand. Hightower raised his brows. "Yes?"

"Darryl, just answer the questions *yes* or *no*."

"But, don't you want to know the details? I mean, there are a lot of facts that ..."

"We'll get to those later. I assure you. But I want to do so in an orderly fashion so that everything I give to the District Attorney on tape flows from one issue to the next. Remember, this is my job; it's what I do for a living."

Hightower nodded. "Okay."

"Just trust me, all right?"

He nodded again.

"Good. Now, getting back to the issue, did you also work on a project for Mr. and Mrs. Potash known as the Illinois Hotel, which was an old abandoned building they had purchased and hired you to convert into six condominiums or rental units?"

"Yes."

"And did you hire a subcontractor by the name of Robert Snow to install a heating and cooling system for the building?"

"Yes."

"Had you used Mr. Snow's services before?"

"Yes, many times."

"And on this particular occasion, did Mr. Snow come to you and request a check from you to purchase heating supplies for the hotel, stating that he would pick them up from Trinidale Builders Supply and deliver them to the hotel jobsite at no charge to you?"

"Yes."

"And you gave him a check for twelve thousand dollars made payable to Trinidale Builders Supply for the supplies."

"That's right."

"And did Mr. Snow purchase the supplies from Trinidale Builders but fail to deliver them to the hotel as promised?"

"That's right. We gave him the check and never saw the materials."

"And did you learn later from his ex-wife that he had returned the supplies to Trinidale Builders Supply, received a cash refund from Scott Sandalman for twelve thousand dollars, closed his business, and disappeared from Trinidale without returning the money to you?"

"That is correct."

Peeps, turned and looked around the room at four sets of eyes, spellbound, before rising and walking from one end of the room to the other and back again. He cleared his throat.

"Now, Mr. Hightower, do you or did you know a woman by the name of Kelli Powell?"

Hightower had to keep from laughing. "Yes. Of course, I did."

"And she worked as an interior design consultant and a salesperson at Trinidale Builders Supply, is that correct?"

"Yes."

"Is it true that the order form for the materials sent to your jobsite was authorized and signed for by Ms. Powell?"

"That is correct."

"Bitch!" Carrie snorted. "I never liked her."

"And did you telephone Scott Sandalman directly when you learned that those materials for which you had no need yet had already been delivered to the jobsite?"

"Yes, I did."

"And did Mr. Sandalman inform you that the material he delivered to your jobsite could not be returned because they'd been specially ordered for you through Ms. Powell at your request?"

Hightower was amazed at how much information Peeps had acquired virtually overnight. But then again, he assumed he had probably gotten it from Omado, who kept one ear to the ground and had snitches scattered all over town. "Yes, he did."

"So, you knew that the materials were not going to be taken back even though you requested them to be removed?"

"Yes."

"After speaking with Mr. Sandalman, did you confront Ms. Powell about the delivery of all those unauthorized materials?"

"Yes."

"And did she tell you that Scott Sandalman had ordered her to deliver the unauthorized materials to your jobsite?"

Hightower felt his brows rise. "Yes, but how did you ..."

Peeps held up his hand.

"Oh, right. Sorry." He took a sip from his wine before setting the glass on the cocktail table. "Yes."

"So, in the end, you decided to keep the materials that had been delivered prematurely for when you reached a stage in construction where they would be necessary, is that correct?"

"Yes. Well, I mean, not exactly. I put pressure on Kelli to have Scott take them back, telling her outright that I wasn't going to pay for them because I never authorized them."

"Realistically speaking, you had to send the materials back because you simply couldn't afford to pay for twenty-two thousand dollars' worth of finish supplies just to have them sit in the garage of the country house you were building for several months until they were needed, is that right?"

"That's correct."

"And did Ms. Powell ultimately convince Mr. Sandalman to take the materials back and credit your account accordingly?"

"No."

"So, it's safe to assume that your account was in serious jeopardy as of that time, is that correct? I mean, if you paid Sandalman's bill, you would have been under great financial stress."

"Yes."

"Can you tell me why that is?"

"Well, we only receive advance payments for a job to the tune of around five or ten thousand dollars a month. That's per draw. That meant it would have taken up to four months of bank draws just to cover the finish materials sitting in the garage, gathering dust."

"In effect, Mr. Sandalman was using your jobsite as a storage facility for the unordered materials while charging you for the privilege of stumbling over them every time your crew went to work, is that correct?"

"Yes."

"And is it true that Illinois Custom Design had suffered other financial losses of a considerable amount at around this same time?"

"Yes."

"And these came from overcharges made by a roofing crew, who ordered three times more roofing materials than called for and then returned the excess materials to Trinidale Builders Supply for a refund, which the individuals received in cash instead of as a credit to your company, is that correct?"

"Yes."

"Is such a refund standard in the industry, a cash refund given to subcontractors or employees instead of a credit made to the company's account?"

"No."

"Would you say it's a rare occurrence for that to happen?"

"It *never* happens."

"Except in this case."

"Yes."

"But there were also other losses you incurred. I understand that someone gained entrance to your office and stole 15 thousand dollars' worth of tools. And that, in another instance, you had completed work on a reconstruction job for the homeowner, who had arranged in writing to pay you after she closed on her mortgage with the bank, is that correct?"

"Yes."

"And who was the owner of that house on which you worked for several months without any appreciable cash flow?"

"Kelli Powell."

"The same Kelli Powell who worked for Scott Sandalman at Trinidale Builders Supply and the same Kelli Powell who authorized the delivery of materials from Trinidale Builders Supply to your rural jobsite before they were needed."

"The same."

"Why did you go so long, working on Ms. Powell's home renovation project without receiving any pay?"

"Because she was strapped for cash. She had hired a general contractor to do the job prior to our coming to town, and he really screwed things up and left her with a mess. Once her money ran out, she was desperate to finish her reconstruction so she could qualify for a bank loan, pay off all her debts, and move into the house as her primary residence with her young son."

"She was divorced?"

"Yes."

"And her ex-husband couldn't or wouldn't help her out financially?"

"She said she hadn't seen him for years, that he just left for work one morning and never returned."

"So, is it safe to say you felt sorry for her?"

"Yes."

"And maybe felt a little attracted to her."

Hightower shrugged. "Maybe. A little. But mostly we were just friends. She'd helped me out when I needed advice on finish products. She looked in her books to find just the right hardware or the best bathroom fixtures or whatever we needed. And sometimes, when the everyday pressures of work got to her, she'd ask if I wanted to go to lunch with her."

"And, in return for her helping you find the right materials for your numerous building projects, you advanced her credit for her own renovation."

"Yes."

"Didn't working on her job for, how long, six months or more, put a strain on Illinois Custom Design financially?"

"Nothing we couldn't handle. You have to remember that, up until then ..."

Peeps held up his hand.

"Sorry."

"So, your arrangement with Ms. Powell was that, upon your completion of the renovation of her home, she would receive funding from her bank, pay you off, have you sign a waiver for payment received, and everyone would be happy, is that right?"

"Yes."

"Did you ever in fact finish that job?"

"Yes."

"And did Kelli Powell ever receive funding upon the completion of the remodel so that she could obtain funding from her bank to pay you off?"

"No. Well, in effect ..." He raised his brows. "May I elaborate?"

"Let me do it," Peeps said. "My job, remember?"

Hightower smiled, took a drink of wine, and nodded.

"Near the time of completion of Ms. Powell's home, she was approved for a home loan, which the lender informed you of directly, saying that he hadn't heard back from Ms. Powell to schedule a date for closing on the loan and for converting her construction loan to a 30-year fixed-rate mortgage, is that correct?"

"Yes, it is."

"So that left you holding the bag for another—what was it? Somewhere around seventy thousand dollars, is that about right?"

"About."

"And instead of closing on her newly renovated home, Ms. Powell bought a one-way airline ticket to a South Seas island where her estranged mother had been working as a teacher for several years. Ms. Powell had apparently established communications with her mother and decided simply to walk away from the newly remodeled home she loved so much, walk away from her obligations to you, and walk away from Trinidale Building Supply, is that your understanding?"

"That's what happened."

"Did Scott Sandalman ever give you an explanation of why Kelli Powell may have quit so unexpectedly, left a high-paying position that she seemed to love, abandoned her house and her home town and her father and stepmother who lived only a few blocks from her new home in Trinidale, and just disappeared?"

"No, he did not."

"And you believe that's because Scott Sandalman paid for all of Kelli Powell's materials, all the upper-end supplies and finishes and all the furnishings she wanted, while she deliberately ran up your tab for labor and other fees, is that correct?"

"Absolutely."

"And in doing so, Scott Sandalman wasn't actually out any money because when Ms. Powell defaulted and walked away, he would have regained legal possession of all the materials he had paid for her to use in her home, is that right?"

"That is."

"All because Scott Sandalman resented the fact that you had recently moved to town, opened up a construction firm, and quickly expanded to carry your own line of building supplies, everything from flooring to roofing, from bathroom and electrical fixtures to windows, doors, and finish materials. All of the same materials that Trinidale Builders Supply had been selling virtually unchallenged—and at much higher prices—for decades, is that correct?"

"Yes."

"As had Sam Omado at Omado Lumber and Supplies."

"Yes, although to a much lesser degree."

"But Sam Omado never pulled a stunt like that on you, did he?"

"No."

"I wonder why *he* didn't object to your rapid expansion the way Mr. Sandalman apparently did." He turned to Omado. "Can you comment on that, Mr. Omado?"

"I like the youngster. It's a shame that this thing happened. He had so much on the ball, so much going for him. I actually thought one day he might even want to buy me out and take over my lumber yard. In fact, I broached the subject with him on several occasions, as I recall."

Peeps turned back to Hightower. "Is that the feeling you had, too? That Stan Omado thought highly of you?"

"Yes, it is."

Peeps looked around. "Any questions? Anything else anyone would like to ask about these matters?"

"I'd like to ask Stan if he can replace for Darryl the heating supplies that Bob Snow stole so we can get back to work. We've already lost more than a week."

Omado stood up, and, grinning, lifted his glass to Hightower. "Whenever the youngster here comes for them, they'll be ready."

The contractor stood up and clinked glasses with him. "That's really first class, Stan. I don't know how to thank you."

"Just win this case," he said. "That's all I ask."

Peeps walked over to the counter, turned off the recorder, and poured himself a Scotch before pouring one for Potash, who had just emptied his glass and held it up for a refill. "After tonight, I can pretty much guarantee you a quick resolution here," Peeps said. "Not a doubt in my mind."

Omado turned back to Hightower. "Just bring your checkbook next time you stop by," he said. "You can post-date a check for whenever you want, whenever you need to. A year. Two years. Six months. Whatever it takes. I'll hold your checks until you say otherwise. When you've gotten your funds back, just let me know, and I'll put them through. Just so our bookkeeper has something for her records, some kind of accounting of what you've purchased."

"It's a deal," Hightower said. "And I can't tell you how much I appreciate this."

"No problem whatsoever," Omado said. "The pleasure's all mine."

"What are you doing?" he whispered.

"What you've been waiting for all evening." She tugged on the end of the tie holding his pants closed and slid them down over his hips. He moaned softly as she slipped her hand down to where she knew he needed attention. He reached out, pulled her closer, covered her lips with his as he cupped first one breast and then the other, rolling the flesh back and forth between his fingers until she let out a soft moan.

"My place?" he asked.

"Certainly not mine," she giggled. "But we'll have to hurry. I'm leaving tomorrow at eight."

"In the morning? For ..."

"Chicago. I've got to get back for business."

He ran his tongue along his lips and nibbled down her neck nearly to her breasts. "For how long?"

"Oh, God ... I think ... probably two weeks."

"Two weeks? How will I survive?"

She giggled again. "Let me give you something to remember me by ..."

Before he could settle into his chair, Carrie threw open the screen door. "Christie, honey, you'd better come to bed, now. It's after one. We're leaving to take you back early tomorrow morning. You have to be there by noon, remember?" She paused, squinted into the darkness. "Oh, Darryl." She hesitated for a moment, a smile creasing her face. "I didn't know you were still here. Sorry about the interruption ..."

She slipped back into the house and closed the door as Christie withdrew her hand. "I'll bet," she said.

Hightower said, "You know what they say about absence."

She drew him closer to her, licked his cheek, covered his lips with her own, exploring his mouth, nibbling on his tongue for an eternity before breaking away. "*Uh-huh*," she whispered finally. "It makes the heart grow horny."

A Chateau Pavie '21—that was the answer to Hightower's prayers. Or so it seemed. He had stopped off at his favorite liquor store, and

Ron—the proprietor who knew more about French wines than Louis XIV—recommended it.

"You taste it once, and you'll never be satisfied with anything else ever again."

Ron had told him of its heritage. Like other vineyards in Saint-Émilion, such as Château Ausone, the Pavie vineyard dated back to Roman times. Taking its name from the orchards of peaches ("pavies") that used to stand watch over the rocky terraces, it sprouted its modern estate under the watchful eye of Ferdinand Bouffard in the late 19th century. He had bought land from several different families. It had been managed separately forever, and the nine hectares he purchased from the Pigasse family retained a separate identity as Château Pavie-Decesse.

But Bouffard's vineyards suffered from a vicious invasion of phylloxera, small, aphid-like sucking insects that feed on the roots of grapevines and sometimes form galls on the leaves, causing severe damage to the crops. With his spirits crushed worse than his season's harvests, Bouffard sold the vineyard to Albert Porte at the end of World War I. Porte, in turn, sold it to Alexandre Valette in 1943. His grandson, Jean-Paul Valette, transferred title to Gérard Perse in 1998 for $31 million.

Perse, a Parisian millionaire and former cyclist, sold two supermarket chains to fund his entry into the wine business. He bought Château Monbousquet in 1993, Château Pavie-Decesse in 1997, and Pavie in 1998. He ripped out most of the old equipment and constructed new, temperature-controlled wooden fermentation vats, a new cellar, and a new irrigation system in the vineyard. He brought in controversial wine consultant, Michel Rolland, who watched the yields cut nearly in half following his severe pruning and green-harvesting while encouraging malolactic fermentation in the wine. The results could have been predictably disastrous except for one thing: they were extraordinarily rewarding. The wine from the vineyard today enjoys a more concentrated and intense taste than ever before in its history.

So much so that, in 2012, Pavie was elevated to the lofty position of Premier Grand Cru Classé (A) status, which made the vineyard one of only four such Saint-Émilion producers in the world.

It was all an intriguing presentation by Trinidale's most renowned connoisseur, but Hightower remained unconvinced that he wanted to be indebted to a wine that cost a figure just south of Venezuela's gross national product. Nonetheless, he picked up a bottle. It was going to be a *very* special night.

At precisely 7:30 that evening, exactly thirty minutes early, the bell rang, and Darryl went to answer the door. He had dressed early and was beginning to prepare dinner when he undid the lock to find not his dinner guest but Carrie standing there.

"I hope you don't mind, but I just had to see you."

Darryl smiled to hide his surprise, instinctively looking out past the front steps to the street. At no one.

"No, of course not. Come on in. I was expecting ..."

"*Umm.* Something smells good. Oh!" she paused. "Oh, God, how awful of me. You're expecting company. I shouldn't have just dropped in."

"It's okay. My guest isn't due for a while yet. Can I get you something? Some wine? Or a vodka rocks with a twist?" He led her into the kitchen and opened up the refrigerator. "Or I can mix up a wine cooler."

He turned around when she didn't answer. "I say ..."

He stopped suddenly, taking in the pained expression on her face. He looked at her more closely. She wore more makeup than usual, with her eyes done to perfection and her lipstick moist and glistening. She had on a lightweight wool sweater with no bra beneath—that much was obvious. Her breasts swelled out and down, the breasts of an older woman, the breasts of maturity, of motherhood, of only God knew what else. The fact that they sagged some only made them appear fuller and larger than they had the previous night beneath her sundress.

"What's wrong?" he asked.

"She shook her head and frowned. "It's Dom. I think he's going to leave me."

He paused. "*What?*"

She nodded "I think we're going to separate."

"Why?" he heard his lips utter. "What happened?" He didn't know why he had asked, but the words had a mind all their own. And a life.

"This whole thing with the hotel renovation and all. I don't know if it's gotten to him, if it's all become too overwhelming or what. But he's talking about just giving up and moving back to Chicago, getting his old job back. Moving in with his son, Dom's child from a previous marriage."

"But you guys are so close to finishing, *we're* so close. We're a couple months away from completion."

"He doesn't think you have any intention of finishing the job."

"Are you kidding me?" Darryl glanced right and left, his mind trying to grasp the words. "What are you saying? Of course, we're going to finish the job. Of course we are. Why on earth would he ..."

"He said that, after talking to Peeps, he's convinced you're going to drain us of the rest of our money and walk away, leaving us stranded and the job incomplete. He thinks you're broke, and you're going to get yourself out of financial trouble by stealing from us. That would ruin us. This is all the money we have in the world—we've sunk every nickel we own into this project. You know that. If that ever happened, if you ever did quit, we'd be destitute."

"You don't think I'd do anything like that, do you? I mean, Peeps ... the interview ... you were there. You heard what happened; you heard what we're up against."

She maneuvered close to Darryl's shoulder and buried her head in his shirt as she started to sob. "I don't know what to think anymore. All

I know is that it looks like my marriage is over." He hoped she wouldn't leave any makeup behind. That wouldn't do. That wouldn't do at all.

"I thought he was all gung-ho," Darryl said. "I mean, we're going to win this thing. We're going to beat Sandalman and the others. We're going to get our money and our materials replaced, and we're going to win. We're going to come out on top. Just the way we were before. I've got money. I've got backup funds. I've got insurance," he lied. "Bedsides, I've already ordered the materials for the hotel's heating system from Omado. They'll be here this week. I don't understand what he's thinking."

"I told him that. I told him I was sure you had enough money personally to finish the job if you had to..."

"And what did he say?"

She shook her head. "He's got his mind made up."

Darryl looked around, stunned. "That's just ... you know, it's just crazy."

"That's not all," she sobbed.

Oh, great. There's more!

"I think he has someone else."

"*What?*"

"I think he's ... cheating on me."

"What do you mean? Why do you say that?"

"It's the way he's been acting these last couple of weeks. Whenever I come into the room and he's on his phone, he hangs up quickly, like he doesn't want me to overhear who he's talking to. And when I ask him who it was, he says something stupid, like it was a wrong number or he was checking the time or something like that."

"Well, who would be having an affair with Dom? I mean, no disrespect intended here, but if either one of you was to get involved with someone else, I'd think it would be ..."

Nice going, asshole, he thought. *Anything else you can tell her? Why not just ask her to climb into bed with you? How much more of an opening could she want?*

"I could never do something like that. I could never cheat on him. No matter what he did to hurt me personally."

"I just meant, you know, he's not exactly Don Juan. And you're so ..." He caught himself, weighing his words cautiously. "—much younger looking. You know. Still attractive. And ... and ... you know. Attractive. Alluring."

Oh-oh. Wrong word. Wrong word. Wrong word. Definitely *the wrong word.*

She looked up into his eyes. "Oh, God, you don't know how that makes me feel. How much more worthwhile it makes me feel. Not like some piece of dead meat you're finished with and throw out with the morning trash or toss to the dogs."

"Of course you're not that. You know that. You know better than that. And I'll tell you. He'd be crazy to leave you. You have a great marriage. Everyone knows that. You two were meant to be together."

"Looks ... can be deceiving," she said, and he swore she batted her eyes once, twice, as she gripped his forearm and squeezed lightly. "We haven't been ... intimate ... in months. Sometimes I feel like he doesn't even think of me as a woman anymore. He doesn't see me as his wife."

"Well, then, he *is* crazy."

"Do you think so?" She drew herself nearer, and before he had time to think, she stood up on her toes, threw her arms around his neck, and pressed her lips up to his. *Hard* He could feel the strain of her nipples through her sweater, feel the heat of her groin pressing against him. Stunned, he tried not to react, but he instinctively felt he was failing. As she pulled back from him, she let out a soft moan and reached down between his legs. "This is another thing I never thought I'd feel again." She squeezed it lightly before her hand clamped down on it so hard, he felt his brows shoot up and his back spring straight up.

"*Whoa.* Carrie. I ... what I mean was ..."

"I can feel what you mean. I think I've *always* felt something special between us. Every time I lay eyes on you. And when I catch you looking at my tits, it sends a shiver throughout my entire body."

Crap, dad always warned me to be discreet.

"I'm right, aren't I? You feel it too, whenever you look at these." She put one palm under each breast and thrust them up, her nipples taut and straining, the blue of the material begging for attention.

"Oh, my God, Carrie. Of course, I feel it. But, I mean, I feel it like a friend. Like a brother toward a sister. I mean, you're a married woman, you know? I think of you as ... as a woman, sure, but as a *married* woman. You and Dom. Together. Just the two of you. Like you were meant to be."

"I'm not saying it will be easy. We'll have to be careful. It would be just like him to twist everything around and make it look as if I was the one out cheating on *him*. But now that we know, now that we understand how we both feel ..."

Panic raced through his frame, a genuine desire to turn and run. But he couldn't risk hurting her. Maybe he was to blame. Maybe he *did* goad her on without even realizing it. Or maybe he *did* realize it but didn't ever think it would amount to anything. *Be careful what you wish for ...*

Suddenly the doorbell rang. He looked in terror at the clock. Eight sharp.

Carrie pulled back instinctively, her eyes never losing contact with his. "Is that the company you're expecting?"

He let out a sudden breath. "I hope ... I ... I mean, I wouldn't be surprised."

He excused himself and went to answer the door. As he opened it, Deidre smiled and stepped in. "Hi. Hope I'm not late. It's not every night that a gal gets invited by her boss to ..." Her voice trailed off, and her brows rose instinctively as she looked behind him at Carrie. "—to have dinner with him."

"Hi," Carrie said, extending her palm. "I'm Carrie Potash. Darryl is renovating our hotel. Down on Commercial? The big old bank building we bought last year."

"Yes, I've heard about it. And I'm sure I've seen you at the office ... with your husband. What's his name again?"

"Well, yes, I think, if that's all we need to discuss for the moment, Darryl, I'd better be running along. Dom is probably holding dinner for me." She smiled curtly, threw one last long, lingering look at Darryl, and turned for the doorway. "I want to thank you again for all you've done ... for us." She stopped, smiled again at Deidre, and added, "You have a very understanding boss."

"Yes," she said, "and he has some *very* understanding employees."

Carrie hesitated, eyeing the woman suspiciously. "I'm sure. All right, then. I'll see you in a couple of days, Darryl. At the jobsite. Bye!"

Deidre turned her mouth up at one corner. "I hope I didn't interrupt anything special, some big business meeting."

"No, no. In fact, I thought when she rang the bell that it was you running a little early. She just had a little ... *stuff* to discuss ... about the replacement materials for the hotel. You know. That last order we placed with Omado?"

"*Um-hmm,*" she said. "I see. Oh, and you might want to take a minute or two to take care of that shirt."

"*Hmm?* What?" He craned his head toward his shoulder.

"Otherwise, that lipstick's going to stain." She smiled. "And that *would* be a shame."

"Oh," he said, feeling himself blush. "Oh, yeah. Yeah. Thanks."

Over the next week, the marketing director for Illinois Custom Design, Trey Salidor, reported three of their clients had decided to halt their jobs. Temporarily, they said. A fourth tore up his contract, claiming that ICD hadn't performed satisfactorily. When Darryl went out to talk to him to find out what was going on, the man told him that he was sorry, but he had to protect himself. He didn't believe Darryl was preparing to go out of business, but that's what the marketing director had shared with him "in private."

When Darryl confronted Salidor, the man feigned ignorance, saying that the client must have lied just so Darryl wouldn't take the guy to court. But Darryl sensed that it went deeper than that. He just wasn't sure how much deeper.

Back in the office, he telephoned Peeps to tell him the latest developments; Peeps was out, his secretary said, and he never called back.

Later that afternoon, he received a call from a woman who identified herself as the district attorney for the town of nearby Lincoln, Illinois. She said that she had received a complaint about a check he had written to a materials supplier that bounced. It was for more than eight thousand dollars.

Puzzled, Darryl said it had to be a mistake—a mistake that the D.A. gave him twenty-four hours to clear up, *or else*. Darryl quickly called his assistant in and asked her about their bank account, and she said it was twelve thousand dollars to the good. When she called the vice-president of the bank for further information, she told Darryl what she'd learned.

"Bad news, boss," his assistant said after the call. "The gal in bookkeeping at the bank said that Stan Omado put through some twenty-four thousand dollars' worth of checks he'd been holding. That put us in the red, so when that check came through from Lincoln, it bounced."

"What? He wasn't supposed to put those through. He was supposed to hold them until we could cover them. Until I told him it was safe to deposit them."

She looked at him sheepishly and shrugged.

"Get Stan on the phone."

But Stan never did answer. The girl who took the call said that he was out. But she informed Darryl that she had checked with their bookkeeping department, and the bookkeeper told her that Stan had instructed her to deposit the checks. *All* the checks. Whatever *that* meant.

Before long, the entire office knew of the problem. With a twenty-thousand-dollar payroll coming up the next day, things were looking dicey. Salidor said he'd go out and try to hustle up some more money, get some clients to issue releases for construction funds from their banks to help see ICD over the hump, but he wasn't sure if he could do anything before Friday afternoon.

Deidre overheard them talking and stepped in to offer Hightower thirty thousand dollars that she'd made from selling some property she had owned. Stunned, he told her it would be for only a short time, and he'd sign a note, naturally. She refused, telling him that she trusted him before she grabbed her keys, hopped in her car, and headed to her own bank to transfer funds to ICD's account by the end of the day.

Somehow, Hightower had managed to dodge a bullet. A second call to Omado ended like the first. Another call to Peeps failed to get a return. He called the D.A. in Lincoln to tell her he'd bring her a replacement check personally the first thing in the morning, and she informed him that would be fine, except that it would have to be cash.

That evening at home, Darryl was praying that the short-term infusion from Deidre would be enough to see them through Friday the Thirteenth—enough to replace the bounced check in Lincoln and meet the looming payroll for their employees. Without his crews, all work would come to a halt, and ICD—and Darryl—would be left hanging high and dry. Along with the Potash's condo job.

As he popped open a bottle of beer, the front doorbell rang. He glanced out back over the patio where all his problems had begun several weeks earlier; it was deserted. When he went to the door, he was surprised to see a uniform standing before him and a crawler with a second cop behind the wheel parked in front of the house.

"Mr. Hightower?"

"Yes, that's right."

"Darryl Hightower?"

"Yes, I'm Darryl Hightower."

"I'm afraid I have to inform you that you're under arrest. We're going to have to take you in for booking."

He looked at the man incredulously. He was a cop. He knew that much for sure. He wore a royal blue uniform and a four-pointed blue hat with a short, black plastic bill and a star on the front. Another star glistened on his chest. His black shoes shone in the waning evening sun. Most of all, Darryl noticed the gun. Big and heavy-looking and black and ominous and still holstered. Thank God!

"Under arrest? You're kidding. Under arrest for what?"

"The warrant here says, passing a bad check. It's signed by the clerk of courts in Lincoln. Dated this morning, 10:52 a.m." He looked up from the paper and handed it to Darryl, who read the words as though they'd been a death sentence. *Insufficient Funds. Failure to Make Restitution. Second Notice. Death by Lethal Injection. No Reprieve. Notify Next of Kin.*

"This must be some mistake. We did have a mix-up with our bank account, but I straightened that all out earlier today. We have the funds to take care of this now. This is all a mistake."

Fully expecting the officer to back down, to apologize for bothering him, and to slither away in remorse, he was unprepared for what came next.

"Hold out your hands, please." And, before he realized what was happening, he felt the cold, hardened sting of steel slapped across his wrists, the tautness of the bindings pinching his skin.

"Well ... I ... if you'll just wait a minute. I have to ... let me lock up at least, will you? I have to ..."

"Do you have the house key?"

He shrugged, fumbling as best he could through his pants pockets before pulling out his ring.

The officer took the key from him, closed the door, and locked it before handing the ring back to him and leading him down the steps to the car.

Along the way, across twenty feet of cracked and heaving concrete to the curb, he spied half the population of Trinidale outside. Staring. At *him*. A neighbor woman watering her flowers. Four kids playing some kind of game on the sidewalk. A couple of painters working on a building across the street, gawking at him from their scaffold. A young couple walking their dog, eyes moving from Darryl's face to the cuffs and back again. He glanced furtively toward the Potash back yard, praying that they hadn't seen him being led away like a common criminal and yet hoping against hope that they *had* spotted him and would come running forward to lend him a hand. Obviously, something had gone very, very wrong. This isn't the way the Lincoln D.A. said it was going to be. She never said he was going to be arrested. How on earth could he make good on the bounced check from jail?

Had the D.A. made a mistake? Had she filed a complaint with the court before he'd spoken to her, promising to make good for the check, and then forgot to notify the court to quash the warrant?

Or did it go deeper than that? Was this yet another client of ICD who decided to put a halt to his job and stick it to the company's owner? And Omado, too? Along with Dom Potash? And Peeps? He was even beginning to wonder about Carrie. And Christie.

Let's see ... am I forgetting anyone?

One call. Just like in the movies. That's all he got, and he prayed he got it right. It was to Deidre, and she said she'd grab her checkbook and be right down. And she was, A little more than two hours after being dragged in, cuffed in Admitting to the tubular frame chair with the black-vinyl seat and back, virtually ignored until someone thought to ask him what he had done and he said nothing he could think of that warranted his arrest.

So, when Deidre came to bail him out, he was more than relieved.

He was grateful.

And stumped.

What had gone wrong? When Deidre told him that Carrie's lipstick-rich visit to him the previous night was a ploy to feel him out, he asked for what, and she told him for money.

"I don't get you."

"She and Dom and Christie have all been working with Peeps to put you behind bars."

"What? Why?"

"Because Peeps thinks that's the best place for you."

"I don't get it. After that night at the Potash's when he asked me everything under the sun, and I answered his every question, why would he want to see me in jail?"

"You're right. You *don't* get it. See, something you haven't quite come to terms with yet is that Stan Omado isn't the only mobster in town. You don't think the town of Trinidale is ninety percent Italian by coincidence, do you? The entire place is loaded with Mafioso. When someone new comes to town and plays ball, plays by the rules, everything is fine. But when someone moves in and starts upsetting the powers that be, all hell breaks loose."

"You mean Omado and Sandalman and all the others? They're all working together? With the Potashes?"

"Bingo."

"Just to teach me a lesson? You've got to be kidding."

"It's not to teach you a lesson. You've already learned that: When you mess with the status quo, you get stomped on. No, what they want from you now is the turnip's blood. That's why Carrie was here the other night, pretending that she and her husband were breaking up, and she was frightened and angry and upset ... and desperate for a shoulder to cry on."

Deirdre looked at him out of the corner of her eyes: he was stunned.

"How do you know all this?" he asked. "You're not as close to them as I am. You haven't been working with them as long as I have."

"I haven't, but the Dansons have."

"Who are the Dansons, and what do you mean they have?"

The Dansons—they own that weird head shop down on Commercial, a few doors down from ICD."

"Oh, yeah. I know who you mean. But how do they ..."

"The Potashes and the Dansons are good friends. The Potashes buy their drugs from them. Most of the people in town do. Dom even does some work for them, printing or something, from time to time. When Carrie got home after crying on your shoulders the other night ..."

"And leaving a little piece of her behind for a remembrance. I had one helluva time getting that out of my shirt!"

"Anyway, she told Dom what had happened. Probably told him you had money. *Lots* of it."

"Shit. I just as much said so outright to calm her fears about our quitting their job before it was finished."

"*Uh-huh*. So, even after the thefts and all the other stuff that's gone on, she told Dom, Dom told the Dansons, and the Dansons told Peeps."

"Peeps? You mean the D.A.'s own investigator is dirty?"

"You know who his closest friend was in town until recently?"

Hightower shook his head. "No. Who?"

"Kelli Powell."

He sat back in his seat. "How do you know that?"

"It's common knowledge. Powell and Peeps, that electrician who keeps calling up and trying to get work from you—Randolph or Rudolph or what's his name—the Potashes, a bunch of Omado's friends and his kids, even Scott Sandalman—they're all a bunch of crackheads. And they all get their stuff from Dansons' Design Works."

"I can't believe it." He stood, feeling his mouth fall.

"Believe it. From dirty judges down to the dirty D.A.'s office, a dirty investigator, and dirty cops. Everyone is either using or peddling drugs. If they're not, they know who is, and they keep their mouths shut and play by the rules. The *Mafia's* rules."

Hightower shook his head, not knowing how to respond. Kelli. Powell. Sweet. Sensitive. Innocent. Fun-loving. Or so she had seemed. Maybe that's what happened. Maybe that's where Powell went wrong. Going to work for Sandalman. Maybe she got in with the wrong crowd over drugs.

"Did you ever hear about that body they found face-down in the river a few years back? The one who had his head bashed in beyond recognition?"

Hightower shook his head. "No. What about him?"

"Well, rumor has it that he tried to muscle in on the Mob here, tried undercutting their drug business. When push came to shove, the Mob called on the police who beat the crap out of him, took him out to the river, and dumped him. Later, after someone discovered him, they investigated and came up empty-handed."

"My God. It's a wonder *I'm* still alive!"

"You're still alive because you're not a threat to them. Not yet, anyway. No, as for now, you're nothing more than a cash cow."

"Or so, thanks to Carrie Potash, they think."

"Or so they think. There was another incident a few years ago. A private plane was coming in for a landing in an unmarked grass strip just east of town. It didn't make it."

"Why not?"

"Blew up on landing. No one knows how. Or why. The FAA sent some investigators down from Washington, but they couldn't tell what went wrong. Speculation is that the guy was bringing drugs in from Mexico, and the Mob wouldn't stand for it. So ..."

"Wow. These guys play rough."

"You're telling me. And that was just for starters."

"Did they ever find the drugs?"

She frowned.

"Yeah, right. Stupid question. I take it back."

"Seems to me as if you've surrounded yourself with all the wrong people. If you don't mind my saying."

"How about Salidor?" he asked. "He's from downstate somewhere, Champagne-Urbana. University of Illinois."

"He's been coming up here for drugs he takes back down with him to sell to the college kids for years. You just happened to stumble upon him when he was looking for a cover. A way to disguise his reason for being here while still maintaining a home in southern Illinois."

"I always thought that seemed a little strange. Owning two homes on the money we pay him. He just told me he could make more money here than down there, so he decided it was worth the weekly commute."

"I'll say it is. He owns a duplex here and a mansion downstate. And he's working on salary for ICD."

Darryl hesitated. "Is there anyone in this town who *isn't* on the take?"

"Besides me and my family? Very few. Unfortunately, this week's Sucker du Jour is Illinois Custom Design and its esteemed and allegedly well-heeled owner, one Darryl Hightower. Or, so goes the rumor."

Sucker of the day? he thought. *Or sucker of the century?*

Hightower set the morning paper on his desk, picked up the telephone, and dialed the *Chronicle*. When a voice answered, he switched it off speakerphone.

"I'd like to speak to Tammy Loosen, please." He waited an obscenely long time before he heard Tammy's voice on the other end of the line.

"Darryl Hightower."

"Oh ... hi, Darryl. What can I do for you?" Her words were empty, hollow, as if she knew damned well what she could do for him and dreaded having to tell him to go take a hike.

"I just read the article on ICD in the paper. You did a good job."

"Thanks. I try."

"Well, next time, try a little harder, will you?"

"What do you mean?"

"I mean, get the story right. You did all this research from the friendly halls of the bureau of records and the office of the District Attorney? And you interviewed some former customers who ducked out on our contract because of some lies someone told them? And you're surprised that I'm upset about it?"

"Darryl, I just tell it like it is."

"No, you just told it like people want you to *think* it is. There's a difference. I thought you were a reporter. I thought we at least shared *that* common bond between us. Our desire to ferret out the truth and bury the ugliness of lies and false information six feet underground where it belongs."

"I'm sorry, but I was assigned an article, and I ..."

"And you did your master's bidding. I understand. But don't you think for a moment you should have come to me first? *I'm* the subject of the story, remember? Source *Numero Uno*?"

"I ... I was going to ..."

"But, no. Instead, who do you quote? People who have an agenda, people with no integrity, morals, or scruples. People who have lived their lives playing their dirty little games in this dirty little town. You just scored a big hit for the Mafia, Tammy. I hope you know that. You've made the Mob very happy this morning. I can just picture Omado and Sandalman grinning from ear to ear."

"You're making a lot of accusations that ..."

"That are going to be proven true, with or without the help of the *Daily Chronicle* and the freedom of the press. And where did you get this information about four criminal charges pending against me? There are no criminal charges, nothing has been filed. But I guarantee you that you just signed a death warrant for Illinois Custom Design. If you think anyone can walk away from reading this hatchet piece and still consider hiring us to build a dog house for his pet pooch, you're mistaken."

"Darryl, I don't know what to say. I had no idea you felt this way. I assumed, since I went to the source—the D.A. and the police department and the clients who used to work with you—and everyone told the same story ... I just assumed it had to be true. I mean, if it walks like a duck and talks like a duck ..."

"Then, it's a damned lie!" he snapped.

"As for those charges, I got that info directly from the district attorney's office. They're working out the details now. One charge for each of four different complainants."

"What complainants? Whose complaints?"

"That I can't tell you. I just don't know. Only that there are four people for whom ICD did work and didn't finish their jobs."

"If we haven't finished their jobs, it's because the clients backed out of our contracts by refusing to pay us our draws. When they refuse to authorize their banks to issue us our money, we can't very well do any more work. I have payrolls to meet. With all the thefts we've had lately, I need to keep the funding rolling if I'm going to stay in business. And as far as the four complainants go, I can pretty much guess. The Potashes and three others who stopped their jobs when Trey Salidor got hold of them and told them I was getting ready to grab the balance of their funds and skip town. Hell, even their own bankers know we're legit. They advised our clients to continue issuing draws as long as we're under contract and continuing with our work. Fucking Salidor."

"I'm sorry, Darryl, I really am. I didn't realize any of that. I just didn't know. I don't think you're a crook. I don't think you ever planned on skipping town. But it's not my job to make that call. My editor sent me out to get a story, and I did. I don't have the luxury of second-guessing the truth. That's what the press is for ... to present the reality of the situation, all the different sides, to the public so they can make up their own mind."

If she'd been there in his office—as she had many times in the past, interviewing the boy wonder and sending out glowing reports on this miracle savior of a construction firm that dropped down out of nowhere, shaking up the apple cart, bringing honesty and integrity to the small Illinois town. If she'd been there, he would have strangled her until the last ounce of blood coursed from her eyes. And then he would have picked up the phone and called her editor to send someone by to gather up the body.

"I don't know how I can make it up to you," she said. "I can run another story, do an interview, get your side out there, if you think that would help. I just automatically assumed that you'd deny all the accusations, and the D.A. has such a strong case against you."

"Forget it. The damage is done. But if you want to help, there's *one* thing you can do for me."

"What? What can I do? Anything. Just name it."

"Get me in to see the D.A. I want to find out what this *evidence* is that he supposedly has. I called Peeps, I called Glenn Davids' office, I called the police department. No one has gotten back to me. It's like I'm *persona non gratis*. But if you set up an appointment with Peeps or Davids, I could just sort of tag along. At least that way I'll get to meet with them and hear first-hand what's going on. They'll be on their best behavior with a member of the Fourth Estate there alongside me."

"If that's all you want, I can save us both the trouble."

"What do you mean?"

"I heard a copy of the taped confession you gave to Peeps. Apparently, at a party that the Potashes threw a few weeks back. You must have been pretty hammered, because you confessed to everything."

"What?"

"Hang on a sec."

Darryl took the phone down from his ear and stared at it for several moments, as if it had made an error in transcribing what Tammy had just said. When he put it back against his ear, she was back on the line.

"I can tell you exactly what you said."

"You have a copy of that tape? The one Peeps made?"

"No, but I have the next best thing. I have the notes I took when Willie played the tape for me. Let me read you a couple things." She paused, the sound of rustling papers in the background. "Here. *Peeps: Did you knowingly and willfully submit a check to Lincoln Servicesmaster in Lincoln, Illinois, even though you realized there were insufficient funds to cover it? Hightower: Yes, I did.*"

She hesitated, more rustling, before continuing. "Here's another. *Peeps: Did you file false charges against a heating contractor in your employ, alleging that he stole twelve thousand dollars' worth of materials from the Illinois Arms Hotel when you actually removed said supplies yourself? Hightower: Yes, I took them.*"

"Wait a minute. What the ... where did you ..."

"Here's an oldie but a goodie. *Peeps: Did you report a theft of twenty-two thousand dollars' worth of materials allegedly delivered by Trinidale Builders Supply to a remote jobsite when, in fact, you had ordered that material yourself and had been anticipating its delivery? Hightower: From Kelli Powell. Peeps: Who was working at the time for Trinidale Builders Supply? Hightower: Yes.*"

Hightower felt a sudden rush of emptiness sweep over him. "Tammy, something is wrong here. Are you sure you took those notes accurately?"

"Verbatim," she said. "I take shorthand, so I get everything down exactly as it's said."

He paused. "Look, I've got to go."

"What's going on, Darryl? I know you. I know you wouldn't do anything like that. But the tapes don't lie. What's the truth, here?"

"I'll tell you," he said, "as soon as I get to the bottom of it. I'll tell you everything," he repeated.

"Promise?"

"You'll be the first to know."

"Thanks. And I just want to say again that I'm sorry I let you down."

"You didn't let *me* down, Tammy," he said. "You let yourself down. Next time, pound the pavement first and hit the keyboard second instead of the other way around. Okay?"

It must have been okay because she said she'd do whatever she could as soon as he gave her something more to go on. If all went right, he'd have a lot more to share with her, and soon.

But sometimes, soon doesn't come soon enough, and later that very afternoon, Hightower answered another knock at his front door. This time, he was prepared. The novelty had worn off. Just as it had for the cops. Except that this time, when they reached Admitting, the cop who had cuffed him and escorted him to the car stopped to read the warrant. His eyes bulged out and he whistled.

"What is it?" Darryl asked.

"Your bond. It's set for $200,000—*cash!* He lowered the paper to his side and looked down. "Who did you kill?"

Hightower shook his head. "Four counts of contractor fraud. That's what they're calling it."

"Contractor *what?*"

"Fraud, whatever that means."

He shook his head. This is a new one on me. Two hundred thou in cash? That's a first."

It was a new one on Darryl, too, as well as on everyone else who checked out the warrant. As the cop who had brought him in loosened Darryl's right hand from the cuffs, he motioned past the contractor to the girl behind the desk. "You know the routine. You get one call. I suggest you make it count."

He did. Within an hour, Deidre had contacted her brother, who worked as an investigator for the D.A. in Chicago. He recommended a good attorney, a guy named Robert Ransom. He had successfully represented some of the highest profile criminal cases in America—"the scumbags of the Universe," as he affectionately referred to them. She hired Ransom on the spot before heading down to the bank to free up more cash.

Four hours later, after sitting for most of that time in a small holding tank with iron bars on the door and only a solitary window and a drunk sleeping off a bender to keep him company, Darryl heard footsteps approaching from down the hall. Finally, a smallish, neatly coiffured cop appeared in front of the cell and opened the door.

"Come on," he said. "You're free on bail."

After Deidre spoke to Ransom, who asked her to drop half of his fifty-thousand-dollar fee in the mail the next morning ("You understand there is no guarantee, and this money is nonrefundable."), the attorney told her that he found the discrepancy between the interview at the party in which Darryl had participated and the taped version Peeps had apparently provided the D.A. "intriguing." When Deidre told him she recalled that Peeps had once worked as a disc jockey for a late-night Trinidale radio station, she thought she heard the lawyer's eyes ignite—a crisp, electrical-like crackling sound that echoed across the line, through time and space, to Deidre's earpiece.

"How did he tape it?" Ransom asked.

"What do you mean?"

"What did he use," Ransom said, "a tape recorder, a videocam, a ..."

"Oh, no, no. Darryl said Peeps used his own cell phone."

"Great! That's terrific! How many cell carriers are there in the Trinidale area? Comcast, I know. Any others? There must be a few more ..."

"*Uhh*, let's see, there's AT&T. I know because I have them. And then there's Verizon; I think that's who Darryl's with. No, no, it's not.

He's with T-Mobile. I remember because he likes to say he's sure they never learned what the word, *mobile*, means. And ... I think that's it. Those three."

"You wouldn't happen to know which carrier Peeps uses."

She felt her head shake instinctively. "No. I think maybe Verizon, but I'm not positive."

"That's all right. I'll find out. Meanwhile, tell Darryl not to get too down. We'll get him out of this thing. I think I have a plan of attack that will work. I'll have to call in a couple favors, but that's what friends are for. We'll put something together in the next week or so, and I'll give you a call."

"A *week*? Not sooner?"

"These things take time," he said. "Meanwhile, I'll call the D.A. and the judge who's scheduled to hear the case and get that cash bond reduced to a surety. He's not a murderer or even a flight risk, for God's sake. Someone really has it in for the guy, I'll tell you that much."

"Yes," she said. "I know. And I know who."

"How many quotes? How many did he play for you?"

"I don't know," Tammy said. "Quite a few. I think all of them. I put some of them in the article ... and the others ..."

"The ones that *aren't* in the article. *All* the ones that aren't in the article. Those are the ones I want."

Deidre listened to the pause, long and painful, on the line. "I guess, since the article has already been published, it wouldn't be like interfering with the independence of the press. I guess."

"Exactly. What it *would* be interfering with is the planned commission of a felony and the robbing of an American citizen of his inalienable rights under the U.S. Constitution."

Another pause, longer this time, so long that Deidre thought for a moment that the woman had hung up.

"Are you there?"

"Yes. Just looking through my files. You want me to drop them off? My notes, I mean. And the tape, although I doubt that it will do you any more good than my notes will."

"That would be terrific."

"And, would some other information be helpful? I have a telephone interview with Christie Potash that I didn't use in the article. And another one with her mom, Carrie. The material I got from them just didn't seem to fit in with the story's flow."

A light suddenly went off in Deidre's head. "Wait. What is it you said about dropping off a tape?"

"Yes."

"What tape?"

"Oh. Oh, well, ever since I got burned once on a story where the guy denied everything he'd told me after the paper ran with it, I record all my conversations. Just so that won't happen again. I have my interview with Peeps on my iPhone."

"If you taped the interview, then you also have the part of the recording that Peeps played for you, implicating Darryl in the felonies. Don't you?"

"Yes, I imagine that would be on it, too. I never shut my recorder off." She paused. "But I don't see how that would do you any good. It's the same stuff as my transcribed notes—and it's all pretty damning against him, tape or transcript."

"Fantastic. Yes, please, if you wouldn't mind. I'd *love* to get the original tape of your interview. *Terrific*. And I'll take good care of it."

"And I get first crack at the story, right? I mean, when you have something solid, if you break something new?"

Deirdre could sense the buzzards circling. "Right. I promise."

She hesitated. "You know ..." She cleared her throat. "I'm not sure if it's my place to say, but you know that Christie turned against Darryl because of you."

"Me?"

"Yes," Tammy said. "She thought she had something going with him. Young. Successful. Handsome. She thought ... well, she and her mother, I guess—both of them thought ... well, that something special was developing there. Until Carrie made a call on Darryl at his place and ran into you."

"Yes, I know, but what does that have to do with their blaming me? He has a free will. He's not married. He can have anyone over for dinner he likes."

"I don't know why, but Carrie said she was ready and willing to back Darryl to the hilt until he showed her he wasn't that interested in her daughter as they'd been led to believe. *Leading her on* are the words she used. And then rubbing her nose in it. With *you*."

"Did she tell you I saw her lipstick on Darryl's collar when I showed up? Or how flustered she seemed to be—how much in a hurry she was to leave after I arrived?"

"No."

"I didn't think so. In fact, I think maybe it wasn't her daughter's broken heart that upset her as much as it was her own. At least, that's the impression I got when I ran into her that night. She looked a little like a woman scorned. As if she had plans for Darryl and her, some kind of a tryst or affair or something, and then I came along and she saw her plans fly out the window ..."

"*Huh!* Wow. I think maybe you're onto something. And maybe I did kind of jump the gun here with my story."

"I think maybe so, too."

"I mean, I never really thought he would do anything illegal. I just thought I was reporting the facts as they existed and that Darryl would be exonerated sooner or later. I never dreamed for a moment that things would turn out the way they have. I never thought they'd have him arrested. He's too decent, too honest to have done anything like what they're accusing him of."

Deidre paused, considered her next remark carefully, and said, "You, too?"

Tammy started to ask what she meant when she stopped. She sighed. "John and I ... I mean, he keeps talking about plans for us to get back together. And talking and talking. I think maybe because my family has money. Then along came Darryl, like a breath of fresh air in this stinking, dirty little town, you know? He just popped into my life, and I guess maybe I had ... some thoughts ... about a future with him."

"I thought maybe you'd felt something like that."

"You won't tell him! You won't say anything!"

"No. Of course not. I'd never do that."

She let out a soft sigh. "Same with you?"

"What ... Oh, you mean what are my feelings toward him?"

"Yes. Are you going to be another one? Just another ship passing in the night? I don't know if he'd recognize the right woman if she came along wearing a billboard strapped to her back."

Deidre laughed. "You may be right. But that's going to have to be his decision. He's going to have to decide who's right for him and who's not. Me? I'm willing to take a chance. Invest a little time. Besides, what's one more heartbreak when you've been through as many as we have, right?"

She laughed. "Yeah. What's one more?"

The 'phone rang, and Deidre checked the clock. *After midnight.* She picked up the receiver. "Hello?"

"Hi," he said. "I saw your light on in the kitchen and figured you were burning the midnight oil."

"Yeah, I'm just going over a few things I've been kicking around."

"I'm not disturbing anything?"

"No, not at all. In fact, I'm working on some evidence for you that I think will come in handy."

"I thought Bob Ransom was doing that."

"Yeah, me, too. But he's in jogging mode, and I think this calls for a full-out sprint to the finish line."

"Sounds like you're really onto something."

"I think I am."

"You want some help? I can come over."

"Yeah, sure. I know what *your* kind of help means. No, thanks. I think I'll just keep plodding along all by my lonesome. That way, at least I know I won't be distracted."

He paused. "Well, okay. But if you need me ..."

"Right. You'll be the first to know."

She hung up, thinking about the night before last—when they were out enjoying a late dinner. A fruity Chianti. Some Italian food. A little soft music. And then, in the car after he drove her home, feeling his lips approaching hers, feeling their warmth, their tenderness as they touched.

Damn, if Tammy only knew what she's missing!

She returned to the work laid out on her kitchen table, piecing together all the different pieces of notepaper and cross-referencing them to the statements the D.A. had made for the article. And becoming more intrigued by the moment.

And then it struck her. *Of course! Why didn't I think of it before?*

She picked up the phone and dialed Darryl, and he was there in minutes. She showed him the article, and he grimaced.

"What are you, some kind of sadist? I've seen this a million times, dreamt it a million more! It's my one recurring nightmare. Remember?"

She told him he'd have to sit through it once more while *she* asked the questions this time and not Peeps.

He shrugged. "Okay, counselor. You seem to know exactly what the hell you're doing, so what else can I say? Let's hit it."

Peeps cleared his throat, unbuttoned his shirt sleeves, and pushed the cuffs up nearly to his elbows. He sat back in his chair and looked out over his desk.

"Now, what can I do for you?" Before she could answer, he shook his head and continued. "You know, I feel terrible about this whole thing. I consider Darryl Hightower a friend, a neighbor. It just cuts me to the quick to have to do what I have to do with this thing. I ... I hope to God I'm wrong. I hope he's innocent, I really do. But, you understand, I don't have any choice in the matter. I have to turn over my findings to the District Attorney."

"Glenn Davids."

"Yes, that's right. He received some complaints from a couple of Darryl's clients who were afraid something like this was going to happen, and they asked Glenn—Mr. Davids—to look into it. That's how I got involved. I wish to God I hadn't, knowing what I know now."

"And what, Mr. Peeps, is that?"

"Well, I know ... well, not *know*. Perhaps that's too presumptuous a word. More like I have seen all the evidence against him, and I had no other recourse but to alert the D.A. to my findings."

"You have a tape recording, I understand."

"That seems to be the worst-kept secret in town." He snickered. "I not only have *a* tape," he continued emphatically, "I have *the* tape. The one on which Mr. Hightower admits to committing the crimes."

Deidre smiled as sincerely as she could and leaned forward, flashing her impressive foundation before him. "And what crimes would those be?"

"Well, why, I'm not in a position to say exactly. Only a judge can determine that." He cleared his throat, obviously affected by her presence. "But it *appears* as though Mr. Hightower committed several crimes—stealing building materials from a number of his clients' jobsites, at a substantial cost to those very clients in time, money, and energy expended to overcome the losses."

"And frustration, I imagine. They must be pretty upset."

"Yes. And frustration. He also attempted to cover up his criminal activities with false statements given to the police and to insurance investigators. And he attempted to defraud Trinidale Builders Supply out of a substantial amount of money, claiming that he had never ordered the materials delivered to one of his more remote jobsites and denying that he knew what became of them."

"Perhaps that was true."

"Miss ... I'm sorry, I didn't catch your name. What was it again?"

"Deidre," she said, her smile widening. "Still is."

"Yes, well, Deidre, if that were an isolated example, one might reach that conclusion, but in light of other allegations and proven facts—for instance, his kiting several bad checks both locally and at a flooring supply outlet in Lincoln—I'm afraid you can reach only one conclusion."

"But, that doesn't sound like anything serious enough to rise to the status of a felony—and certainly not a series of them. All you have are a number of accusations by people whom you might say had a great deal of incentive for lying. After all, if Darryl is convicted, he'll have to pay his clients a lot of money as reparation, won't he? Free money to them. Money they won't have to borrow from the bank to finish their jobs. See what I mean? So you have their accusations pitted against Darryl's statements in his own defense. It sounds a lot like a *he said/she said* situation to me. Hardly conclusive evidence that a series of felonious acts have been committed."

He smiled, his face bearing that familiar *Okay, gotcha!* look. "*Ahh,* but it's a little more conclusive than that. We have the *coup de grace* here." He opened his top right-hand desk drawer and pulled out his cell phone. "We have the recording."

Her brows rose, and her eyes widened as she tried to look impressed. "And you say that Darryl actually confessed to committing those criminal acts before you? And on tape?"

Peeps patted the phone like he would an obedient puppy. "That's right. And it's all right here."

"And you have no doubt about the interpretation of what he said? I mean, perhaps, in your haste to get to the bottom of this thing, you misunderstood some of his comments?"

He shook his head and smirked. "No."

"But why would anyone sitting in front of a bunch of people, some of whom were clients of his and one of whom he knew to be an investigator for the D.A.'s office, confess to committing a number of serious crimes?"

Peeps looked pleased to hear the question, as if expecting it for some time and pleased to be able to regurgitate an answer.

"Call it criminal ego, if you will. We see it all the time. Even Jeffrey Dahmer opened up once he was cornered, apparently quite proud to have gotten away with as much as he had for so long. Perhaps Mr. Hightower is similar in that respect to Mr. Dahmer."

Deidre cocked her head and squinted.

"Or, perhaps he'd had a little too much to drink that night—we all did—and simply didn't realize what a poor light he was casting on his own actions."

Deidre let out a short, crisp breath.

"Or maybe he was just ready to get caught. You know, sometimes criminals are like that when they figure they've gotten away with just about all they can, so they think they'd might as well give it up."

"Or, perhaps," she said, "mistakes were made in transcribing the information on the tapes into a transcript for the District Attorney to read?"

He scoffed.

"No chance?"

He shook his head. "None."

"So, you transcribed the tape yourself?"

"Absolutely."

"And that's how you know that no mistakes were made in the transcription process."

He nodded. "Miss ... *uhh* ... Deidre, I told you that already. May I inquire as to what you're getting at, here? Why you're asking all these questions?"

Deidre stared into his eyes for several moments until he began to squirm. He reached under his left armpit to scratch, adjusted himself on his chair, and set both hands on his desk before hiking his shoulders and dropping them down again. "Well?"

She opened her purse and extracted another cell phone. It was different from Peeps' a newer iPhone with a larger screen and a better speaker.

"I'd like you to listen to this, if you would."

He stared at it curiously as if he were seeing a two-headed turtle. "What is it?"

"It's an audiotape. The same audiotape that you recorded on your own phone. Same time, same place, same party, same people present. All unedited, untouched, and un-transcribed. Would you like to hear it?"

He shrugged. "I've already heard it. Several times."

"I know you did. But I'd like you to hear it again. This time, the way it really happened."

He raised his brows, his eyes widening, not quite sure what to say in response. Deidre hit the *play* button, and Peeps' voice spilled out:

Did you knowingly and willfully submit a check to Lincoln Servicesmaster in Lincoln, Illinois, when you knew there were insufficient funds to cover it?

Hightower's voice answered: *No, I did not. Our account would have had more than enough money in it if Stan Omado hadn't broken our agreement to hold our checks without depositing them until we straightened out this theft thing. Oh, right. Sorry. I mean, no, I did not.*

Deidre fast-forwarded to the next bookmark. Peeps said:

After speaking with Mr. Sandalman, did you confront Ms. Powell about the delivery of all those unauthorized materials?

Yes.

And did she tell you that Scott Sandalman had ordered her to authorize the shipment of the unordered materials to your jobsite?

Yes, but how did you …

She glanced at Peeps, who was turning a luminous shade of green, before jumping ahead to the third bookmark:

And is it true that Illinois Custom Design had suffered other financial losses of a considerable amount at around this same time?

Yes.

And these came from overcharges made by a roofing crew, who ordered three times more roofing materials than called for and then returned the excess materials to Trinidale Builders Supply for a refund, which they received in cash instead of as a credit to your company, is that correct?

Yes.

Is such a refund standard in the industry, a cash refund given to subcontractors or employees instead of a credit made to the company's account?

No.

Would you say it's a rare occurrence for that to happen?

It never happens.

Except in this case.

Yes.

But there were also other losses you incurred. I understand that someone gained entrance to your office and stole 15 thousand dollars' worth of tools. And that, in another instance, you had completed work on a reconstruction job for the owner, who had arranged in writing to pay you after she closed on her mortgage with the bank, is that correct?

Yes.

And who was the owner of that house on which you worked for several months without any appreciable cash flow?

Kelli Powell.

Peeps suddenly pushed his chair back from his desk and threw up his arms. "All right, so, you made your point. Now, you'd better tell me, where did you get that tape?"

She sat back in her chair. "Does it really matter?" She folded her arms across her chest, never taking her eyes off him. "My question is a little more relevant. Where did you get *your* tape?"

"I ... I recorded it." He hesitated. "At the party at the Potash residence."

"Yeah, and then you transcribed it yourself, according to you. Which means you listened to the accurate tape and deliberately distorted it, and then you gave that distorted transcription—a pack of lies—to the D.A. and to the press and to, let's see, who else can we imagine, here? How about the Potashes and Stan Omado and Scott Sandalman and anyone else who you thought might find your fabrication interesting."

Peeps' face turned red. "I ... I didn't transcribe it myself. I ... I sent it out. We always send all our tapes out for transcription."

"Out where?"

"What?"

She could see him stalling for time, sense the wheels turning in his head, smell the skid marks they'd left behind. "Where did you send it for transcribing? Because wherever it was, I suggest you find someone else to do the job from now on. Seems as if they're not all that reliable."

"We send them ... you know, different places. Look ... I said when I said that, I mean, what I meant when I said that was I handled it myself—I sent them out for transcribing, not that I did the work myself. I'm not a ..."

"How drunk were you the night of the party at the Potash residence when you taped the interview with Darryl?"

A gleam struck one eye. "Yeah. I guess. Plenty. I had too much to drink, that's for sure. I thought the tape ..."

"You thought you were going to stack the deck against the best, most honest contractor this town has ever seen. You thought you were going to tar and feather him right along with everyone else who has something to gain by seeing him arrested and convicted. What I want to know is, what's in it for you, Mr. Peeps? What do you get out of dirtying your soul? The undying admiration and gratitude of Stan Omado? Of Scott Sandalman? How about Robert Snow? You know him, too, don't you? The heating contractor who started this whole mess rolling ... with your blessing?"

"No. How would I know him?"

"How *wouldn't* you? You were once married to his ex-wife."

Peeps got up and took a slow turn around his desk, stopping next to Deidre's chair. He reached out just as she stood up. She held up her phone, clicked on "speakerphone," and said, "Heard enough?"

"I think so."

Peeps looked stunned. "What is this?"

A deep, strong voice resonated from the phone. "Hello, Mr. Peeps? Bob Ransom here, in Chicago. I'm Darryl Hightower's criminal defense attorney. And, unless I'm mistaken, you're going to have a lot to answer for to your District Attorney. In fact, so will he when the disciplinary board of the Illinois State Supreme Court looks into this matter, which they're sure to do after I file a complaint with them. They're going to want to know why no one investigated this matter more thoroughly. And why the chief investigator for the Town of Trinidale falsified court evidence to elicit a bad indictment of one of its citizens. After all, a man's life is literally at stake here, what with a total of 80 years' worth of prison time on the line. I'm sure the two of you will be hearing from the board shortly. In fact, you can count on it."

"That's it, then?" Deidre asked.

"That's it," Ransom said. "Nice job, Deidre. Talk to you soon."

She clicked off, picked up her purse, and turned toward the door. "Why, Mr. Peeps, you've been a veritable smorgasbord of colors this afternoon. Now, you're absolutely ashen." She paused, feigned concern, and continued. "But don't feel too bad. If you need a good defense attorney, I suggest you give Mr. Ransom a call. I believe he just wrapped up one case. He just might be in the market for another client soon. And I can highly recommend him."

"What gave you the idea?" Hightower asked. "How did you ever come up with it?"

"Well, to be honest," she said, "it wasn't until Tammy let slip the fact that she'd taped her interview with Peeps the other day. Once I knew that, I listened to her tape closely and picked up on Peeps' original questions to you. When you stopped by the other night, I got the idea of asking you the same questions he did at the party, and I taped them. After you left, I combined the two tapes—the one with his original questions and the one with your reconstructed answers. I have to say, you have a great memory. Peeps never even suspected you had reconstructed your answers for me to dub in on Tammy's tape."

"Why, you little schemer. Isn't that illegal? Editing two tapes into one that way?"

"Absolutely. But that's exactly what Peeps did to set you up. Sometimes, you know, you just have to fight fire with fire." She paused as she slowed the car down to make a turn. "All I can say is thank God Tammy kept her tape with Peeps after she transcribed her notes."

Darryl rubbed his chin. "So, we have Tammy to thank, then. I mean, in reality. Except for her, I'd still be behind the eight ball."

"You've got that right."

"Maybe I should get her a bottle of wine ..." He paused, watching her from the corner of his eye. "Or maybe take her out to dinner to some nice restaurant or something. You know, just to let her know how grateful I am."

"*Not* a good idea."

"It's not?"

"In fact, it's a horrible idea."

"It is?"

"I'll tell you what. Why don't you let *me* come up with a way to thank Tammy. You know what I mean. Women just have a knack for understanding other women so much better than men."

He shrugged. "Could be you're right."

She paused as she steered the nose of her car into the driveway leading to her garage, mumbling nearly incoherently beneath her breath, "Damned straight I'm right."

"Tell you what, then," he continued. "Let me at least take *you* out for dinner. To thank you for all *your* help. I mean, there's no way on earth I would have survived this whole, sordid mess without you."

She nodded her head before pulling to a stop and turning off the ignition. She leaned closer to him. "Now, *that's* more like it," she said, pressing her lips to his for several seconds before finally pulling back. "But I think you're going to owe me a helluva lot more for this one than *dinner.*"

Don't miss out!

Visit the website below and you can sign up to receive emails whenever D. J. Herda publishes a new book. There's no charge and no obligation.

https://books2read.com/r/B-A-PKCL-SLLHB

BOOKS 2 READ

Connecting independent readers to independent writers.